BLOWN AWAY

Blown Away is the sixth novel in G. M. Ford's acclaimed Frank Corso series, following *Fury, Black River, A Blind Eye, Red Tide* and *No Man's Land*. G. M. Ford lives in Oregon.

Also by G. M. Ford

The Frank Corso series

FURY

BLACK RIVER

A BLIND EYE

RED TIDE

NO MAN'S LAND

The Leo Waterman series

WHO IN HELL IS WANDA FUCA?

CAST IN STONE

THE BUM'S RUSH

SLOW BURN

LAST DITCH

THE DEADER THE BETTER

G. M. FORD

BLOWN AWAY

PAN BOOKS

First published in the United States of America 2006 by William Morrow
An imprint of HarperCollins Publishers Inc., New York, USA

First published by Macmillan 2007

This paperback edition published 2007 by Pan Books
an imprint of Pan Macmillan Ltd
Pan Macmillan, 20 New Wharf Road, London N1 9RR
Basingstoke and Oxford
Associated companies throughout the world
www.panmacmillan.com

ISBN 978-0-330-44199-5

3 5 7 9 8 6 4 2

A CIP catalogue record for this book is available from
the British Library.

Printed and bound in Great Britain by
Mackays of Chatham plc, Chatham, Kent

Visit **www.panmacmillan.com** to read more about all our books
and to buy them. You will also find features, author interviews and
news of any author events, and you can sign up for e-newsletters
so that you're always first to hear about our new releases.

1

"The head landed over there."

Corso turned and watched the guy trace an arc in the sky with his finger.

"Right where that red Honda is parked," the guy said.

"Where was Marino sitting when the bomb went off?" Corso asked.

This time the guy pointed to the area in front of Corso's boots. "Right there. See? There where the pavement's been patched."

"I don't see anything."

"You have to look close," the guy said. He pointed. "See the little rectangle there?"

Corso bent at the waist. In the gathering gloom, he couldn't make out the supposed patch in the pavement, so he dropped to one knee and used his hands. He found the outline with the tips of his fingers. Traced it. Maybe five feet by three. Done very neatly, as if by a landscaper rather than a road crew.

"Didn't even need to be fixed," the guy said. "Didn't have a mark on it."

Corso looked up. The guy was in his middle thirties, working on a potbelly. He needed a haircut almost as badly as the herring-bone sport jacket needed a trip to the dry cleaners. Other than grooming problems, however, Carl Letzo seemed like a pretty nice fella . . . more or less what Corso had come to expect from small-town newspaper reporters. What he hadn't come to expect, however, was for small-town newspaper guys to meet him at the airport. Especially when he hadn't told anyone he was coming.

"It was like the spot had cancer or something," Carl said. "Something that needed to be cut out before it could spread. Something to be expunged . . . you know, so the body could get about its business."

Corso rose from the pavement. He dusted off his hands and looked around. Something about these places out on the edge. A sense of whiteness . . . a sense of the void . . . of something vast and impenetrable just beyond the horizon. He'd felt it before, many times, that sense of impermanence. Like the place was a line of demarcation rather than a home . . . a sentinel rather than a respite . . . like the only thing left to those who stayed behind was to witness the passing of the parade.

"So, Carl," Corso began, "I appreciate you bringing me down here and all, saved me a bunch of time, but ahhh . . . just for the record, how was it you knew I was flying into your fair hamlet here?"

"Dorry."

"Who's Dorry?"

"Your publicist."

"Ahhhhh." Corso exhaled. It all made sense now. He'd changed publishers since his last book. Taken more money than he once could have imagined and run like hell. Hadn't occurred to him they'd assign him a publicist. He made a mental note to call his new editor . . . Greg was it? . . . yeah . . . at night . . . at home.

"So . . . you were here when it happened?"

Carl pointed at the Bank of Commerce, in whose parking lot they now stood. "Right there by the corner of the building. That was as close as they'd let me get."

The one-story rectangle of a bank was only slightly more adorned than the pavement had been. The lack of pizzazz seemed determined to convey a sense that these people were not wasting your money, or theirs either, for that matter.

All that remained of the surrounding trees were the black trunks set in the frozen grass and, spread above the ground, the gnarly, arthritic remnants of branches, quivering in the early-evening breeze.

To the west, the sky was leaden, backlit, as if somewhere in the reaches of the heavens a long-shuttered window had been opened, announcing to the senses . . . before the first scent of salt air . . . before the first crab shack . . . announcing that terra firma was about to end and that, like it or not, Plan B was about to become the order of the day.

Corso checked his watch. Four-ten and the late-fall light was already slipping into the lake for the night. Out on the road, streetlights sputtered to life as traffic crept along. It was cold enough to snow. Cold enough to keep people indoors for long periods of time. Suicide weather.

Behind Carl, a forest green Acura slid across the lot, its studded tires snapping the bare pavement like castanets. Malingering remnants of dirty snow huddled beneath the shrubbery.

"I figured there'd be a lot more snow."

Carl nodded. "Usually is. Up until a few weeks ago, we had it piled halfway up the fences. Then we got a warm spell. Rained like crazy for a whole week. Melted everything."

"What was the weather like last year?"

Carl Letzo thought about it. "About like this. 'Cept snow on the ground. We got about six inches the night before." He looked around, seeing it all again in his mind's eye. "Pretty much business as usual. People around here don't let a little snow get in their way."

Corso gestured toward the back door of the bank. "So he comes out that door with the money."

Letzo nodded. "He's got the money in a white plastic bag," he said. "He doesn't get more than a coupla steps out the door and the cops grab him."

"He try to break away from the cops?"

Letzo shook his head. "That was right before I got here, but I don't think so. I've never heard anybody talk about him resisting."

"So what then?"

"From what I hear, he's wailing about how he's going to blow up if he doesn't follow the directions in the note. The cops are scared to be close to him, so they set him out in the parking lot and wait for the bomb squad to arrive."

"And?"

"That's when I got here." He pointed at the pavement. "He was sitting here on the ground . . . cross-legged."

"Doing what?"

"Crying. Begging for somebody to help him."

"And then?"

Letzo's eyes narrowed. "Kerblooie. The bomb went off. Blew parts of him all over the place."

"Where was the bomb squad while all this was going on?"

He tried to control his tone but didn't manage it. "On their way," he said.

"How late were they?"

"Something like ten minutes," Letzo said without hesitation.

Corso looked him over. "Do I take it that their failure to arrive in time has been subject to some local debate?"

"There was plenty of blame to go around."

"From the time somebody called for the bomb squad, how long did it take for them to arrive?"

"Depends who you ask."

"Why's that?"

"Because there's some debate as to exactly when they received the call."

Corso waited for him to continue. He did. "The folks in the bank claim it was twenty minutes or so before they got here. Bomb squad claims the call came later. They say they made it in nine minutes flat."

"That's quite a discrepancy."

"A genuine bone of contention."

"And nobody ever followed up on it?"

"On what?"

"On the discrepancy. Last time I looked, that's what the press does. They poke their collective noses into the nooks and crannies of dissension. They point fingers. They assign blame."

Letzo shrugged. "There's still a lot of raw feelings around here."

"So?"

Corso watched the man's cheeks flood with color. "I guess you could say the town's kinda closed ranks around the incident."

Corso stared in disbelief. "That mean they all tell the same story or they don't tell the story at all?"

Carl Letzo looked embarrassed. "Mostly both," he joked.

"Sounds to me like there's an investigative report around here someplace."

"Be my last report," Letzo said.

"Really?"

When he shrugged again, Corso sensed the gesture must have become habit, a way of lessening the sting of his journalistic ineffectiveness, a sad coming to grips with his personal and professional limitations. "And you're hoping I'll turn over rocks until something crawls out." Corso barked out a dry laugh.

"I didn't say that," the younger man said.

"Because, I hate to tell you this, Carl, but coming up here wasn't my idea. My new publisher thought the whole 'bomb around the neck' thing was cute. He insisted I come up here and nose around for a book. I usually pick my own subjects, but you know . . ." This time, Corso looked embarrassed. ". . . guy'd just given me enough money to buy my own jetliner . . . what was I going to do? . . . say no?" Corso didn't wait for an answer. "Believe me, Carl, getting railroaded into writing somebody else's idea of a story doesn't appeal to me, so what I'm going to do is spend tomorrow seeing the local sights, then bright and early next a.m., I'm going to jump on the first flight out of here. No muss, no fuss, no bother. I'll tell him there just wasn't enough for a book, then get on with my life."

Letzo pulled a hand from the warmth of his jacket pocket and ran it down over his fleshy face. "You gotta understand," he began. "This place . . . it just made it. Just missed joining the rest of the rust belt. We had just enough going on to avoid going under. Folks around here are proud of that. They don't want to be hearing anything negative right now."

Corso made a rude noise with his lips. "That's what newspapers do, Carl. They tell people things they don't want to hear."

Corso watched Carl Letzo's facial expression change from to sullen to resigned and back to sullen. The tick-tick of tires on pavement pulled Corso's head around.

A brown-and-white police cruiser nosed into the parking lot, wheeled left toward where they stood and stopped directly behind Corso. The low angle of the sun and the tinted windows made it difficult to see who was inside.

After a moment the driver's door swung open with a groan. The door was still bouncing on its hinges when she stepped out. Somewhere in her early forties, she was stocky without being fat. A beer keg of a woman. Maybe five-foot-ten and about half that wide. In the right light, in the right mood, the right person might have called her pretty. Not today though.

Today she was all business, all hard cop eyes and hard cop attitude.

"You peddling your papers down here, Carl?" she asked.

Something in her tone set Corso's teeth to gnashing.

"Carl's safeguarding the public's right to know," he said.

She neither acknowledged Corso nor moved her eyes from Carl Letzo.

"This your attorney, Carl?"

Carl used his hand to gesture toward Corso. "Actually, Chief Cummings, this gentleman is a writer. His name is Frank Corso. He writes . . ."

"I know what he writes," she interrupted. Her words hung in the air like smoke. Carl folded his arms over his chest.

"This has the feel of that old Rod Steiger movie," Corso said. "You know where Sidney Poitier comes into town and gets warned off by the Southern sheriff . . . the old 'you in a heapa trouble now, boy' kind of thing."

She offered a thin insincere smile. "In case you haven't noticed, Mr. Corso, we're about as far north as we can get."

"Must explain the weather," Corso said, matching her tooth for tooth.

After an awkward moment, she relaxed her shoulders, softened her face, and very nearly managed to sound affable. "Come on, Mr. Corso. Jump in. I'll give you a lift to your hotel."

Corso was shaking his head before she finished the sentence. "No thanks," jumped from his mouth. "I try to stay out of police cars."

"Unofficially, of course," she added with a warm smile.

"I particularly try to stay out of unofficial police cars."

"Why don't we . . ." she began.

"Am I under arrest?" Corso countered.

"Would you like to be?"

"Not if I can help it."

"You and I have a few things to get straight."

"Such as?"

"Such as the possibility that you may be guilty of withholding information vital to a murder investigation. Such as your stated intention to poke around in an ongoing felony investigation, which I'm here to tell you, isn't gonna happen."

"Stated where? Where did I ever say anything like that?"

She looked at him as if he must be kidding, ducked her upper torso back into the cruiser and came out holding a magazine that she flipped Corso's way. The pages flopped open about halfway to Corso. He had to take a step forward and bend at the waist in order to keep it off the ground.

The minute he got it turned right side up, he sucked in his breath and winced. This week's *People*. He was on the cover. Standing on Saltheart with his shirt off. Liberal computer enhancement had produced a tightly muscled, Mr. Bad-ass look. The headline read: *Cold Case*. The bold white type suggested the bestselling author was going to solve a mystery that had baffled even the FBI. Bestselling book to follow. See page nine.

He rolled the magazine tight, walked over, and handed it to the chief of police. Her narrow gray eyes demanded an explanation.

Corso shrugged. "News to me," he said.

"How can that be?"

"I've got a new publisher. Apparently he's a bit more gung ho than I'm accustomed to."

"So you had nothing to do with this? You *just happen* to be here in town this week? In a week when you *just happen* to be on the cover of *People* magazine."

Corso sighed. "I'll tell you the same thing I told Carl. I'm here because my publisher sent me." He gestured toward the magazine. "Apparently, this is an idea he's had in the works for some time. Also apparently, I'm going to have to have a few words with him regarding keeping me in the loop." She started to speak, but Corso raised his voice and kept talking. "So . . . just so we're clear with each other . . . ready?" She didn't respond. "I have no intention of writing about this place. Not now. Not ever. This isn't my kind of story. I like 'em easy, and if this one were easy, somebody would have figured it out by now. I've tried solving the big mystery before and ended up looking like an idiot."

"With your history, Mr. Corso, it's kinda hard to know which incident you're referring to. Are you talking about the time you were fired by the *New York Times* for fabricating a story and the subsequent twenty-million-dollar judgment against the paper?" She didn't wait for an answer. "Or that time you led Texas authorities to believe you knew the whereabouts of a murdered woman. Or maybe the incident in Minnesota when . . ."

"Take your pick," Corso snapped. With a curt nod, he turned and strode away, toward the back of the parking lot, where they'd left Carl's Honda. For a dozen strides, the only sounds to reach his ears were the sounds of his boots on the pavement and the brittle clatter of the wind in the bare trees. Then he heard the slapping of soles and the huffing and puffing as Carl jogged up even with him, his breath rising toward the sky in plumes. "You've sure got a way with people," Carl panted.

"It's a gift," Corso said.

2

" I keep telling you, I don't work this way," Corso rasped into the phone. "I can't operate with people looking over my shoulder."

"We like to think of ourselves as a team."

It was like talking to a wall. No matter how many times he told the guy he didn't need any help, all he got back were corporate platitudes.

With his free hand, Corso massaged his temple. He walked to the window and used the plastic rod to pull the gold curtain aside. Beyond the hotel parking lot and the rocky beach, the expanse of gray water loomed immense. Even in darkness, he could make out the whitecaps churning this way and that in a frenzied stew of wind and weather.

"I'm out of here first thing in the morning," Corso said.

"Kevin's going to be very disappointed."

"Kevin's a big boy. That's how you get to have 'publisher' painted on your door. He'll get over it."

A pin-drop moment passed.

"Of course, you'll be in violation of your contract."

"I'll what?"

"The performance clause."

"Which says what?"

"Which says that you will take assignments as directed and pursue them with all professional dispatch."

"Professional dispatch?"

"If memory serves."

Corso turned his back to the window and paced to the center of the room. "I quit," he said. "I'll have my accountant return your advance. Tell Kevin I'm sorry we couldn't do business." He pulled the phone from his ear and started to push the disconnect button when he heard squawking.

"What?" he said into the mouthpiece.

"Plus the eight-million-dollar default payment."

Corso drew a shallow breath. "You're telling me that . . . that if I quit now, I owe you eight million dollars."

"Plus legal expenses, of course."

Corso felt the blood rising in his cheeks. Twice he started to speak but thought better of it. The muscles along the side of his jaw twitched. He pulled the receiver away from his mouth and took several deep breaths. "You'll be hearing from my attorneys," he said finally. "In the meantime. I'll be pursuing the matter with . . . what was it . . . ?"

"Professional dispatch."

"Yes. That's it. Professional dispatch."

Corso used his thumb to break the connection. He threw the cell phone onto the bed, where it bounced twice before coming to rest.

Corso crossed the carpet in two long strides, picked up the house phone and dialed fourteen. Four rings, then, "Housekeeping."

He asked to have a pair of feather pillows sent up.

"Oh . . . well . . . I'm not sure if we . . . I'll . . ."

"Buy them if you have to. Put them on my bill, but get a couple of feather pillows up here."

"Oh yes . . . I'll . . ."

Corso hung up before he cursed. Angry with himself for taking his frustrations out on the help. Angry about his arrogance. Angry about the effect money seemed to be having on his life. He cursed again before he snatched the cell phone from the bed. He extended the antenna and walked over by the window.

"Sandstrom, Ellis and Taylor." A voice as smooth as honey.

"Peter Sandstrom please," Corso said.

"I'm afraid Mr. Sandstrom . . ."

"This is Frank Corso." More of that damn arrogance, but who cared?

As he waited, Corso wondered if the phrase "on the line" was relevant anymore. Whether any kind of tangible connection existed between two people conversing on cell phones. Was there a line? A beam? A something? Four minutes and half a dozen electronic clicks later, Peter Sandstrom came on the line.

"Frank," he said.

Corso skipped the pleasantries and platitudes and got to the point. When he was finished talking, a silence settled over the line. Then suddenly Corso could hear raised voices in the background. "Where are you?" he asked.

"On the fifth tee at Ballantine. You know . . . that wicked up-hill dogleg to the right."

"You've got to get me out of this contract."

Corso thought he might have heard a short dirty laugh before Sandstrom began to speak. "I'm up next on the tee, Frank, so I'm going to make this short and sweet. You're swimming in the deep end of the pool, baby. Maybe a dozen people in the whole country make as much money writing as you do now. And . . ." He drew it out. "In case you've forgotten, there's no such thing as a free lunch. You've put them in the position where the only way they're going to see their money back is to promote you like the second coming of Christ." Background voices again. "I'll look at the contract, Frank, but I'm telling you the same thing I told you at the time. It's all very much status quo, comes with the territory kind of stuff. You have an obligation to follow up on their suggestions, and they have an obligation to provide you with the necessary resources. It's that simple. Don't make this any harder than it needs to be." The voices again. Louder this time.

"But eight million bucks?"

Peter Sandstrom made a dismissive noise with his lips. "That's a piss hole in the snow compared to what they gave you, man. Relax. They're just covering their collective asses in case you're a complete bust like that Graham woman. You remember her? With the Margaret Thatcher hair? Took all that up-front money from Random House and never wrote another line. Not a syllable. You remember?"

Corso's grunt suggested the possibility of recall. A knock sounded from the hall. Corso shifted the phone to his left ear as he skirted the bed and made his way to the door, where he pulled back the safety lock, at which point the door burst open.

Had Corso not been six feet six, the initial onslaught would have convulsed his solar plexus and the action would have been over before it began. As it was, the big one's ski-masked head hit him right in the belly, bending him at the waist, driving him backward across the carpet, with the cell phone twirling off into space as Corso let himself be propelled across the room where he finally planted a foot, grabbed the guy's red plaid jacket with both hands and pistoned up a vicious knee to the groin.

The knee found a home. The guy groaned and staggered. Corso went down onto his back, pulling his attacker with him, using the guy's weight and momentum to propel him up, over and out into space. Wasn't until the guy came down on the desk with a horrendous crash that Corso saw the second one.

Same ski mask . . . different intentions. This one had a hypodermic syringe locked in his right glove. The steel-wire point glistened with a drop of something silver as it rocketed downward toward Corso's throat. A cry escaped Corso's mouth as he threw his body hard to the left. The needle missed. The guy cursed.

His assailant brought the hand back up by his ear and was about to make another plunge when Corso put his full weight and his considerable length of bone behind a kick to his antagonist's knee, the impact of which drove the joint sideways in a direction in which it had never been intended to flex. Sounded like somebody snapped a twig. The guy dropped the syringe, lowered his seat onto the carpet and reached for his knee. A high-pitched keening sound filled the room as he rocked back and forth in pain.

Corso was in the process of scrambling to his feet when a heavy boot caught him squarely in the ribs, driving the air from his lungs with a great whoosh and sending a wave of pain flooding throughout his body. He rolled again, moving his face in time to deflect the sole of the boot, sending the force raking down over his ear and onto the carpet below.

He went fetal and waited for the boot to crash into his head. He felt blood on the side of his face as he peeked out through the crook in his elbow, then rolled to his knees in time to see the bigger of the two helping his maimed partner out through the door.

Sitting on the floor, just inside the jamb, a heavyset Hispanic maid had her head thrown back like a coyote baying at the moon. Her wavy black hair shook slightly as she howled for all she was worth.

3

Corso flinched as the medical technician worked on the tear in his right ear. "You really ought to go to the hospital," the tech said again. "Get this thing fixed right."

"I'll get it looked at as soon as I get home," Corso assured him.

The guy's face said he didn't believe a word of it. He shook his head as he sat back on his heels, peeled off his surgical gloves and looked up at the cop who'd been hovering over the two of them for the past ten minutes. "That's all I can do from here," he announced. "Long as he don't tear it open while he's sleeping, he ought to be all right." The cop nodded and helped him to his feet.

They'd pulled an armchair out into the hall, where a Spanish-speaking officer had managed to get the maid calmed down enough to answer questions.

Corso got to his feet. The room reeled and gamboled. He reached down and put a hand on the bed to steady himself. After a moment, he crossed the room, went into the bathroom and closed the door. His legs felt unsteady, so he sat on the closed lid of the commode and put his face in his hands. After a while, he got to his feet, put both hands on the rim of the sink and looked into the mirror. A trio of medical staples held the top of his ear in place. A thick red scrape ran from his hairline to his jawbone.

He turned on the cold water, scooped up a double handful and splashed it on his face. He sputtered, took a deep breath and repeated the process. Then again and again, until the frigid water began to clear his head.

Someone knocked on the bathroom door. Asked if he was okay. He said he was fine, dried his face and hands with a towel and stepped back into what had once been his hotel room. The pair of cops was comparing notes over by the door. On the far side of the room, the forensic team was packing up its gear and getting ready to leave.

The flattened remnants of the desk were decorated here and there with the remains of Corso's room service steak dinner. Someone had opened a window, allowing a stiff lake breeze to fan the curtains across the floor like long, gold fingers.

A guy about thirty slipped into the room. He wore a gold badge on the pocket of his blue pin-striped suit. He limped over to Corso and put a concerned hand on his elbow. The badge said his name was Randy Shields, hotel manager. The facial expression said his leg hurt and he'd rather be elsewhere.

"I can't tell you how sorry we are, Mr. Corso," he whispered.

"Nothing to be sorry about."

Corso's largesse seemed to relieve him. "We have a new room for you," the guy said. "Two floors up on the lake side. Whenever you're ready just call the desk and . . ." He held up a hand. Boy Scout's honor. "On the house, of course."

Corso nodded his thanks and pocketed the new plastic key. If there was anything the hotel could do . . . anything . . . just anything . . . Corso kept nodding and trying to smile.

"You from here?" Corso finally asked. "I mean like born and raised."

The guy laughed. "I'm *from* here, but been gone for the past eighteen years."

"You know Nathan Marino?"

"Not personally. I knew *of* him. Knew his older brother James. We were in the same high school class. Nathan was a few years behind us."

"What happened to your leg?"

"Kuwait. Shrapnel from a booby-trapped car."

The cops ambled over. As cops go, these two were a bit long in the tooth. By the time they got to their midforties, most cops were either so burned-out they couldn't function or so corrupt they didn't need the pension. These two still shined their brass and polished their shoes, and both wore sergeant's stripes. That's where the similarities ended. The bald one had the palest blue eyes Corso had ever seen. Made him look like a vampire. The one with the mustache was Hispanic. Not a Mexican. Something else.

"Guess we got everything we're going to get," mustache said.

His partner checked his notepad. "You and Mrs. Casamayor agree right on down the line. Two guys. Blue ski masks. One noticeably bigger than the other. The shorter of the two being helped along by the other guy on the way out."

Corso nodded. The movement caused his head to spin. He sat down on the bed.

"You're sure nothing's missing?" mustache asked.

"This wasn't a robbery," Corso scoffed.

The notion seemed to startle them. "You think they meant to harm you?"

"I think they meant to kidnap me," Corso said. "I think the idea was to render me unconscious and take me away somewhere."

"You're basing that on the syringe," mustache said.

"And the fact that they had a key."

"I thought you said you unlocked the door."

"I said I took off the safety bolt. The door should have still been locked, but it wasn't."

They snuck a look at each other. Corso didn't need prompting.

"And the whole way they went about it. You want to assault somebody, you show up with a baseball bat. You want to rob somebody, you jam a gun in his face, you don't try to wrestle him to the floor and stick a needle in him."

Separately, they each snuck a look out through the open door.

"What's in the hall?" Corso demanded.

The bald guy cracked first. "A laundry hamper," he said. "Nobody from housekeeping has any idea how it got there. They keep them locked in the maintenance closets at the ends of the halls. The maids use those little carts of theirs. They get full, they dump them in the hampers. The hampers themselves are not permitted in the corridors."

"Ever," added mustache. "According to Mrs. Casamayor it's a firing offence."

"Besides which they quit making up rooms six hours ago."

"That's what I'm telling you. Those guys were trying to kid-nap me."

For the first time, the bald cop seemed to consider the possibility that Corso might be onto something.

"We don't get many kidnappings in Edgewater," he said finally.

"But then again, we don't get many celebrities either," his partner added.

Something in his tone caught Corso's attention. "So you're figuring this must be something I brought with me," he said.

"Only makes sense," mustache offered.

"How'd they know where to find a laundry hamper?" Corso asked.

The cops gave a collective shrug.

"You said the maintenance closets were locked."

"Same key the maids use to get in the rooms."

"They force the door?" Corso asked.

"Doesn't look like it."

"How'd they know I was in my room?"

They shrugged in unison. Corso kept at it.

"Sounds to me like they had a lot of inside help. It was me I'd start with the hotel staff . . . past and present."

"But it's not your call now, is it, Mr. Corso?" The voice came floating in from the doorway. Corso had to crane himself around the officers to catch a glimpse of Chief Cummings walking across the carpet. She wore a black wool overcoat buttoned to the throat, over some kind of dress or skirt. The cops began primping like schoolboys as she ambled over their way.

"You boys about finished here?" she asked.

They assured her they were ready to go. She encouraged

them to do so. They didn't have to be encouraged twice. They were in the doorway when she said, "Have the report on my desk for start of business tomorrow."

She watched them disappear and turned her attention to Corso. She reached out and put her fingers on his chin, turning his head to the right so she could see his damaged ear. "Could have been worse," she mused.

"Could have been better too."

"You gotta be careful who you open your door to these days."

"I'll try to keep that in mind," Corso assured her.

"In the meantime . . . you go back to your boat and do whatever it is you writers do. We'll look into the assault. We need anything, or we have any information for you, we'll be in touch."

"It wasn't an assault," Corso said. "Those guys were trying to kidnap me."

She waved a dismissive hand. "We'll see." She said the words in the tone an adult would use on an unruly child. Corso felt his anger beginning to rise.

A pair of liveried porters showed up at the door. Corso directed them to his belongings. He and the chief stood in silence, watching the young men load Corso's suitcase and garment bag onto a brass luggage dolly and wheel it out of the room.

A moment after the door clicked closed, Corso fished the new room key from his pants pocket and started for the door.

"I think maybe I'm going to stick around for a few days."

The news stiffened her spine. "I don't think that would be a good idea, Mr. Corso. Seems like the forces of evil have drawn a bead on you. It's probably best you move on."

Corso laughed. "You probably won't believe this, Chief, but all of a sudden I've got eight million reasons to stay," he said.

4

"That's all," she said. Corso took the clipping from her blunt fingers and glanced at the date. The article was slightly more than a year old. The byline read Carl Letzo. *Marino Mystery Remains Unsolved* read the modest headline.

"Nothing since, huh? No follow-ups. No anniversary reminder or anything like that?"

She shrugged. "I just work down here in the newspaper archives," she said with a wan smile. "Mondays, Wednesdays and Fridays. You'd have to talk to Mr. Blundred if you wanted to . . ."

Corso cut her off. "Thanks for the help," he said.

She smiled, revealing a mouthful of braces but made no move to leave. Corso waited for a moment, then sat back in the chair and looked at her quizzically. She fidgeted and turned her face away. Her thick brown hair was held back from her face by a red plastic clip. She used one chubby hand to pick at the cuticles of the other.

"I read all your books," she blurted. "As soon as they come out. In hardback," she added quickly.

Corso thanked her. "It's always nice to know somebody's reading the damn things."

Corso's expletive brought a rush of blood to her cheeks.

"My mother and I . . . I . . . we read them together. She reads them while I'm at work."

Corso kept smiling. The silence seemed to unnerve her.

She giggled. "Sometimes when I come home, she won't give it back to me. She's . . . you know . . . she's so into the story she's just got to keep reading."

"Sounds like you need to buy two."

Her eyes widened. "Hardbacks? Are you crazy? I mean . . ." She stopped herself. "Oh I didn't mean to . . . I . . ."

"No problem," Corso assured her. His insides tightened. The grin threatened to slide from his face and shatter on the floor. This time, it was he who turned away, picked up his notebook and pen from the table and opened it to the first blank page. "Tell you what," he said. "You write your name and address in here, and I'll have the publicity department send you a couple of signed copies whenever a book comes out."

"Really?" she wheezed. "Really?"

"No problem," he said again. A voice emanating from the back of his head asked him whether or not he used the phrase "*no problem*" with an uncommon regularity. He watched her scratch out her name and address and decided he did. Decided he threw the phrase around like rice at a wedding, then wondered why that was so.

Claudia Cantrell. South East Admiralty Avenue. Corso cleared his throat as he turned the page. "Thanks again for the help," he said.

Took her a minute to catch the hint, at which point she excused herself on the pretext of work to be done and sidestepped from the room in a flurry of apologies.

Corso sat back in the wooden chair and gazed at the modest pile of yellowing news stories on the table in front of him. The dusty odor of old newsprint brought him back. Back to his early years at the *North Carolina Nation*. Back when they'd referred to the paper's dank basement as "the morgue." Before microfiche, before microfilm . . . *way* before digital information storage, back when they kept hard copies of everything. Back before the past was subject to revision.

The paper was beginning to stiffen with age, the stock color moving from blond to beige. Another ten years and it would take an archaeologist to pry it open.

In the kind of banner bold type generally reserved for World Wars and Terrorist Attacks, it asked, "*Suicide Bomber*?" A grainy photo of the parking lot where he'd spent yesterday afternoon covered the center of the page. Slightly right of center, a quartet of cops surrounded a shrouded bundle of something as it lay on the pavement among the piles of fresh snow and rotting leaves. The bold print asked: "*Madman or Victim*?"

Despite his best efforts, Corso's lip curled at the irony. That was the question, wasn't it? Whether Nathan Marino had willingly taken part in the criminal activities leading up to his demise or whether, as many thought, he'd just been some poor slob who'd had the great misfortune to have been at the wrong place at the wrong time and had ended up paying for his bad luck with his life.

Assuming one was the kind of person who believed in such things, the facts could surely be described as *simple enough*. On the night of March 24, 2003, a thirty-nine-year-old delivery driver named Nathan Marino had left Aunt Bee's Country Fried Chicken at about ten-fifteen in the evening with six take-out orders to deliver. Five were pretty much par for the course. Three Deluxe dinners, which included three pieces of Aunt Bee's "justifiably deeelishious" chicken, a thigh, a wing and a breast, along with a pair of chewy biscuits and a small plastic container of coleslaw.

Two more were for the Mountain Man dinner, which was the same as the Deluxe but with a bucket of mashed potatoes and gravy thrown in. The sixth order had been a matter of some debate. Came from way out, nearly over in Cartell County. Two Super Buckets and four large Cokes. Any regular order from anything like that far away would have resulted in a polite refusal to deliver. Fifty-three dollars' worth of chicken, was, after all, fifty-three dollars' worth of chicken and so, with the understanding he could go home when he finished the run, Nathan Marino had been dispatched.

Thirteen hours later, a disheveled and disheartened Nathan Marino appeared at the counter of the Bank of Commerce, where he'd passed a note to a teller explaining that he'd been taken hostage and had a bomb wired around his neck, and that any deviation from his instructions would result in his being blown to kingdom come. As if to punctuate the situation, he'd pulled open his jacket wide enough to reveal an oversized handcuff locked around his neck. From the handcuff hung a black metal box the size of a camera case. A dozen or more wires ran down over his uniform shirt into the box. His red puffy eyes suggested he'd been crying. "Please," was all he said.

As she'd been so recently trained, the teller, one Mary Lou Tabakian, had immediately activated the silent alarm and complied with the demand for money, stuffing the entire contents of her cash drawer into the white plastic bag she'd used to transport her lunch.

Branch manager Phil Conley had long contended that the alarm buttons were poorly placed and ripe for inadvertent activation, so when he sidled over to Mary Lou's window, his assumption was that his newest teller had unknowingly bumped the button with her knee, thus validating his well-known concern regarding their whereabouts.

The sight of Nathan Marino wiped the smug smile from Phil Conley's face and sent the hairs on the back of his neck to full attention. His worst fears were realized when Mary Lou handed him the note.

Conley read it twice. When he looked up, Nathan gave him a quick peek at the bomb and said, "All of it. They want me to get all of it."

Corso sat back in the seat and imagined himself facing the bank manager's dilemma. What was he going to do? The threat wasn't directed at the bank or its customers but rather at the guy with the note. On one hand, his job was to guard the bank's assets. On the other hand, choosing money over a man's life wasn't something he wanted on his permanent record. The bomb looked real enough, but what if it wasn't. What if it was some half-wit contraption this guy had put together in his garage. A device whose greatest danger was in making the bank look the fool, a possibility not destined to sit well with his ultraconservative superiors, but one which, he decided, was far more desirable than its gruesome alternative.

Phil Conley looked Nathan Marino in the eye and said, "Just a moment please; I'll take care of this for you."

Although his hands were visibly shaking, he kept his face pretty much intact as he moved down the line of tellers, emptying cash drawers and whispering instructions to close the windows as he went along. The process took the better part of five minutes. By the time he got back to Nathan and Mary Lou, he'd appropriated another white grocery bag, this one with a red Safeway logo on the side, and packed it as full of cash as the first. As the bags wouldn't fit through the slot, he hefted them over the top of the cage, where Nathan Marino took them from his hands and headed for the back door without so much as a by-your-leave. The rest, as they liked to say, was history.

Three steps outside the bank's back door, Nathan Marino had been tackled and quickly subdued by a squad of policemen. By the time they had him splayed and handcuffed, somebody'd finally noticed the contraption wired around his neck and allowed discretion to become the better part of valor. After carefully patting Nathan down and extracting a block-printed, multipage set of instructions from his coat pocket, they'd marched him out into the center of the parking area and forced him to sit on the pavement as they began to clear the area of both civilians and themselves.

Sitting cross-legged on the asphalt, Nathan Marino emitted an unending and seemingly unpunctuated stream of pleas and exhortations to the effect that they mustn't do this to him. That he must be allowed to complete his mission or else he'd surely be blown to bits by the unnamed kidnappers who had committed this heinous act. He begged; he cried; he blubbered all the way to the end. Never showing anything less than complete certainty regarding his doom were he not allowed to fulfill his instructions to the letter. Whoever these real or imagined people were, they'd certainly made an impression on Nathan Marino.

Corso sat back in the chair again. He crossed his long arms over his chest and closed his eyes, trying to imagine the terror Marino must have felt as he sat on that frozen patch of ground waiting for the bomb to explode. He'd thought about dying before. More times than he could count, but never like this. His death dreams revolved around stopping bullets or hurtling into concrete from behind the wheel. Always quick. Always final. Above all, always heroic. Never just sitting there like a side of beef waiting for a sudden surge of electricity to work its way down some anonymous wire where it would trigger an explosion whose sudden fury would tear him to pieces. He shuddered at the hopelessness and futility of Nathan Marino's passing.

The question of how long Nathan Marino sat in that parking lot before oblivion struck did not become an issue, at least not in the pages of the *Edgewater Ledger*, until a couple of days before the coverage stopped altogether. Apparently, Carl Letzo's assessment of the situation had been correct. At the first whiff of incompetence or impropriety, the local powers had completely shut down the information pipeline.

By April 6, thirteen days after the event, the story had altogether disappeared from the local papers, returning lead stories to such heady matters as sewer and water levies and the gala opening of a new "executive" golf course on Lake Prichard, wherever the hell that was.

While the amount of time Marino waited before the device detonated was subject to some debate, the specifics regarding the moment of truth itself were uniformly agreed upon. According to bystanders, a tearful Nathan Marino had been rocking back and forth, filling the air with pleas when, all of a sudden, the air was split by a sharp crack, followed by a deep thud, as if something thick and wet had been dropped from a great height and rendered asunder by the impact.

What witnesses seemed to most uniformly recall was the manner in which the concussion blew Nathan Marino over backward so violently as to make his torso bounce twice before finally coming to rest beneath a cloud of blue smoke. That and the sight of his head arcing across the sky.

5

Despite law enforcement's best attempts to control the flow of information, the details of the autopsy made the Internet within a week. Unnamed sources detailed how the explosive device had been cleverly designed to wreak maximum damage to the wearer. On the three sides the enclosing box had been formed of fiber-reinforced steel. On Nathan's side, however, the box had been constructed of less exotic material. Taking the line of least resistance, the explosion had mangled Nathan Marino's chest and torso, the concussion killing him instantly by blowing his heart to bits in the nanoseconds before launching his head across the parking lot.

As a bank robbery, attempted or otherwise, ran afoul of a number of federal monetary regulations, it fell under the general purview of the FBI. Before the week was out, the Bureau had entered the scene and, as was always the case, the flow of anything akin to new information ground to a halt.

Corso made a note to inquire as to whether the Bureau had come into the case on its own behest or whether their presence had been requested by local authorities. Probably the former, as most law enforcement agencies had been burned at least once by the Bureau's tactics and were loath to deal with them except under the most extreme circumstances. The Bureau's MO in a case like this was to arrive with smiles and fanfare, then immediately take over the micromanagement of the investigation while assessing the situation.

As far as the FBI was concerned, that the perfect case was one with sufficient media appeal to keep it on the evening news, one that had heretofore baffled local law enforcement agencies and could, in the Bureau's opinion, be resolved in a timely manner, while, at the same time, affording no possibility of the Bureau looking anything but stellar in its efforts.

Apparently, it had taken the Bureau less than a week to decide that the strange death of Nathan Marino consisted of far more questions than it did answers, primarily the question of whether Marino had been a victim, a coconspirator, a dupe or, as some thought, the suicidal sole proprietor of a bizarre bank robbery scheme. Unable to answer this most basic question to their satisfaction, the FBI had done what they always did when the prospect of glory was judged to be too costly or too remote—they disappeared, leaving local authorities holding the bag.

The following three weeks of media scrutiny had done little to resolve the questions surrounding Nathan Marino. A thorough check of his background and employment history had revealed him to be the son of a large local family from whom, in recent years, he had grown estranged. A mediocre high school student, Nathan had taken five years to graduate. Teachers and guidance counselors had often described him as affable but prone to daydreaming, as untroublesome but unmotivated, as average but lacking in ambition.

Upon graduation, Nathan had embarked upon an extended series of service sector jobs that had kept him economically afloat for the past twenty years. He'd delivered flowers for a couple of years. Mowed the grass out at the golf course for a couple more. Worked as a security guard down at the shipyard. Spent time washing dishes at the local Shari's restaurant. The list numbered eighteen jobs in twenty years. From all accounts, Nathan had been completely satisfied with his position in society, never expressing a desire for further education, never hanging around one job long enough to begin the climb up the company ladder. At the time of his death, Nathan had been delivering chicken for just under eleven months. His direct supervisor, one Harley Dewers, had described him as "an easy guy to get along with," willing to take shifts on nights, weekends and holidays because, Harley speculated, "he didn't seem to have a lot going on with his personal life," an assessment that, by any measure, had to be considered something of an understatement.

Nathan had neither married nor sired children. Nor, for that matter, ever so much as gone on a date, as far as anyone knew. Local women with whom he'd attended high school had described him as ordinary-looking but "sweet" or "kind and thoughtful" or . . . "nice" . . . in, as each had been compelled to add, "a brotherly sort of way" . . . rather than . . . "you know, anything romantic."

Thus pigeonholed, he'd apparently resigned himself to the life of a confirmed bachelor, living a solitary existence in a series of rented dwellings, the last of which, according to the paper, was somewhere out on Lowell Road, a wild unincorporated area of the county just west of town. Those whose duty it had been to sort through his meager belongings had described his domicile as spare but neat, neither spit-shined clean nor hog-wallow messy, but more or less what one would expect from a man who was not expecting visitors.

Nathan's sole concession to acquisition had been paperback novels . . . Westerns . . . nearly a thousand of which had been re-trieved from his one-bedroom rental. As he didn't own a televi-sion, it was assumed that Nathan must have frittered away the cold dark nights of winter dreaming of saloons and stampedes, somewhere in the Wild Wild West.

In what Corso assumed had been an attempt to maintain some semblance of dignity in the face of chaos, the Marino family had closed ranks, offering nothing more to the press than a series of statements, each read in a monotone by James Marino, Nathan's eldest brother and designated family spokesman, to the effect that the family believed their son Nathan had been the victim of a horrible crime, that they were united in that belief and were ap-palled by the way the authorities were treating both Nathan and the Marino family as suspects. Other than that, the family was not prepared to speak about the situation and should that deci-sion change, they'd be sure to let everybody know. Wham bam good-bye. That was it.

Had the blue-collar Marino family been more media savvy, they'd have understood how the lack of grist never stops the wheel. That as long as the stream kept running, the wheel kept turning around, that selling newspapers, not providing accurate coverage, was the object of the exercise and that, without facts, the fourth estate felt entitled to resort to speculation, rumor and hearsay, all of which were what filled that great void called the Evening News. Veiled rumors of violent family intrigue, whispers about possible childhood abuse, questions about Nathan's possible sexual preferences, interviews with friends, neighbors, schoolyard chums and former classmates . . . as was to be expected, they ground it all to dust, then went on their way.

Nationally, the story had been chewed up and spit out in just under a week. Locally, it had seemed as if the story would surely have had more legs . . . and it did . . . for a while. Long enough for the byline to change from Carl Letzo to somebody named Mary Anne Guidry.

What first caught Corso's ear was the quality of the writing. How out of the blue it seemed like Carl Letzo's flinty prose had been replaced by the breathless meanderings of somebody from the society pages, which, in fact, was precisely what had happened, although Corso didn't know that at the time. All he knew was that he was having so much trouble reading the article, he turned back to the front page to make sure he was reading the same guy, only to find he wasn't.

The switch was sufficiently radical and ill conceived as to get Corso's antennae twitching. He thumbed his way through the remaining collection of news stories. All Mary Anne Guidry. No Carl Letzo.

After several moments of thought, Corso reached back atop the stack of newsprint at his elbow and began to reread what had apparently been Carl's last piece on the Nathan Marino story. He read it twice. Wasn't until he was right down at the end of it on the second pass that he picked it up. A brief mention of the discrepancy regarding the time line for the arrival of the bomb squad and a promise that he'd have more to reveal tomorrow, a promise circumstances had apparently made impossible for Carl to keep.

Corso levered himself to his feet and stretched. He wondered whether he should leave the news articles on the desk or return them to somebody upstairs. Before he was able to make up his mind, the sound of approaching voices pried the question from his mind. Sounded like Claudia Cantrell and somebody who'd sandpapered his larynx. A third voice entered the chorus as the approaching footsteps rounded the final corner.

Claudia Cantrell and Carl Letzo hung back along his flanks like pilot fish on a shark, alert for scraps, but keeping well away from the mouth. He was about sixty, going bald slowly but all over; he moved awkwardly, like a man with bad knees. He walked right up to Corso, a foot or so inside the normal space people reserve for themselves. His breath smelled of Certs and stale coffee. The expression in his eyes said nobody'd told him "no" in years. Apparently, introductions were not required.

"Get your ass out of here," he said.

Corso eyed him with amusement. "Just my ass? Does that mean the rest of me can stay?" he asked with mock gravity.

In the shadows behind the guy, both pilot fish winced.

"Do you know who I am?" the guy demanded.

"No, but I'll bet you're going to tell me."

"I own this newspaper, and I don't want you here."

Corso started to reach for his hip pocket. "I've got a valid press credential. Access to the files is generally considered a professional courtesy. I don't see . . ."

The guy cut him off. "Not to you," he said. "You're a disgrace to the profession. I know all about you. The *New York Times* . . . the lawsuit and all of that."

The timbre of Corso's voice rose. "First off, you don't know one damn thing about what happened to me in New York. You and everybody else are just talking out of your collective asses."

The guy opened his mouth to speak. Corso poked him in the chest with a long finger. The mouth stayed open in disbelief. "Secondly . . ." Corso finished, ". . . the only thing you and the chief of police and the local criminals are accomplishing with your 'get outta Dodge' crap is you're starting to get my attention."

The older man closed his mouth and swallowed. Corso kept at him. "Yesterday all I wanted to do was to get back to my boat. As far as I was concerned, this jerkwater town had absolutely nothing to offer in the way of a story. Now I'm starting to wonder. I'm starting to wonder what kind of bone you all are so damned determined to keep buried." Corso threw an angry hand in the direction of the paper's archives. "It's not like any of this stuff is a mystery or anything. It was all over the evening news there for a while. It's one of those odd stories half the people in the country can recall with a little prodding and"—he stretched the word out—"being warned off so repeatedly just piques my interest, Mr. Dithers . . . just piques my interest."

He would have liked to have gone nose to nose with Corso but found himself a good eight inches short of the task. "Hargrove," he said in a shaky voice. "My name is Grant Hargrove and don't you forget it, mister." The sound of his own voice seemed to revitalize him. He reached out to return the favor . . . to poke a finger into Corso's chest, but something in Corso's steady gaze suggested he think better of it. He hesitated, finger stiff in the dusty air and instead, he took a short step backward before jamming the hand into his pants pocket. "Carl," he barked. "Show this smart-ass the door."

Carl didn't move. His eyes were the size of saucers as they bounced back and forth between Corso and the older man. When obedience was not immediately forthcoming, Hargrove turned his back to Corso and his attention toward Carl Letzo, whose face fell into a wearied expression of resignation, suggesting this wasn't the first time Carl had played the role of Hargrove's whipping boy.

The air was alive with emotional electricity. It occurred to Corso that he was quite possibly witnessing Carl's last moments as a reporter for the *Edgewater Ledger*. Behind Hargrove's back, he nodded and pointed at the stairs, telling Carl he'd go along peaceably. Making it easy for him.

"Well?" Hargrove bellowed.

Carl kept his eyes locked on Corso. "We better go, Mr. Corso," he said, hoping he'd interpreted Corso's acquiescent gesture correctly. Hargrove had twisted his gaze back to Corso, so he missed Carl's sigh of relief as Corso turned to the desk and began to gather his things.

Hargrove's confidence was on the rise. "Miss Cantrell . . . check the clippings. Make sure everything you gave him is there."

Corso let the aspersion slide. As he snapped his notebook closed and dropped it in his jacket pocket, Claudia Cantrell came clomping down the last few stairs and did as she was told. Her hands shook as she rifled through the pile of yellowing newsprint. She kept her eyes straight down like a frightened mouse in the shadow of the cat.

Corso headed for Carl and the stairs. Hargrove couldn't resist. "Make sure he's completely off the premises," he said as they started up. Carl said he would.

6

Snow was falling, coming straight down, thick and puffy like inside a paperweight. Corso pulled the collar of his coat up around his ears. Carl Letzo rubbed his hands together. His cheeks were red with embarrassment.

"Thanks for helping me out in there," he said to Corso.

Corso felt his discomfort and changed the subject. "You're a good writer," he said to Carl. "I just spent most of the past two hours reading your work. Your prose is economical. It's transparent . . . just like it's supposed to be in a reporter. You could write for any paper I've ever worked at."

Carl Letzo nodded his thanks but kept his eyes averted. "Yeah," he muttered under his breath. "Yeah, well thanks again."

The tinkle of tire chains reminded Corso of sleigh bells. The snow was coming harder now, spilling from the sky as if heaven had sprung a leak. Corso held out his hand, watching the snow-flakes land in his palm and slowly turn to water. He shifted his weight as he tried to come up with the right words. "You could . . . you know . . . New York really isn't that far from here. I'd bet you could . . ."

A bitter laugh cut him off. "Sure didn't work out too good for you," Letzo said.

This time it was Corso who turned away, looking out at the street through a plume of frozen breath, out where the ceiling had fallen below the tops of the buildings, out where noise of traffic had been muffled by the accumulating snow, where most of the cars had their headlights on in broad daylight as they moved slowly about, poking their noses here and there like blind moles.

"Hey . . . sorry," Carl Letzo said. "I didn't mean . . . I . . ."

"No problem," Corso said, wincing at the sound of the phrase.

Carl's shoes squeaked in the freshly fallen snow as he walked around to face Corso again. He shook his head in disgust. "Shows you how screwed up I am right now," he said. "Somebody does me a favor and I say stuff like that to him."

Corso waved him off. "You were right," he said with a wry grin. "Taking journalism advice from me is kinda like trading cooking tips with Jeffrey Dahmer."

They shared a guilty laugh before Carl spoke again. "You're right too, man. I've sunk down about as low as a body can get." He peered out through the wall of falling snow, as if he were ex-pecting a sail to show on the horizon. "Seems like just the other day it was all so full of promise." He looked straight up for a moment, allowing the snowflakes to fall on his crimson cheeks. "Fresh out of the university. Engaged to the girl of my dreams.

Landed a job on a small daily paper in upstate Pennsylvania." He lifted his hands in an exaggerated movement, then let them fall to his sides with a slap. "Look out world, here I come," he intoned with far too little joy.

"What university?"

"Penn State."

"Hell of a good school."

"I had it all worked out in my mind, man. Start out here. Rise in the ranks. Couple more small towns, then on to the major markets. Big time, big city, win the Pulitzer, retire to writing my memoirs on Martha's Vineyard." He snapped his fingers, but they made no sound. "All planned out. One, two, three like birds on a wire."

"What happened?" Corso asked.

Carl made a world-weary face. "What happens to people's lives?" he asked. "They go by. What was it John Lennon said? 'Life is what happens while you're busy making plans.'"

"Something like that."

"Seemed like it was just yesterday I walked into that newsroom for the first time."

"How long has it been?"

Carl thought about it. "Thirteen years," he said after a moment. He heaved a deep sigh. Snow was beginning to collect in his hair.

"What brought you here to begin with."

"My wife . . ." He stopped himself. ". . . my ex-wife Nancy. She came from here. Her parents owned McClendon's Home Store. Her brothers run it now." He nodded toward the newspaper building. A bitterness crept into his voice. "She's Hargrove's niece." He waved a hand in the air. "It's all very inbred around here. Everybody's on the payroll. Everybody knows everybody else's business." He looked north toward the lake. "Funny thing is . . . Nancy and her parents moved away and I'm still stuck here."

"Where'd they move to?"

"Pensacola, Florida." He looked over at Corso who was bent at the waist brushing the snow from his hair. "Couldn't take the weather anymore."

"What's she doing in Pensacola?"

"Going to school." Carl shook his head in disbelief. "Ocean-ography."

"Divorce is rough," Corso said. "Never been through one myself, but I used to work with a guy whose first wife died back when they were still in grad school. Few years later, he got re-married, had a coupla kids. House with a picket fence and all that. Everything under control until he gets served with papers . . . he told me the divorce was way harder to deal with than the death. At least death is final. You may have some issues about what hap-pened, but at least they're not walking around the same sidewalks you are. They're not suing you for the kids. He said there was a sense of closure to death that divorce doesn't have."

"We couldn't have kids," Carl said. "That was a big part of the trouble between Nancy and me. She really wanted kids." He flicked a gaze over at Corso as if daring Corso to disagree. "Turns out, I'm shooting blanks. Only thing lower than my current stock with Hargrove is my sperm count."

Corso wondered if it was true and decided to change the sub-ject. "How come Hargrove took you off the Marino story?" he asked.

Carl stamped his feet on the snow-covered sidewalk. "The whole timing thing with the bomb squad. He told me to leave it alone. When I didn't, he pulled me off the story." His eyes, which up until that moment had expressed mostly sorrow, were now narrowed in anger. "Had me in the doghouse ever since. He'd have fired me if he could, but we've got a professional association . . . you know . . . run by the same organization runs the pressman's union . . . I've got what amounts to tenure . . . firing me would be a problem, so he's just going to keep feeding me garbage work until I either move on or die from boredom."

"What's in it for him? Why's he squashing the story?"

"One hand washing the other. Nobody wants to look bad around here. Nobody wants to look like a bunch of hicks who can't take care of their own business." He looked around, as if making sure he wasn't going to be overheard. "This is a tightfisted little community," Carl said. "Lots of older folks, living on fixed incomes. They're the only ones still here. Younger folk move out as soon as they're able. Come back and visit on the holidays." He looked around again. "You don't want these people getting wind of their public officials failing to provide the kind of services they paid for. That happens, it'll be back like it was in the nineties . . . school bond elections failing . . . sewer levies going down by four-to-one margins. This place damn near shut down."

"So . . . what now?"

"If I could sell the house, I'd get the hell out of here." His words came quicker now, as if they were being recited. "I wanted to make it easy for my . . . for Nancy, so I bought her out of the house. Used my 401(k) money to do it. Now I'm stuck in a dying town with *no* and I mean *no* real estate market whatsoever." His voice rose. "I mean . . . who in hell is going to move to a place like this? Half the town is for sale. People are taking pennies on the dollar just to get out."

Corso shrugged the snow from his shoulders. "You're a young man. Start over."

Carl started a retort but changed his mind. "You'd be the one to know, now wouldn't you."

Corso nodded. "I was just about your age when the whole *New York Times* thing came tumbling down around my ears. I wasn't just out of work; I was a pariah. The scourge of the entire newspaper business. I got turned down for a job writing a weekly newsletter for the meat packers' union. My fiancée packed up and left without so much as a note. I was about to get evicted from my apartment."

"What happened?"

"Some crazy lady who owned a newspaper in Seattle offered me a job. I'd like to say it was the best offer I had at the time, but, truth be told, it was the only offer I had, so I took it, packed up one suitcase of my stuff, trashed the rest, and headed out West."

"And now you're on the cover of *People* magazine."

"I got lucky. We hit a couple of investigative stories right out of the gate."

"I need to get lucky."

"It'll come." Corso said it with more conviction than he felt.

Carl Letzo noticed the disparity.

"I gotta go," he said.

Corso nodded his understanding. "If Hargrove put you back on the story, where would you start?"

"Two places," Carl said without hesitation. "I still want to know what happened in the dispatch office. I want to know where the ten-minute gap came from."

"And?"

"The Marino family. They've never said a word."

7

Corso sat on the edge of the bed and removed his frozen shoes. He carried them across the room and spaced them out along the top of the heater . . . facedown for maximum drying efficiency. This snow kept up and he was going to have to give in and buy himself a pair of those clunky things the locals were clomping around in . . . men in those hideous moon boots, women in those fringed après siege units.

He made a move to drape his coat over the back of the chair but changed his mind and crossed to the closet, pulling out a hanger and wiggling it into his jacket, which he then took into the bathroom and hung on the showerhead, allowing the collected snow and ice to melt and run down the drain rather than onto the carpet.

As he smiled at his own prissy nature, an image passed before his inner eye, sending him back to his days at the *Atlanta Journal-Constitution*. Twenty-three years old, sent out on the road to cover a rock band named NOMAD as they thrashed their way across the South, opening for acts like Ozzy Osbourne, Alice Cooper and Black Sabbath. Although his memory had divested itself of their names, Corso could vividly recall the casual manner in which they'd trashed and torched nearly everything close at hand, especially hotel rooms. Something about hotel rooms brought out the very worst in those lads.

As witness to their trail of destruction, Corso had, for the first time, been forced to come to grips with the middle-class nature of his own values. Prior to the tour, he would have described himself as being as rebellious and taciturn as any other young man his age, which was, after all, precisely why the paper had given him the assignment. His two-week encounter with NOMAD had, however, made it plain to him that, regardless of his somewhat backward upbringing, somewhere in his heart he was pure bourgeoisie.

And it wasn't about niceties or legalities or respect for other people's property. In his neck of the woods, such notions, when they weren't being openly sneered at, were most often simply ignored. No . . . it was about waste. Where Corso came from, waste was the eighth deadly sin. And not for any highfalutin philosophical reason either but sinful simply because resources of any kind had always proven so terribly difficult to acquire and nearly impossible to retain, that people of Corso's ilk considered wasting anything to be the zenith of disrespect and to border on insanity.

To this day, Corso still heard his mother's harumph of disgust every time he paid $150 for a silk shirt. He recalled how he'd

seen her face on the yacht broker's wall on the day he'd purchased
Saltheart. The disapproval in her eyes had punctured his joy like a
needle and had diminished the luster of the moment.

And how, when he'd hit it big with the second book, how
he'd offered to buy her any house in town and how she turned
him down, holding out for years, insisting her house had been
good enough for his father and the rest of the family and was
good enough for her too, until she finally relented, but even
then preferring a modest ranch house out at the end of Per-
kins Lane to the newer, glossier palaces closer to town. What
the hell was it she was gonna have to say to those town people
anyway?

Corso ambled over to the desk and sat down. He sorted
through his notes, sifting for everything he had about the Marino
family. Three brothers, James, Nathan and Paul, and a sister,
Hannah. Parents, Herm and Diane, still alive and all of them
still living right here in town, at least as of a couple of years
before.

While Carl had proved respectful of the family's privacy,
Mary Anne Guidry had been less circumspect. In a futile attempt
to spice up her otherwise puerile columns, Ms. Guidry had included a number of folksy little details, such as the fact that older
brother James was a longtime employee of the Karlin County
Road Department. That sister Hannah, last name now West,
had given birth to a fine baby boy back in December of 2001.
That the boy had been named Henry Lee after his father. Guidry
also related that the parents were among the first residents of the
now-long-established Conger Hills neighborhood. Just the kind
of information any self-respecting investigative reporter could
and would use to find his way to their doorsteps.

Corso pulled the phone book from the desk drawer and

fingered it open to M. Sure enough, Herm and Diane were still at 359 Conger Hills Road. Henry and Hannah West lived on Flowering Tree Lane and the Karlin County Road Department . . .

The bedside phone began to ring. Corso glared at it, demanding it stop. It didn't. Five, six, then seven times. He stood up, bent over the desk and snatched the receiver from its cradle. "Yeah," he said.

"Frank." The voice was intimate, almost jovial.

"Yeah," Corso repeated. "Who's this?"

"Greg."

"Greg who?"

"Greg. You know . . ." He recited Corso's new publisher's name.

"Ah," was all Corso could come up with.

"I just got off the line with Kevin."

He made it sound like the last word was "heaven."

"Yeah."

"He's firm on this, Frank. He believes in this story."

"Then tell him to come out here," Corso said.

"What?"

"I need some help. Tell him to come out here and give me a hand."

A pause ensued. "Er . . . I mean . . . Kevin doesn't . . . he's in the Caymans at a con . . ."

"Yeah . . . those conferences in the Caymans will just wear a body out."

Greg searched for an appropriate response. Corso threw him a bone.

"If you guys are so gung ho about this thing, I'm going to need some help out here."

"What kind of help?"

"Serious investigative reporting help. The kind of help who can watch my back and take care of himself at the same time."

"I thought you always worked alone."

"I've got no cover here. Thanks to that goddamn magazine, everybody in this town knows who I am and what I'm here to do. Everybody in this burg knows everybody else. Everybody knew Nathan Marino. The way I figure it, somebody around here probably does know something they've been keeping to themselves, but one person slogging around in the snow by himself isn't going to turn over the right rock unless he gets real real lucky. Also I need somebody who can watch my back while I'm turning over rocks."

"Why would you need your back watched?"

"I've been meeting some resistance."

"What kind of resistance?"

Corso told him. Starting with the sheriff, the pair of policemen and Hargrove, before segueing into his little wrestling match with the ski-mask brothers. The latter recitation seemed to catch in Greg's throat. He coughed once, then went silent.

"Now . . . if this is dangerous . . ." he hedged.

"All good stories have an element of danger to them," Corso said. "That's what makes people buy the books."

Silence filled the airways again. Finally, the editor said, "If you don't mind my saying, Frank, you seem to have had a complete change of heart in the past twelve hours or so. If I recall correctly, last evening you had no interest in this story whatsoever. Exactly what precipitated this sudden attitude shift?"

Corso mulled it over. "I guess I don't like being told to leave town . . . no matter how professionally it's done. I don't like being denied access to generally available sources of information. And, you know, call me crabby, but getting manhandled and having needles poked at me just seems to bring out the worst in me."

Greg made a noise as if to speak, but Corso cut him off. "Given a little time, I'm betting there are a whole lot of things I could learn to dislike about this place. And, contract or no contract, *a little time* is all I'm prepared to spend in this godforsaken hamlet. So send me out some serious help and we'll see exactly what it is these people are so damn preoccupied with keeping out of sight."

"I know *just* the person," his editor said. ". . . Chris Andriatta . . . freelances for our television news department . . . lives over in Hoboken . . . just got back from an assignment in Afghanistan."

"See now . . . that's exactly the kind of experience I'm looking for."

"I'll put things in motion," Greg assured him.

"*With all dispatch*," Corso added before starting to hang up the phone. He stopped midway and brought the receiver back to his lips. "Hey," he said. "Gary."

"Greg."

"Right. Eh . . . Sorry. So listen."

"Yes."

"For the time being anyway, it's probably best Chris and I not be seen together. Get another car. Book another room in this hotel. I'll be in touch."

"Okay."

"And from here on, if you want to call me, use my cell phone."

8

The snowflakes were smaller now. This morning's flakes had turned to shards of windblown ice, slanting in from what seemed every direction at once. The kind of snow that freezes the end of your nose and squeaks under your feet. The kind of snow that stays long past its welcome, ending its life as black ice, hiding in the shadows of walks and stairs, crouched and waiting for its moment of mayhem to come round at last.

The wind had freshened since morning, and now rolled off the lake in gusts . . . icy spurts licking the piles of freshly fallen snow, sending it skyward again, mixing the new with the old, creating a landscape of suggestion.

The storm had fully mobilized the Karlin County Road Department. By the time Corso pulled to a stop in the parking lot, the last plow was roaring out the gate, engine bellowing, orange lights ablaze, hurrying to join the dozen others Corso had spotted as he'd white-knuckled the last seven miles up State Route 67.

The rented Chevy Suburban had been rock solid on the road. Nearly six thousand pounds of plastic and rubber and steel, it shrugged off the buffeting of the wind and just kept lumbering on through the maelstrom, Corso clinging to the wheel like a tick.

The faint hiss of the falling snow became audible as Corso peeled his stiff fingers from the wheel and used them to shut off the engine. The Karlin County Road Department occupied a one-story brick building sitting at the center of what looked like about ten fenced acres. The yard was nearly empty as Corso popped the door, stepped out into the storm and picked his way over the snowy sidewalk to the front door. At the extreme back of the yard, a front loader was scooping sand into the bed of a dump truck, its shrill electronic beeper sounding every time it was shifted into reverse.

A blast of warm air massaged Corso's face as he stepped into the room. The lights were on, but nobody was home. Half a dozen desks were scattered about the walls, but other than the insistent ringing of a telephone, the only sounds were distant voices . . . two maybe three . . . coming from a brightly lit room running along the back of the building.

Corso weaved his way through the furniture toward the voices. Turned out to be the lunchroom. Redwood picnic tables with attached benches. A couple of coffee stations. A bunch of vending machines. Two guys in short-sleeved shirts and ties. One sitting at a table peeling an orange, the other feeding coins into a Coke machine. Whatever it was they'd been chatting about came to a stop the second Corso entered the room.

James Marino set his orange on the table. He was older than
Corso. Fifty or so, with a fair complexion and bright blue eyes
behind rimless glasses. Corso walked over and sat down opposite
him. He waited as James rolled the orange peel up in a paper
towel and began to tear the fruit into segments.

"My name is . . ." Corso began.

"I know who you are," the man said.

Over by the wall, the Coke machine disgorged a can of pop.
The other guy scooped it up and walked past them on his way out
to the office area, where the phone was still ringing its plaintive
song. James Marino read the question in Corso's eyes.

"It's just somebody wanting to know when we're going to get
their street plowed," he said. "Everything we own is already out
there, so there's no sense making any promises we aren't going to
be able to keep."

"Seems like folks around here would be used to this kind of
thing."

"They are," Marino said. "Except they forget they're the very
same people who voted down the county budget three years in
a row. Then they're the first to complain about the potholes we
can't afford to fix or when the snow removal service isn't as good
as it used to be." He popped an orange segment into his mouth
and eyed Corso while he chewed. "You don't look much like your
pictures in the magazine."

"I'll take that as a compliment."

"I've got nothing to say to you."

"Why's that?"

"Because . . . that's how we've decided to handle it."

"I should think you'd be the first people to want to see whoever did this to your brother brought to justice."

James Marino ate another orange segment, then dabbed at his

lips with another paper towel. "When the family is ready to make a statement, we'll make one."

"And you-all don't wonder how come the police department made your brother sit there in that parking lot until the bomb went off?"

Marino held up a hand. "We wonder about a lot of things, Mr. Corso, but we do it privately. That's the way we handle our business."

"It's been over a year," Corso offered. "How are your parents holding up?"

"You leave my parents out of this."

Marino looked up from his orange. "You'll have to excuse me," he said. "We've got a lot of equipment out in the field to-night."

"What about your brother?"

"Whatever problems Nathan had are over now."

He chewed the last three segments, dabbed at his lips again and got to his feet. Corso stood up with him. "You think it was him, don't you?"

"Pardon me?"

"You think Nathan rigged himself to that bomb. That's why you're keeping mum on the subject, instead of what any other family would be doing . . . instead of demanding justice for your brother."

"How would you know? Have you ever lost a brother?"

"I have."

The answer startled him. "To what?" he asked after a moment.

"To booze. To methamphetamines," Corso said. "I guess . . . in the end to despair." Corso paused, took a deep breath. "Michael hung himself in a jail cell down in Georgia where I come from."

"When was this?" he asked suspiciously.

"Six and a half years ago."

"Folks still talk about it?"

"My mother says they do."

"What do *you* say?"

"I can't say. I haven't been there in a long time."

An accusation hung in the air like smoke.

Somebody had come into the office area and was having a conversation with the other guy. Marino began to ease himself out of the room.

"Then you know what this kind of thing can do to a family."

Corso nodded. "My youngest brother . . . Ronnie . . . I hear he's pretty much determined to take up where Michael left off."

"Then you know why I insist you keep away from my parents." He started to say something else but stopped himself.

"The FBI doesn't think Nathan's guilty," Corso said.

James Marino stopped moving. He turned back to face Corso. "The FBI hasn't said anything one way or the other."

"I know a couple people in the Bureau. I made a few calls. They're still very tight-lipped about the whole thing. All they're willing to say is that the Bureau's satisfied that Nathan Marino did not have the wherewithal to build the explosive device on his own."

"That doesn't make him innocent."

"What it means is that whatever happened to Nathan that day is out of the realm of the obvious. Nathan is the obvious. If the Feds could have made any kind of case on Nathan, they would have. They like the obvious. It's what they're set up to do. They catch the easy bounce, get their picture taken with the locals and ride out of town on a wave of gratitude. The fact that they're still not saying anything . . . the fact that they're offering a hundred-thousand-dollar reward for information leading to the arrest and conviction of the guilty parties tells me they don't have a clue."

"That still doesn't make Nathan innocent."

"As far as I'm concerned it does. I mean . . . what are the alternatives. If he wasn't an innocent victim . . . what? . . . He let somebody talk him into wearing a bomb to rob a bank? Who's gonna agree to something like that?"

James Marino started to move again. "I've got to go," he said, gesturing toward the office area.

Corso got to his feet. "You think it's possible, don't you. You think maybe somebody talked him into taking part in some hare-brained bank robbery scheme."

"I think I've got work to do," James Marino said.

"You must think your brother was pretty goddamn stupid."

The other man spun to face Corso, his face beginning to redden. "What I think of my brother is none of your business. Nathan was . . ." Again he stopped himself. "Nathan was what he was. Nothing's going to change any of that. I can't stop you from poking your nose into it, but I can refuse to be part of adding any more misery to the load my family is already carrying. Now . . . if you'll excuse me." He turned and walked to a desk over in the right-hand corner of the room. Before zipping up his coat and heading for the door, Corso watched him dial the phone and begin to speak into the receiver.

9

The Bullseye Diner had one of those neon signs they don't allow outside of Nevada anymore. As a shimmering silver arrow pierced the center of a red-and-white target, neon sparks flew upward in delight. Then the whole thing blinked like a Keno machine and started over. Repeated itself about every fifteen seconds or so. A real eye-catcher it was.

It was two-thirty. Late for lunch. Early for dinner. Except for a waitress whose name tag proclaimed her to be Ruth and a cook she'd called Myron, the place had been deserted ever since a pair of long-haul truckers had settled up their bills and rolled off into the storm.

Corso used a piece of toast to sop up the last of the egg yolk. He was running over his conversation with James Marino, replaying the moment he'd lost any chance of breaking him open. It had happened in the second when he'd admitted he hadn't been back home for a long time. Something about being that far from one's roots had created a gulf between the two of them, a fissure that even the specter of mutual loss had been unable to span. Corso wondered if James Marino had ever dreamed of leaving. Ever seen himself making conquests on faraway fields or whether his life here in the place of his birth was truly enough for him. As if familiarity, fellowship and a sense of place were sufficient salve for the call to adventure.

It was a phenomenon Corso had puzzled over for years. Seemed like some folks were destined to stay at home while others were just as destined to leave. The notion of his mother living anyplace other than where she'd always lived was laughable. "Why would I want to go someplace else?" she'd want to know. "I got everything I need right here. Why go anywheres else?" Corso, on the other hand, had always been destined to leave. From his earliest memory, he'd always felt like an alien in that place. As if he'd fallen off a wagon and been taken in and raised by the family. The rest of them knew it too. Just from the way he taught himself to talk. Like the people on the TV. Not like anybody they knew.

Frank was going places. Wasn't like he wasn't one of them or anything like that. No . . . he looked too much like Papa before he went off to war for there to be any doubt as to his lineage. It was more like Frank'd been born knowing he was gone and wasn't about to be coming back. Like he was telling you to take a good look while you had the chance because it was going to be a while before you caught sight of him again.

Corso suddenly recalled the summer of his seventeenth year as he'd stood in that dirt bus stop with a cardboard suitcase in one hand and a GI knapsack in the other. He was on his way to college. Going away on a full-ride scholarship he'd won in an essay-writing contest sponsored by the *Atlanta Journal-Constitution*. "What Democracy Means to Me." For all the family knew about going off to college, he might as well have been going off on a lunar expedition.

His mother waited until the bus came into view and threw her arms around him. "You make us proud, Frankie," she said. "This is the beginning of whatever you was born for." He remembered feeling like Clark Kent leaving Smallville. His mother stepped back a pace and fixed him with her hawklike gaze. She'd worn her teeth for the occasion. Her eyes filled with water. "I ain't gonna say good-bye," she said. And she didn't either. His mind's eye watched out the back window of the bus as she'd faded to a faraway dot, then all of it to black.

Deep in thought, Corso had his nose about two inches above the grease in his plate when he heard shoes squeaking his way. He looked up. Ruth had abandoned her newspaper at the other end of the counter and was moving his way with the kind of splay-footed shuffle relegated to those whose lives were spent on concrete floors.

"It finally come to me," she announced. "You're that writer guy. One come to town to clear up that bank robbery deal." She shook her head. "I mean I knew you wasn't from around here the minute you asked me if you could still get breakfast this timea day. Everybody round here knows we do breakfast twenty-four/seven."

Corso smiled and stuck out his hand. She took it. "Frank Corso," he said.

"I'm Ruth Hadley. And you want to know about Nathan Marino . . . well, you maybe ought to start by askin' me."

"You knew Nathan?"

She leaned her elbows on the counter. Gave him a wink. "What if I told you Nathan used to work here?"

Corso went back to sopping up egg yolk. "No kidding," he said.

"Used to bus dishes." She pointed at the pair of polished-steel doors. "Right back there in the kitchen where Myron is. Myron," she called. No answer.

"Afternoon shift. Four till closing," she went on. "Showed up every day like clockwork. Worked hard."

"How long ago was this?"

"Four or five years before he got . . . you know . . ."

"Blown up."

"Yeah," she said. "Guess that makes it darn near six or seven years ago doesn't it?" She threw Corso a lopsided grin. "Time flies when you're havin' fun."

Corso held up a finger. "Let me guess," he said, raising his pitch two octaves. "Nathan was a nice boy. Quiet. Kept to himself."

"Now how'd you know?" Ruth asked right on cue.

"That's what the neighbors always say about serial murderers. After the guy's been captured and the authorities have been digging up the backyard for a week, that's when the TV stations send people out to see what it was like living next to a cannibal. The neighbors always claim he was just the sweetest boy."

Ruth was nodding thoughtfully. "Why do you suppose that is?"

"I think . . . you know . . . no matter how crazy you are . . . if you've got a couple fifty-five-gallon drums filled with body parts hanging around your apartment . . . I think maybe a low profile . . . easy come, easy go kind of attitude might be the order of the day."

The notion made sense to Ruth. "Well . . . Nathan *was* a nice young man."

"I'm sure he was."

"Liked to read his little Western books." She gestured toward the kitchen with her head. "Out back there in the summertime."

"How long was he here?"

"Oh . . . a year or so. Called up one morning . . . said he was taking a job doing something else . . . I don't remember exactly what." She smiled. "That was like him though. Call and tell you he was done. Not just leave you hanging like so many of them." She turned her head and eyed the kitchen area again. "Myron," she bellowed. Still no response.

"He's probably out back smokin' one of those cigarettes of his." Her face softened. "I worry about him. He's got this nasty cough won't go away." She read the question in Corso's eyes. Waved his wonder off.

"Myron's my old man. We bought this place from old man Kilmer back in '78, when it wasn't much more than a shack." She looked around, taking in everything, the stools, the booths, the ceiling; her eyes got as shiny as the stainless-steel walls. "Had in mind leaving it to our girls to take over and run after we was gone, but they got no interest in running a diner . . ." She made a disgusted face. "Whole idea of running a diner is just way beneath their collective dignities, if you know what I mean, so I guess we'll just sell it and head for the sunshine like everybody else."

"Back in the midseventies in Seattle, there was a sign on the interstate asking the last person leaving town to be sure and turn out the lights."

"Getting that way around here too," she said. "Nothing left around here but old-timers like Myron and me. Kids all grow up like ours . . . get out of school and move someplace else first time they get a full tank of gas."

Corso used his hands to lever himself up from the stool. He

pulled his wallet from his hip pocket, extracted his debit card and handed it to Ruth, who straightened up, patted herself down for her order book. He stretched as she squeaked back down toward the register, then followed along. "You got any deep dark secrets about Nathan Marino you want to share with me," Corso asked as he ambled along in her wake.

She shook her head as she spindled the check and jabbed at the cash register.

"There's no secret. He was just a quiet man with his own ideas. Different drummer type. Maybe a couple of ants short of a picnic, if you know what I mean. And if there *was* some deep dark secret, it sure as heck wouldn't be secret anymore. Between the Staties and the Feds and the local yokels, they must have interviewed just about everybody in town. Everybody had their chance for fame and fortune. If there was something there, somebody would have spoken up."

Corso swiped his card, punched in his code and waited for a bank on the far edge of the continent to confirm that he was indeed possessed of $7.16. For some reason or other, he found the process insulting.

"How much longer are you and Myron going to be slingin' hash?" he asked as he signed the receipt.

She checked the room and gave him a conspiratorial wink. "You heard of Burger Barn?" Corso indicated it was news to him. She leaned in closer and lowered her voice. "They're buying us out, lock, stock and barrel. Gonna tear it down and build one of those drive-ins of theirs." He watched her eyes as they morphed from sadness to hope. "We got us a hell of a deal on a place in Fort Myers," she said. She looked around again. "Kinda deal you gotta know somebody who knows somebody else, if you know what I mean."

10

Corso stood still and watched as she thought about slamming the door in his face. He kept a smile welded to his lips and hoped her sense of hospitality would refuse to permit such rude behavior. She looked him up and down, shook her head in disgust. "If you're gonna be tramping about in this kind of weather, mister, you best be getting yourself some decent gear," she said, while still holding the storm door in her hand. She pointed to his shoes. "You keep wearing those little loafers of yours and frostbite's gonna be taking off more than just the tassels."

Corso shifted his weight from foot to foot trying to maintain feeling in the soles of his feet. "Yes, ma'am," he said. In the hour since he'd left the Bullseye Diner, the temperature had dropped another fifteen degrees. The snow was sliding sideways in sheets, except now it was brittle under the feet as a northerly wind began to transform the landscape into a solid block of ice.

She sighed. "I guess you might as well come on in," she said finally. "I don't want anybody finding you dead on my doorstep."

She was pushing seventy, a big thick woman with the air of a survivor. Her hair was dyed a shade of brown unknown in nature. She stepped aside, shepherding Corso through a double-doored vestibule and into the front room of the house. What his mother would have called the parlor. The room was upholstered in worn flower prints and smelled of dust. A gas fire hissed as it licked up among the stone logs in the fireplace. Corso watched Oprah's mouth moving on the TV screen. He rubbed his hands together.

"James called and said you might be coming around. I been expecting you for the past hour or so."

"I ttttried your daughter first." Corso shuddered inside his jacket.

She shook her head. "They're down in Orlando. Got them a time-share down there." She rolled her eyes. "Take the kids for a week twice a year. Just pop 'em out of school and drag 'em down there with 'em." Her disapproval settled over the room like a slipcover. She looked Corso over again. "But I suppose the neighbors told you that, didn't they?"

Corso nodded. "Yes, ma'am," he said.

She held out a hand. "Let me have your coat," she said.

Took Corso a couple tries to get the frozen zipper all the way to the bottom. He shouldered himself out of the coat and followed her over to the fireplace, where she hung his jacket from a brass hook on the mantel.

She pulled a plastic bottle of hand lotion down from the mantel, squirted a dollop into one palm and massaged it in before turning Corso's way again. "So . . . that what you're here for, mister? You here to prove that my boy Nathan got himself mixed up in something got him killed. Sell more books. Make an ever bigger name for yourself."

"Nothing I've seen so far suggests your son was anything but a victim."

She took him in all over again, her eyes running over him like a chill wind. She returned to her seat on the couch and used a freshly lotioned hand to direct him toward the red-and-white love seat on her left.

"It's because he was different, you know."

"What was because he was different?"

"That's how come everybody seems to think he was"—she hesitated—"how come they think he was involved in some way."

"I don't understand."

"He was . . . Nathan was just outside of what they were used to." She looked at Corso, hoping for a glimmer of understanding. When a spark failed to flicker, she went on. "Nathan just wasn't like other kids. With my other children, I mean you look at 'em now and you think back and realize you could see who they was going to turn out to be practically from the very beginning. James was always going to be in charge of something or other. When he was knee-high, he was just like he is now, very serious. Everything had to be in order. Everything in its place." She made a little dividing movement with her hand. "Hannah . . ." She shook her head in wonder. "That girl was always Suzie Homemaker. Played with dolls till she was darn near twelve. Never once heard her say she wanted to be a teacher or a nurse or an actress or anything else for that matter. All that girl ever wanted to be was somebody's wife and mother." She spread her hands in wonder.

"Little Paul used to wear his daddy's boots and helmet around the house whenever Herm wasn't using them himself. Never wanted anything more than to work in the mine like his daddy. But Nathan . . . now that boy was another matter altogether."

"How so?" Corso prompted.

She thought it over. "He never played with the other children. Not even his sister and brothers. Didn't like any of the games kids played. He liked to make up his own games." She checked to see if Corso was listening, then continued. "He had a million of those little toy action figures. He made up his own little world. They all had different names and different voices."

"What did he want to grow up to be?"

"That was just it," she said. "He didn't want to *be* anything. He just wanted to *be*." He face went dark. "What's so bad about that? Is that something so terrible? Do you have to be ambitious to be a good person?"

Corso shrugged. "No matter what kind of lip service gets paid to the idea of self-expression, our society doesn't encourage a person to follow his own path. Our society encourages him to get a job. To strive. To be independent and not be a burden on society. If you can find some way to follow your bliss while working nine to five, well then that's okay. Feel free to have a hobby."

She was shaking her head. "Nathan was never a burden. He always took care of himself. He never came to us for money or anything."

"Then why this notion something was wrong with him?"

She leaned forward now, as if she'd been anticipating that very question. "It started way back when he was in grammar school. He just didn't seem to have any interest in what they were teaching. The school wanted us to have him tested." She scrunched up her face. "Herm was against it. Wouldn't hear about any such thing. Took me darn near two years to get him to come around."

"And?"

"Nathan tested out normal. Not smart, not dumb, just normal."

Corso detected something ironic and nearly mocking in her tone. "How'd your husband feel about that?" he asked.

She wagged a finger Corso's way. "That's the funny part. Here Herm was worried and all that they were gonna say his boy was some kinda . . . and I'm using Herm's word here, not mine . . . some kinda *retard* and when they don't . . . when they find out he's just a regular kid like everybody else, that's when, all of a sudden, far as Herm's concerned Nathan can't do anything right. Not from that day to this."

"Why do you suppose that was?"

"You know, I've thought about that. I think as long as it was possible there was something wrong with Nathan, Herm kinda felt like he didn't want to be picking on anybody with a disability, but the minute those tests come back normal"—she snapped her fingers—"then it was like, okay . . . if there's nothing wrong with this boy, well then he's just lazy, and if there's anything my husband can't and won't abide, it's lazy."

"Was he?"

"Was he what?"

"Was he lazy?"

She frowned. "Not at all. He worked hard all his life. One little job after another, but he was always employed."

Corso stayed silent for a moment. "So how come he never found himself. Never found anything he wanted to pursue?" he asked after a moment.

"He wasn't looking?" she said. "Do you have to be chasing something to be happy?"

"I guess not," Corso said.

"My Nathan was a dreamer," she said. "To him a job was just something you did because you had to. Something to spend time at so's you could spend time at your own things."

"Which were?"

"He liked to read and watch old black-and-white movies. He liked to play with his cats. He was really fond of sitting down by Harris Creek . . . out behind that house he rented . . . just sit there all day dreaming his dreams." She leaned forward. "I don't want to make it sound like he was perfect or anything. He had his scrapes growing up." She caught wind of Corso's next question. "Boy things, growing-up things." Her tone made it obvious the subject was closed.

"Doesn't sound like a bank robber to me," Corso said.

Her eyes misted over. "Of course it doesn't," she said.

"What's his father think now?"

She made a rude noise with her lips. "Herm don't think much at all anymore," she said. "Since this . . . since all of this . . . he spends his days and nights down at Charlie's Bar." She nodded toward the door. "Down at the junction. You passed it on the way up here." The muscles along the side of her lower jaw rippled with tension. "Bunch of his old buddies from the mine hang out there all day and night. You want to know what Herm thinks, you're gonna have to go down there and ask him yourself."

11

From the look of it, Charlie's Bar and Grill had occupied its present location prior to the invention of pavement. The cracked and yellowed ceiling undulated overhead as Corso crossed the floor toward the bar at the back end of the space. He threaded his way among the dozen or so wooden tables and chairs filling the center of the room. On the left, a pair of pool tables, their felt tops worn slick and shiny, had attracted a small crowd of players and onlookers.

The real action was on the right, where an old-fashioned shuffleboard table elicited whoops and hollers every time somebody sent one of those little metal discs sliding along the hardwood toward the far end. The clicks of colliding discs and the dull thud of pieces falling from the table were occasion for a rowdy buzz from players and onlookers.

The tops of the windowless walls were lined with neon beer signs. Storz, Stotz, Schlitz, Pabst Blue Ribbon . . . must have been fifty of them, some of which Corso had never seen before, others he knew to be long defunct.

Corso bellied up to the bar. He watched as the bartender cleaned off one of the tables over by the shuffleboard machine and returned with the dirty plates and glasses balanced in one hand. He moved like he was walking barefoot on broken glass. The guy set the dirty place settings in the sink and turned on the water. His age was tough to gauge. Sixty plus anyway. Thinning hair combed straight back. Wrinkled dress shirt and a little bolo tie.

"Help ya?" he asked without looking up.

"How about a Pabst?"

"Can, bottle or draft?"

"Draft."

The guy dried his hands on a small white towel and picked up a clean glass. The line coughed air and spit foam as he began to fill the glass. He spilled out the foam, waited for beer to appear from the tap and filled the rest of the glass. He found a paper coaster and set the bubbling glass in front of Corso. "Buck fifty," he said. His eyes were red and watery. He had a small mustache, neatly trimmed but yellowed here and there by nicotine. From four feet away, he smelled like an ashtray.

Corso pushed a five-dollar bill onto the bar. "I'm looking for Herm Marino," he said.

The bartender picked up the five and pushed a button on the old-fashioned cash register. Kerching. He flicked his eyes to the right, toward the guy sitting alone down at the far end of the bar. Big bulky guy with hands the size of waffle irons. Last of the flat-top crew cuts, combed straight up. He was staring into a fresh beer like he was afraid it was going to escape and smoking an unfiltered Lucky Strike.

Corso left the change on the bar and sidled over to the end. He slid onto the corner stool and set his beer down. "You Herm Marino?" he asked.

All he got was a short, sideways glance. "My name's Frank Corso. I'm a writer. I'm doing some research on what happened to your son."

Marino took a long moment to process the information.

"Don't waste your time," he said finally. "He's not worth the effort."

"Why's that? He was your son, wasn't he?"

"He was a bum."

"That's not what I hear."

Marino swiveled his stool to the left, taking a sudden interest in the rows of potato chips hanging from a white metal rack. Corso kept talking. "I've been asking around town. I hear he was reliable and considerate and self-supporting. Always had a job. People say he was a nice guy, a hard worker who showed up every day."

Marino did a slow swivel. "What kinda job?" he asked with a sneer. "Some menial . . . backroom . . . cleanup kinda delivery thing?" He dismissed the idea with a wave of his big hand. "Nathan had no more ambition than a stray dog. Had no pride. No drive."

"Not everybody needs to be a doctor or a lawyer."

Herm Marino slid over onto the stool next to Corso. His face was so close Corso could make out the veins in his nose. "I ain't no snob, and don't you make me out to be one neither. All my life I worked with my hands." He held them up for emphasis. They looked more like roots than hands. "Thirty years for the

Thurston Company . . . mine number six, so don't be talkin' to me about no doctors and lawyers." He smelled of cigarettes, stale beer and Aqua Velva. His blue eyes were filigreed with red. The color had begun to rise in his cheeks. "All I wanted was they had some kind of plan for what they were gonna do with their lives. Just pick something and get on with it." He cut the air with the edge of his hand. "Take care of yourself and your family. I never asked nothing more than that."

"And Nathan didn't do any of that?"

"Nathan didn't do a goddamn thing." He spit the indictment out like a pit, then ran a hand through his bristly hair. "I'm always amazed at you press guys. What it is you find so interesting about my no-account son is beyond my imagination. Only interesting thing the kid ever did was die."

His own words seemed to take Marino's breath away. Corso clamped his jaw closed. He felt Marino's words settle onto his shoulders. For a moment he felt the disappointment of every parent whose dreams for their child had been splintered by circumstance. When Corso looked up, Herm Marino had him fixed with a withering stare. Their eyes met and stayed that way.

Half a minute passed before Marino broke the connection. He slid back over onto his original stool, picked up the pack of Lucky Strikes and began to tap it on the bar, as if to pack the contents more tightly. Corso noticed the lamp behind the bar. The fringed shade vibrated a little as the brass hula dancer swiveled her hips in mechanical rapture.

Marino stared straight down. "That sounded pretty harsh, now didn't it?" It was somewhere in between a statement and a question.

"Sounded disappointed," Corso offered.

"Parents got a right to be disappointed sometimes," Marino

said without looking up. "They go the route. They do it all for twenty years. They feed 'em and clothe 'em and take 'em to the doctor when they need it. They got a right to a few expectations."

"What if kids weren't put in this world to live up to anybody's expectations but their own?"

"You sound like my wife," Marino said.

"It happens the other way too."

"What happens?"

"Some kids grow up and become something their people could never have predicted. Something good . . . something famous . . . but something the home folks know so little about, something so far from their personal experiences that this person they once loved might as well be from another planet now."

Another silence. "That what happened to you?" Marino asked.

"Something like that, yeah."

"Your folks . . ."

Corso interrupted the question. "My folks have absolutely no idea what to make of me. The idea that I went to college, that I make my livelihood writing, that I live on a boat in some place called Seattle . . ." Corso shook his head, as if in disbelief. "I mean, they love me and all, but I might as well be Polynesian as far as they're concerned." Marino was about to speak. Corso silenced him with a raised palm. "Only thing they know for sure about me is that I'm not one of them anymore. Some of them aren't sure I ever was."

"I loved Nathan," the other man said out of the blue. It was the kind of statement that inspired silence. Corso gave it its due.

"I love all my children," Herm Marino said.

"How could you not?"

"But loving him's not the same thing as being able to tell people"—he banged a big hand on the bar—"no . . . my kid would never do anything like that. He just wasn't the type. No way he'd do something like that. No sir." He looked over at Corso. "I *never* had any idea where that kid was coming from. He wasn't like any kid I ever met. Didn't even like to be picked up as a child." He hesitated, making sure Corso was listening. "Can you imagine that? He run off if you tried to pick him up. Never seemed to listen to anything you tried to tell him. Just stared off into space making those little noises of his. When people started asking me whether he could be part of a bank robbery, I didn't know what to say."

"What do you think now?"

"I'll tell you the same thing I told those FBI guys. If you're asking me whether or not I think my son was part of a scheme to rob a bank, I got to tell you it's possible." He spread his big hands in resignation. "Not because he could come up with a scheme like that on his own, but because he was just gullible enough to get talked into a half-assed idea like that. Just gullible enough to believe the bomb wasn't real and just gullible enough to believe that whoever was in it with him wouldn't really hurt him." He waved his big hands again. "Every single time that kid ever got into trouble, got himself suspended from school, got brought home by the cops for stealing beer from the Elks Lodge . . . every single time it was because somebody else talked him into doing something stupid." He pointed a crooked finger at Corso. "I think maybe that's why he gave up on people. I think maybe he lost faith in his ability to tell whether people were being truthful or not, so he decided to just not take any chances."

"How isolated is that?" Corso sighed.

"Desert island isolated."

Corso was still ruminating on their assessment of Nathan's life when a movement at his shoulder brought his head around. James Marino wore a tan goose down jacket, so full of feathers it made him look like the Michelin Man. His head was covered by a red wool hat whose earflaps were folded down and tied beneath his chin. "Come on, Pops," he said. "I got Harvey and one of the trucks outside. We'll give you a ride home."

He looked over at Corso as if daring him to object. "What did I tell you?" he demanded.

"Not a hell of a lot, as I recall," Corso said.

"Leave my family alone," he said.

"Just doing my job."

By that time Herm was already on his feet. Corso thanked him for his time as he shuffled by and watched from his stool as James pulled his father's hat and jacket down from the coatrack, helped him with both, then took him by the elbow and propelled him slowly out the front door. "Yeah baby," someone shouted from over by the shuffleboard table. Corso turned back to his beer.

12

C orso sat in the seat revving the engine. He kept his arms folded across his chest and his hands inside his jacket, hoping the warmth of his armpits would bring some feeling back to his fingers. By the time he'd gotten the ice cleared from the windshield and the back window, his hands were numb and very nearly unable to operate the door handle. The defroster roared like a freight train. The wipers thumped back and forth at warp speed, clearing little crescents in the ice and snow as he rocked back and forth in the heated seat trying to keep the blood from freezing in his veins.

He stayed that way for the better part of ten minutes before the shuddering subsided and his hands felt capable of aiming the rental car back to his hotel. The rest of the cars in Charlie's parking lot looked like a string of pearls, opalescent in the purple-hued lights, names and brands now nothing more than interconnected mounds of snow and ice. Corso wondered what their barflies were going to do when they came out at closing time. Or maybe they didn't, he thought. Maybe that was the trick. Eliminate all this freezing-your-ass-off stuff. Maybe they just stayed inside swilling suds, shooting pool and playing shuffleboard until the spring thaw rolled around.

He used the switch to move the transmission from two-wheel high to four-wheel high. He dropped the shift lever into gear and started around in a wide circle. The cold rush of evening had formed a layer of ice on top of the snow; the tires crunched as they plowed furrows in the surface of the parking lot. He followed a double set of tire tracks out onto the highway and turned north toward town.

The highway was deserted. The overhead lights more like dim distant stars than terrestrial navigation aids. The snowplows had removed the bulk of the storm, leaving the sanded road surface slick and shiny with ice. Corso could feel the car scratching for traction as he accelerated. First time the transmission changed gears, the SUV started to go into a full slide. Corso slowed, snapped on the emergency flashers and crept along at twenty-five, keeping an eye on the rearview mirror, making sure nobody was going to total him from behind while he was looking the other way. The car started to go sideways again, caught a patch of sand and righted itself. Corso cursed himself for staying too long at the fair and leaned farther out over the dashboard.

Dim lights coming from the other direction turned out to be a snowplow, its blade angled off to the right, pushing a wave of dirty snow up onto the shoulder. The pulsing yellow light seemed more like a warning than it had earlier in the day.

What on a dry night would have taken ten minutes to drive, took him thirty-five. Half hour in, he started to wonder if he'd turned in the right direction. Wondered whether or not the storm had gotten him turned around. Whether he was driving farther out into the wilds rather than toward town. The thought tightened his neck into a burl and made his mouth go dry. He checked the gas gauge. Almost full. He gave a sigh of relief just as the dull glow of lights appeared in the distance.

He tried to roll his neck, but it was locked tight. He massaged it with one hand as he crawled toward the distant lights. To his left, down at the far end of town, he thought he could make out the red sign on top of his hotel. He squinted and tried to be sure, but the falling snow made the red glow little more than an intermittent smear of color in the sky.

And then the roar started. About five blocks before where he planned to turn. Sounded like an airplane was landing on top of the car. All of a sudden everything was bright white. And then the first impact, the blow from behind breaking the back window, sending the SUV wiggling all over the road. Corso held on to the wheel for all he was worth. He flicked his eyes at the rearview mirror and was temporarily blinded by what must have been enough lights for a football stadium.

The roar of the engine got louder. Corso could hear strips of safety glass falling into the back of the SUV. Cold air swirled around his head. He heard the fan belt squeal and braced himself. Bam . . . another blow from behind. That's when the carnival ride started. Not one of those newfangled super coasters at Six Flags. More like the kind of thing they used to drag to county fairs and such way back when he was a boy. The Whip was the ride he most remembered. Half a dozen brightly painted cars darting this way and that on narrow iron rails, whirling in a tight clover-

leaf pattern the mechanics and geometry of which were designed
to induce screams and occasionally separated vertebrae.

The rental car was spinning out of control, the frozen world
flashing by Corso's eyes like a bad music video. He feathered the
brakes, but his efforts had no effect. Before he could try again,
the terror hit the SUV from the side, crushing the driver's door in
onto Corso's hip, wrenching a scream from his lips, sending the
car pinwheeling sideways down the ice-covered road.

Corso recognized where he was. Another revolution and the
car was going to be pointing right down Main Street . . . toward
the lights . . . toward home . . . Corso dropped the transmission
into low . . . pulled his neck down into his shoulders like a turtle
and waited . . . waited for the SUV to complete another circle as
the lights got brighter and the roaring got louder, before he put
his foot to the floor, sending all four tires spinning back and forth
as the car crabbed forward at an angle, heading for the intersection, slithering back and forth as one wheel or another found a
purchase and propelled him on.

He missed the intersection by six feet. The driver's side wheels
bounced up over the curb, skidding the car sideways across the
meridian, frozen bushes scraped along the sides of the vehicle,
before the SUV suddenly bounced to a shaking, steaming halt
when the other two wheels refused to leave the highway.

Corso clawed at the seat belt, found the button and pushed.
That's when he realized that some part of the crushed door had
pierced his hip; he bellowed in pain and threw himself to the
right, tearing himself free of the jagged metal. He felt something
warm running down the outside of his leg as he dove across the
console toward the passenger seat and the seeming safety of the
far door.

He got about halfway there when the next impact threw him

face forward onto the passenger floor. Upside down, feet banging off the headliner, he felt the rental car leave the ground, teeter on two wheels, and flop over onto its side with a bang and the tinkle of broken glass. And then the car was moving again. Being pushed backward along the icy street.

Scraping along on its side, bits of dirty ice and snow coming in through the broken window, the car was beginning to fill as Corso struggled to right himself, forcing his torso up and over the seat until he could get one hand on the steering wheel and begin to pull himself upright. The screech of tearing metal assaulted his ears. He had one foot on the doorpost and another on the armrest. His face was jammed hard against the driver's side window. He forced his eyes to the right, away from the lights, peering out through the shattered back window in the direction they were moving.

A metal railing, then nothing but water. He could smell the frothy saltiness of the lake. The word "no" rose in his throat as the car sheared through the railing, hung for a moment on nothing more than pretense, then, with a piteous sheet metal groan, began to somersault downward toward the dark water below.

13

The SUV landed wheels down in the water, rocking back and forth, nose to tail and back again; the impact drove Corso's solar plexus into the console, forcing the air from his lungs, causing a glittering galaxy to appear before his eyes as he gasped for air. After two, three, four unsuccessful attempts to inhale, the knot in his chest abated enough to allow him a single great gulp of air. And then another. And a third. Until his vision cleared. Until the sound of rushing water invaded his consciousness, causing him to look around.

The car undulated gently on the waves, allowing a stream of water to pour in the back window whenever it rocked in that direction. For a moment, Corso watched dumbfounded as the rhythmic stream of water got thicker and thicker. As the rear of the vehicle began to sink, Corso came alive, scrambling across the passenger seat to the broken-out window on the far side of the car. The edges of the frame were festooned with bits of broken glass. He forced himself to ignore the pain as he pulled the top half of himself out into the freezing night air. He sat for a moment collecting himself, then got a foot on the window frame and slithered belly down up onto the roof of the SUV.

Almost immediately he began to shudder. The roof was a solid sheet of ice. His teeth began to click like castanets. The car had floated about ten feet out into the lake. The street was about the same distance above. On the right of the breakwater, a flight of snow-covered stairs led to the sidewalk above.

The rear of the car gave a wet belch and began to sink beneath the water. The flopping of the windshield wipers reminded him the engine was still running. For whatever reason, he took solace in the powerful vibration emanating from the engine compartment, as if the engine's idle and the beating of his heart had inexplicably become a single entity.

The headlights pointed nearly straight up, scouring the blackness of the heavens for help as Corso eased himself across the hood. Moving with great care, he first hooked his toes onto the front bumper, then, as the car tilted completely onto its rear end, managed to pull both knees up onto the grille, where he sat sidesaddle shaking uncontrollably.

The engine ticked quietly in the darkness. The partially submerged car seemed to have found some semblance of stability, rolling contentedly in the slushy waves like some giant fishing bobber. Half-in, half-out of the water, moving neither closer nor farther from shore. Corso thought he heard the muted whoop whoop of a siren somewhere in the distance, but before his senses could confirm or deny, a sharp hiss emanated from beneath him. The sound of cold water reaching hot metal.

Corso held his breath and tried to control his shaking as if his actions alone could keep the car afloat. It took everything he had to unknot five of his fingers from the grille in the moments before the hissing got worse, more constant, more insistent this time. Even Corso's addled senses knew the score. Despite the momentary sense of stability, the car was sinking and so was he.

He looked toward shore. His muscles contracted; the flesh tightened on his bones at the sight of the ten or so feet of black water between the bottom step of the stairs and himself. A groan escaped his lips as the hissing became even more intense. The water reached the back end of the motor, sending it shuddering and spitting, enveloping Corso in a pungent cloud of coolant steam. The car began to shake. The engine gave a final death rattle, lurched once and stopped altogether.

A look back over his shoulder confirmed his worst fears. The water was working its way over the windshield. He was maybe three feet above the surface and sinking ever faster. The siren was closer now. He was sure even before the pulsing red lights began to dance all over the snowflakes.

He reached out as if to touch terra firma one last time, then the water was at his hip, scouring a line of frozen agony along the outside of his leg. Numbing the whole side of his body, spurring Corso upward. Standing on the grille now as his shoes filled with icy water, his cramping muscles were unable to straighten his spine. He stood stooped and ancient as he bent his knees and pushed off the car for all he was worth.

Which was about three feet. The icy water took his breath away. The floating snow and ice made it like trying to swim in beef stew. He flailed with all his might, kicking his legs, trying to pull himself forward, toward the stairs and the circling red lights. Beating the water to foam as his clothes became saturated and began to pull him downward into the inky abyss.

A song. One he used to sing with his mother began to play in his ears. For reasons unknown, something about John Brown's body lying moldering in the grave began to pump through his mind. He could hear her thin voice. Feel the warm glow of the old coal stove on his cheeks. He was swinging his arms but couldn't remember why. She got to her feet. Turned off the kerosene lamp and held out her hand to him. He stretched his arm as far as it would go but could not find the comfort of her hand in the frozen darkness. He closed his eyes and went to sleep.

He didn't dream of anything. No long passageways. No bright white lights. No welcoming relatives at the end of the journey. No harps. No wings. No halos. None of that stuff. Just the restful blackness and the calm quietude in the floating moments before he heard the words, "I've got a heartbeat here," and he was born all over again.

"He may be some famous author or something, but that's one tough son of a bitch," he heard a deep voice say.

"Fucker was dead for five minutes." A different male voice.

"He's not out of the woods yet," somebody female admonished. "It's quite likely he's nothing but a vegetable with a heartbeat. And watch your language."

"Brain function is erratic," another voice said. "Vital signs are marginal."

"He's carrying an organ donor card," said the woman. "Healthy young specimen like this could keep a lot of other people alive for a long time."

"Anybody looking for next of kin?"

"Records is working on it."

"Famous guy like this . . . they're gonna want to keep him alive till he grows moss on his north side," one of the men said.

Corso wanted to speak. Wanted to reach out and take somebody's hand. To say, "Hey there. It's me here. Frank Corso. Don't give up on me. I'm right here." He wanted to, but his muscles wouldn't cooperate. He couldn't force so much as a syllable though his lips. Couldn't get his eyelids to twitch. Couldn't wiggle a finger.

"Core temperature is rising," said another woman.

Corso strained in the darkness.

"Let's get him down to ICU," the skeptic said. "We'll find out what next of kin has to say about keeping him alive and go from there."

Corso felt a warm hand on his chest. Right over his heart. Then the cold metal of a stethoscope. "Heartbeat's getting more regular, but it's brain function I'm worried about."

Corso put every fiber of his being into bending his elbow. He felt it move. Incrementally at first. A millimeter at a time. His shoulder muscles twitched from the strain. The hand on his chest began to slide out from beneath whatever he was wrapped up in. Made it all the way up to his throat before Corso caught the wrist in his hand. His arm shook uncontrollably, but his grip was iron.

"I'll be damned," he heard her say.

14

"They said it would be a week . . . at least," Randy Sheilds sputtered.

Corso waved the hotel manager off. "Another day in that place and I'd have been dead," he growled. "There's no way to get any sleep in a hospital." He held out his hand. "I seem to have misplaced my key."

Took Shields two minutes to program another keycard. He limped out from behind the desk, then went back and retrieved a white envelope from one of the little cubicles. "You have a message," he said.

Corso jammed the envelope in his pocket and started for the elevator.

"Let me have one of the bellboys . . ." Sheilds began.

"I'll be okay," Corso said with a great deal more conviction than he felt. Halfway to the elevator, his shoe caught on the carpet, sending him staggering for a couple of steps before he regained his equilibrium. He pushed the button and waited for what seemed like an hour before the elevator car appeared.

In the nearly sixty hours since he'd left the room, nothing much had changed except the weather. The snow had stopped altogether. The storm now nothing more than a dark line of clouds far out over the northern expanse of the lake. He double-locked the door behind him and walked over to the bed. He sat on the edge and ran a hand through his hair before allowing himself to lean back onto the flowered print bedspread for what he envisioned to be a few minutes' rest.

When he opened his eyes again, it was dark outside. Sometime during the intervening hours he'd kicked off his shoes, crawled all the way up onto the bed and wrapped himself in the coverlet.

He pushed himself upright and started for the bathroom. He felt like the tin man. His joints felt rusty. His mouth was so dry his tongue stuck to his teeth. He moved slowly, holding on wherever he could.

He started the shower, closed the lid on the commode and sat down. By the time he managed to get fully undressed, the room was filled with steam. He used both hands to raise his leg high enough to clear the edge of the tub. He held on to the showerhead as he brought the other leg into the tub and pulled the plastic shower curtain closed.

He bent low, allowing the steaming water to cascade down the back of his neck. The heat melted whatever glue was holding him together. He dropped to one knee, then to both, and finally sat in the middle of the tub with his hands locked around his knees, as clouds filled the bathroom and the steaming torrent rained down from above.

He lost track of how long he sat there. All he knew for sure was that it was the longest shower of his life. His hands and feet were pinched and white by the time he dried off and found another set of clothes. He was moving better now, more fluid, less spastic. Still a little tremor in the hands, but otherwise no worse for the wear than a real bad hangover. That's what he was telling himself anyway.

He was cleaning up his own mess. Some people would have just left it for the maid, but Corso couldn't do that. He knew from experience that the little twinge of guilt he felt every time he thought about acting on whim . . . he knew how it made him feel . . . knew that little twist in his gut, knew it was a signal to be reckoned with. He was stuffing clothes into the plastic bag intended for the hotel's valet service, when he noticed the white envelope protruding from the pocket of his jacket.

He pulled the package from its hiding place and looked it over. Purple ink on hotel stationery. His name printed on the front in angular letters. He turned the envelope in his hands a couple of times and thumbed it open.

A phone number. Two one three area code. He knew it well. L.A. Took him a full minute of going through his clothes and looking around the room to realize his cell phone hadn't survived the swim. He cursed under his breath and picked up the hotel phone from the bedside table. Dialed nine to get out, then dialed the number.

"Yeah," a voice said.

"You leave me a message?"

"You Frank Corso?"

The voice was husky but definitely a woman.

"Where are you?" he said.

"Right where you told me to be."

Corso thought it over. "I'm in 1273," he said finally.

"Five minutes," and the connection broke.

Wasn't that long. More like three when a single knock sounded on the door.

Corso was careful this time. Peering out through the little spy-hole in the door. Pushing his face over to the side so he could see up the hall in both directions. Satisfied it was a she, and she was alone, he unfastened both security devices and opened the door.

Somewhere around forty. Five-foot-six or -seven. Didn't take much imagination to see the girl in her, but the lines around her eyes told a different tale. Gave the impression there wasn't much she hadn't seen. Hard to tell whether her short brown hair had been streaked by the sun or by a beautician. She wore jeans and a simple blue shirt. Wasn't much in the way of fashion, but it looked good on her. She clutched a pile of books and papers to her chest.

Corso stepped aside and allowed her to enter the room. When he'd finished double-locking the door, he turned around. She was a pace away, holding out her hand.

"Chris Andriatta," she said.

Corso took her hand and introduced himself. Her hand was callused and dry. Her grip was firm. "Hospital said they were keeping you for a few more days," she said.

"I had other plans," Corso replied.

She looked him up and down. Shrugged. "Except for the ear, you don't look much worse for the wear."

"I absorb punishment well."

Her laugh was deep and rich. "I wouldn't make it a hobby if I were you."

"God knows I'm trying not to. Believe me. You got a cell phone I can use?"

"I thought I was the only Luddite left without a cell phone."

"I took mine for a swim." He nodded toward the phone on the bedside table. "That one makes me nervous," he said.

She looked around the room, then headed over to the desk, where she dumped the armload of books and papers she was carrying. She pulled out the padded chair and sat down. "I thought you were going to be out of commission for a while, so I started doing a little preliminary work," she said.

"Like?"

She rummaged through the pile. Came out with what looked like a high school yearbook. "The Wilson High School Vikings," she said. "Nineteen eighty-seven."

A paper clip marked the spot. She flipped back the cover and pointed at the first picture in the third row. Nathan Marino. Kinda looked like his father. All slopes and angles, the face looked like it had been assembled from spare parts.

"Where'd you get the book?" Corso asked.

"From the high school."

"They just gave it to you?" he asked incredulously.

"Speak softly and carry a big purse."

Corso sorted through the pile of papers. "You didn't let any grass grow under your feet now, did you?"

She shrugged. "I was here. New York's paying me. It's not like there's anything else to do around here."

Corso nodded his approval. "Anything interesting?"

"What's interesting is what's not there."

"Like?"

"Like everything. He didn't join anything. Didn't do anything. He was like a shadow or something. One of those kids who just never found his slot."

"A wall hugger."

"I called just about everybody in his high school class." She waved a dismissive hand. "Everybody remembered him of course . . . you get blown to pieces by a bomb and folks tend to recall . . . but you know, when you got past the bomb and the stuff that was in the newspapers, he was just as big a mystery to them as he was to me." The hand again. "Same old, same old. Quiet guy, kept to himself. Yadda yadda."

She thumbed to another paper clip, nearer to the back of the book. Nathan in a Madras tuxedo jacket. A thin young woman with a wan smile was attached to his arm.

"As far as anybody knows, this is the closest Nathan Marino ever came to an actual date. Her name is Nancy Weldon. She lives alone and teaches eighth grade at one of the local elementary schools."

"She any help?"

She shook her head. "It was a parent thing. Nancy was a wallflower. Nathan was a nerd. The parents put it together. The prom was the only time they were ever in each other's company."

"That's it?"

"She said he was . . ." She used her fingers to make quotation marks in the air. "She said he was 'nice.'"

Corso rolled his eyes. "What else have you got?"

"Everything." She rummaged through the pile of documents. "Birth certificate. Graduation announcement. Twentieth reunion picture . . ."

Corso picked up the photograph. Maybe seventy or eighty people squinting into the lens. Corso was still trying to find Nathan Marino's face when a loud knock sounded on the door. "You expecting anyone," he asked.

"Not me."

Corso moved gingerly toward the doorway, checking the locks

again before bending over and putting his eye to the peephole. He straightened up and looked over at Chris Andriatta. Something in his expression tightened her jaw muscles.

"What?" she said.

Corso snapped the bolt and pulled back the security lock. The door opened on its own. Half a dozen men in suits and topcoats came rolling into the room. The one in front held up an ID case replete with gold shield. "FBI," he said.

The other guys fanned out over the room like ants at a picnic. Scooping the pile of papers from the desk. Collecting Corso's toilet articles from the bathroom. Throwing everything into his suitcase and snapping it closed.

A pair of burly field agents took Corso by his elbows and began to move him toward the door. He tried to dig in his heels but didn't have the strength.

Corso jerked his arms from the agents' grasp and braced himself in the doorway.

"What kind of bullshit is . . ." he began.

"The kind where you're coming with us," gold shield interrupted. "You are being held as a material witness to a federal felony investigation."

By that time, the agents had reannexed Corso's elbows and skidded him out of the room. "What about her?" one of the others wanted to know.

"Bring her along," the lead guy said.

15

In flight, the little jet was nearly silent. Only the occasional buffeting of the wind reminded Corso they were above the clouds. Across the aisle, Chris Andriatta had kicked off her shoes and spread herself out over both seats.

She'd been asleep for an hour, when one of the field agents emerged from the front cabin with a pair of sandwiches in plastic wrap and two Diet Cokes.

"Ham or turkey?" he asked Corso.

"Turkey," Andriatta suddenly answered from across the aisle. She sat up and held out her hand. The agent dropped the sandwich and the can of pop onto the seat next to her and turned and handed Corso the remainders.

"You know," Corso said, "this G-man thing doesn't work out . . . you might consider a career in food service."

The guy kept his face rock hard like Rushmore. "I'll keep that in mind," he said before turning and heading back up the aisle.

"You still busting their chops I see?"

"Helps pass the time," Corso said.

Corso picked at the plastic wrap and watched in awe as she consumed the sandwich in four mouth-stretching bites before downing the Coke in a single pull. By the time she'd crushed the can down to the size of a hockey puck and wiped her mouth with her sleeve, Corso's face had broken into a full-blown grin.

"A woman of her appetites," he commented.

She laughed and wagged a finger at him. "Don't get your hopes up," she said. "I've spent the past five months in Afghanistan. In that part of the world, you eat when you can, where you can and as fast as you can." She muffled a belch with the back of her hand. "It's a hard habit to break."

She slid over to the window and pulled up the plastic shade.

"What are we over?" Corso asked between bites.

"Desert," she said. "Lots of desert."

Corso sat back in the seat and ate his sandwich while she peered out the window. The sandwich tasted more like cardboard than food. He rolled the plastic wrap into a ball, started to slip it into the handy pocket and then changed his mind and threw it on the floor instead. He took a couple polite pulls on the Coke and asked, "When was the last time you spoke to New York?"

"Day before yesterday."

"What'd they say about my being in the hospital?"

"I didn't tell them."

He stopped chewing. "Really?"

Something in his tone got her attention. She turned back his way. "I decided not to say anything . . . you know . . . what with the DUI aspect and all . . . .

Corso held up a hand. "Whoa . . . whoa . . ." he said. "What DUI aspect is that?"

She searched his face for duplicity. Didn't find any. "I mean . . . they didn't come right out and say it or anything. Just said you'd been drinking in some bar before the accident and . . ."

"Accident? Who said it was an accident?"

"Everybody. The local news. The local paper. Said you'd been drinking and you know . . . lost control of the car and skidded into the lake."

Corso's laugh was devoid of humor. "I'll be damned," he said. "If somebody threw me out of a speeding car in that town, they'd charge me with littering."

She stopped picking her teeth with her finger. "You're saying it wasn't an accident?"

He told her the story. Everything he could recall. "That's all I remember," he finished. "I'm told a woman in the hotel across the street called 911 and that a coupla firemen in survival suits pulled me out of the lake, but all that's strictly hearsay. I don't remember anything after I started swimming toward shore."

She mulled it over. "I tell you one thing," she said. "I'm certainly glad there was another side to the story. 'Cause I'm telling you . . . the idea of flying out to some frozen wasteland only to find out my contact's managed to drunk drive himself into a lake . . . I'm telling you I had thoughts about doing a one-eighty and heading right back the other way."

"Wouldn't have blamed you a bit."

She slid over into the aisle seat. "As long as we're in the vicinity of the subject . . ." she began.

"What subject was that?"

"The subject of us working together."

"Okay."

"As a journalist . . ." She made an amused face. "As a journalist anyway, I've got a spotless reputation. I'm known for my 'no bullshit' reporting. People in the business believe what I tell them. They know I'm not going to make them look bad and they pay me accordingly. I like it that way and don't want to be involved in anything that detracts from my credibility. Is that clear?"

"Perfectly," Corso said.

"I mean . . . if you don't mind me saying, Mr. Corso . . . your profile is all over the place. You're the recluse who's on the cover of *People* this week. With you it's either spectacular success or spectacular failure. No middle ground. And to make matters worse, you tend to do both in the full glare of the public eye."

"Not by choice."

"Well then . . . you'll understand what I'm saying."

"Which is?"

"Which is that . . . whatever the hell is going on here . . . I want to stay in the background. It's best for me if people don't recognize my face. Anonymity works for me. I'm not looking to change that."

"I'll do the best I can."

She looked him over again. "And you don't have any idea why we've been picked up and spirited off by the FBI?"

"None. The only thing I'm working on is Nathan Marino."

"You're leveling with me?"

"I'm sorry I got you into this."

It was her turn to laugh. "Hey . . . listen . . . I've been questioned by the Taliban. By the Cuban secret police. By the Russians . . ." She gestured toward the front of the plane. "These guys are Boy Scouts. I just want to make sure I'm not getting myself into anything I can't get out of."

Corso met her gaze. "Swear to God . . ." He held his fingers in the Boy Scout salute. "I've got no idea what's going on here or where we're headed."

"West," she said.

16

The overhead speaker hissed. Corso pushed himself upright in the chair and rubbed his eyes. After spending most of the night in flight, he barely remembered the airport or the half hour ride to the federal building in downtown Los Angeles. He threw his arms straight up, as if signaling a touchdown, stretched his legs and groaned. On his left, Chris Andriatta shifted in the seat without either raising her head or opening her eyes.

An amplified voice crackled from the ceiling. "For reasons that will become apparent, we're going to brief you on these incidents in the reverse order in which they occurred." A click and a pause. Andriatta sat up and looked around. The electronic voice came again. "The second call was an automated distress signal from a Washington Mutual branch in northeast San Bernardino. Came at 9:03, just as the bank opened." The lights dimmed.

Somewhere in the back of the room somebody flipped a switch, sending the big flat-panel TV sputtering to life. Grainy black-and-white. Time and date in the upper left-hand corner: 05:06:05; 8:59 A.M. Bank exterior. Hispanic guy about thirty using the cash machine. Looks like he's making a deposit. A woman walks behind him and looks up at the camera. The picture freezes, then zooms in. "This is the first picture we have of her," the amplified voice said. "We've enhanced the face, but the age of the tape and the quality of the equipment severely limit the degree of resolution."

The face could be anyone female with teeth and a full head of black hair. "Her name is Constance Valparaiso. She's an RN for a hospital in Pomona. Been there nine years. Competent and reliable. Nothing at all to suggest she's anything but a victim." Pause. "According to both Ms. Valparaiso and her husband, she left for the hospital at 7:15 A.M. That time of the morning, it's about half an hour to work. She's not expected until eight but likes to get in a little early. People she works with confirm."

"This was Wednesday, the sixth?" somebody asked from the darkness.

"Yes," the voice confirmed.

The view on the screen changed. Color film this time. Suburban setting. Little yellow house with flowers out front. "She drives an '89 Toyota Corolla. Parks it out front of the house in the street."

"Why not the garage?" somebody asked.

"Hubby's got a brand-new Ford Ranger pickup."

"Figures," a female voice said. A couple of people laugh.

"Perp is waiting in the car. Puts a gun to her head, tapes up her hands and face and stuffs her down on the floor of the car."

"She get a look?"

"Male in a Spider-Man mask. White, she thinks."

"Why white?"

"The voice."

Somebody makes a rude noise.

"Around 10:00 A.M. hospital calls her house. They figure she's sick and hasn't remembered to call in. When they don't get an answer, they check her contact info and call the hubby. Who calls the San Bernardino PD. Everybody agrees it's not like her at all. SBPD takes it seriously. Puts Ms. Valparaiso and her car on the want list."

"But . . ." somebody prompts.

"But we don't see her again until . . ."

"Twenty-five hours later."

"Give or take."

"She have any idea where they took her?"

"At least an hour away."

"Who says they don't drive around in circles?" somebody asks.

"She says she thinks the traffic got lighter as they drove."

"Could be anywhere. An hour from San Bernardino could put you in Yucca Valley or up at Big Bear Lake."

"Who's debriefing her?"

"SBPD."

A buzz of conversation swept across the room. "Needless to say, she's quite upset. They're taking it easy with her. The Bureau's got a shrink from Quantico on hand. They're hoping she might come up with something once she calms down." A hum from the crowd had its doubts.

The viewpoint changed. Black-and-white again. Bank interior now. Same female, third in line. She's nervous, looking around and moving her weight from one foot to another like she needs to pee. She's got a canvas shopping bag in each hand.

The conference room was full. At least a dozen cops. Several kinds of G-men. A couple ATF ops and a handful of strong silent types whose affiliation was anybody's guess. Corso and Andriatta are up at the head of the table, sitting close to the screen.

"If you check the folders on the table in front of you, you'll find a copy of the note she handed the teller."

A rush of ruffled papers filled the air. The voice begins, "Please . . . I've been kidnapped. I'm wearing a bomb." Corso looked up just in time to see Constance Valparaiso push the canvas bags through the slot. With her hands now free, she pulls open the white sweater to reveal some sort of apparatus . . . a one-foot-square metal box hanging down over her chest. The film stops. The voice continues. "Please do exactly what the note says or they will blow me up."

Even with the poor film quality, it's obvious she's crying. Her eye shadow is running down her cheeks like an oil slick. The voice reads the rest of the note. "Large bills. No cops. No tracking devices. No helicopters. They will know if she's being followed. They will kill her if all instructions are not followed. Do as you're told and she'll be returned safely."

The tape moves for another minute as the teller begins stuffing the bag. Guy in a good suit and a bad tie arrives. Reads the note. Says something to the Valparaiso woman, who again pulls open her sweater to reveal the bomb resting on her chest. This time, more of the device is visible. It hangs from her neck by what appears to be an oversized handcuff.

"Well, I'll be damned," Corso said, leaning forward. Andriatta put a questioning hand on his arm. "Just like the one Marino was wearing," Corso whispered.

The guy in the suit moves the other customers way down the other end of the bank. Once everyone's settled, he ducks into the vault. Three minutes later, he reappears, both bags stuffed to bursting with bills.

The narration continued. "Bank manager's a guy named Mauro Bonillo. An Argentinean. He'd seen Monday's bulletin, so he knew what to do. Does a nice job of keeping things under control."

The videotape started up again. Constance Valparaiso heading for the door; she can barely walk straight from the weight of the bags.

"How much did they get?" someone asks from the darkness.

"Two hundred sixty-three thousand and change."

Somebody whistled. "What's money weigh?" somebody else asked.

"Four hundred ninety bills to a pound," the guy behind Andriatta answered. "A million dollars would weigh more than a ton if you used all one-dollar bills. Use hundreds and it's just over twenty pounds." Another buzz from the audience.

Valparaiso's outside now. Half a dozen San Bernardino police cruisers are spread out in a semicircle around the parking lot, but nobody makes a move to stop her as she exits the bank, wobbles over to her car and drives off. The videotape backs up to where she turns to leave the bank. The focus zooms in to the back of her head. A laser pointer highlights the area behind her right ear, where a pigtail of wire is clearly visible.

"Ms. Valparaiso was wired for sound," the narrator says. "We think it's at least possible she was wired for pictures also."

"That means the perp was somewhere close by."

"Maybe," says the narrator.

The image of the back of Ms. Valparaiso's head remains on

the screen. The voice-over resumes. "The victim followed directions. North on the 215 freeway all the way up to Victorville,
then back south on State Route 247 for forty-six miles to the
town of Landers, at which point she was instructed to turn onto
County Road 316. Six miles up, the voice in her ear tells her to
stop the car and get out. She does as she's told." The picture
on the screen changes back to the second time Valparaiso pulled
her sweater back to reveal the bomb. Zoom in. The laser pointer
indicates a small keypad on the front of the black box. Zero
through nine. "She says the voice in her ear gave her a number
sequence. Told her if she wanted to live to push the buttons in a
specific order. She doesn't remember how many numbers or what
the sequence was."

The level of side talk in the room was beginning to rise.
"We're almost there," the amplified voice admonished. "The
voice in her ear tells her to take the device off, earpiece and all,
and put it on the roof of the car and to start walking back the
way she came. Takes her an hour and a half to walk back to State
Route 247. She flags down a truck. The rest is history." The buzz
rises to a dull roar.

"Questions," the voice asks.

"The car?"

"Right where she left it. No money. No bomb."

"Prints?"

"Hers, her husband's and a set we're still processing. Whoever
they belong to is not in IAFIS. The Bureau's working on it."

"Gonna end up belonging to somebody they know."

"In all probability," the voice agreed.

"Anybody with a grudge against this woman?"

"Not that we know of."

"Any political affiliations?"

"They're Democrats."

"That explains the bomb," somebody quipped.

A ripple of laughter crossed the darkened room.

"Do we even know for sure that the device was real?"

A pause ensued. "That brings us to the prior incident," said the voice.

17

C risp black-and-white images. Split screen. Another bank. Much smaller than the first. One view from high above the teller stations. One from a wide-angle camera mounted above the front door. Both cameras agree it's 8:58 A.M. on March 5 and that the bank is empty. The voice returns to the overhead speakers. "This incident is considerably shorter than the other, so I'm going to let it run. We can go back over it later." A hum of acquiescence rolled around the table. "What you're seeing, ladies and gentlemen, is the Republic of Vietnam Bank. It's located in a strip mall catering to recent immigrants on the corner of First Avenue and Foothill Boulevard in La Crescenta." A young Asian man appears at the teller station closest to the door. White shirt, striped tie, no jacket. He's carrying a cash drawer.

"The teller's name is Don Keodalah. He's thirty-one years old, has a wife and three kids. He lives four blocks away and walks to work regardless of the weather." Another man appears on the screen. Dark suit and tie. Trim nearly to the point of emaciation. Thinning hair combed straight back.

"The bank manager's name is Andrew Nguyen. Sixty-eight. Single. Lives with his younger sister in Glendale." Nguyen says something to the teller, gets an answer, then hustles over to the front door, which he proceeds to unlock.

"We know what he said?" somebody asked.

"He asked the teller if he was ready."

Nguyen walks to the far end of the counter, opens a little gate and lets himself in. He's still got his back to the door when the customer comes in. Southeast Asian. Maybe forty, running to fat. Thick horn-rimmed glasses. Wearing dark slacks and a wind-breaker. He looks around furtively, then walks over to the window, pushes a piece of paper through the slot. From the higher camera, you can see Keodalah's scalp twitch as he reads the note. He reaches out with the toe of his left foot. A blinking icon appears in the upper left-hand corner of the screen.

"Silent alarm."

"We got a make on the vic?"

"Not as of this morning."

Nguyen appears at the teller's shoulder. The younger man hands over the note. Looks like Nguyen reads it more than once and starts yelling, rapid fire, mouth moving like a machine gun. He crumples the note and throws it back through the slot.

The customer looks like he's in agony. He unzips his wind-breaker. Pulls the nylon wide apart, revealing the same type explosive device as Valparaiso wore the day before now locked around his neck.

Nguyen's yelling at the customer, waving his arm like crazy. Looks like the customer's yelling back, but the camera angles don't show his mouth.

"We have a translation?" the same voice asked.

"The Bureau says he's telling the vic to get the hell out."

"Not much gets by the Bureau," somebody comments. Laughter ripples around the room, then catches like a hook in their collective throat as the bomb goes off. Big puff of smoke, then Bam! Both cameras oscillate violently. Something gooey smears itself over the overhead lens in the second before the right-hand side of the screen goes black. The camera over the door keeps running. When the cloud of airborne debris clears, most of the counter is gone. So is most of the guy wearing the bomb. Amid the rubble a leg moves. Everyone around the table holds his breath and leans forward, hoping for a miracle, but as the point of view zooms in, it become apparent that the leg is just that . . . a leg . . . and that the movement is nothing more than the last spasm of a vaporized nervous system.

"Jesus," somebody whispered.

"Three fatalities," the voice-over intoned.

The tape rewinds to where Nguyen pushes the note back through the teller slot, then starts again . . . superslow motion this time. They watch in horror as the victim's mouth trembles as he tries to speak. Whoever's running the machine stops the action in the frame before the bomb detonates. The victim has his hands up at shoulder level . . . like he's pushing against something . . . when the first puff of smoke appears from the black box on his chest. After that, even the miracle of videotape can't slow things down much. In a heartbeat, the frame is filled with smoke, mercifully obscuring the horrific moment when the victims are torn asunder by the force of the blast. The tape runs back to the close-up of the twitching leg and the screen goes blank.

The disembodied voice from the ceiling started again. "A pair of county units were the first responders. Thinking it was maybe a gas leak, they cordoned off the whole shopping center, which has allowed us the past couple of days to carry out our investigation with little or no interference. Yesterday's incident, however, makes it impossible to keep the situation under wraps any longer. The media isn't buying the gas leak story. The locals are fielding a couple dozen Freedom of Information requests. They've got a press conference scheduled for eight this morning. Questions?"

"The lab make the explosive?"

"Military grade C-4. Could be part of the material stolen from Twenty-Nine Palms."

"We know how the vic got to the bank?" the guy behind Corso asked.

"The locals came up with an unclaimed Nissan Pathfinder in the parking lot. It's registered to a Mrs. . . . ." He struggled with the Vietnamese name. "As of this a.m. they've been unable to contact Mrs. . . . ."

He butchered the name again. "If Mr. Morales of the FBI is still with us, perhaps he could share the Bureau's actions to this point."

A light-skinned Hispanic rose from the back row. He wore a well-cut tropical suit and a two-hundred-dollar haircut. He was handsome to a fault. He surveyed the crowd as if he owned it.

"At this point, the Bureau is concentrating on known terrorist groups. This morning, we questioned seventy or so suspects." He anticipated the obvious question. "We're not limiting ourselves to foreign terrorists. We're including everyone from Nazi skinheads to right-wing antigovernment types. We believe this line of inquiry is the one most likely to bear fruit."

"Anybody taking credit for it?" somebody asked from the audience.

Morales cleared his throat. "The San Bernardino office received a call last night. The caller claimed the bombings were retribution for the capture of Eric Rudolph. They say the bombings will continue until he is released."

Another buzz ran through the crowd. The questions and answers continued for the better part of twenty minutes before the lights were flipped back on. The buzz reached a crescendo, then, in ones and twos and fours, the conference room emptied, until only Corso, Andriatta and a knot of people at the back of the room remained.

Wasn't until the room cleared that Corso caught his first glimpse of the guy in the wheelchair. One eye, one hand and one foot missing. Right side of his face looked like a pepperoni pizza. Corso watched as the guy used his remaining hand to operate the joystick on the chair. The soft whir of electronics floated above the muffled conversations coming from the back of the room.

The horror in the wheelchair had made a quick right turn and huddled up with Special Agent Morales and the rest of the FBI contingent. The other suit took his time getting to the front of the room. He leaned his backside against the table and folded his arms.

"Which brings us to the two of you," he said.

18

He gave Andriatta a polite nod and fixed his tinted lenses on Corso. He was pushing sixty. Nearly as tall as Corso, but with a little more bulk. He pinched the sharp creases in his trousers as he settled himself into the chair. He tilted the chair up onto two legs and laced his fingers behind his head with an air of cordial informality.

"I don't guess I have to tell you why you're here," he said with a distinct Southern drawl. Like they were just a pair of good ol' boys on the porch.

"I'm guessing Nathan Marino."

Another nod and a boyish scratch of the head. He smiled. "Must be why you're getting the big bucks, Mr. Corso."

Corso found it difficult to maintain eye contact with the guy.

A quick flick told him Andriatta was having the same problem
The approach of the ghastly apparition in the wheelchair was sufficiently compelling as to hijack even the best intentioned gaze.

He picked up on their dilemma. "My name is David Warren.
I'm the assistant deputy director for the ATF for this region."
He gestured toward the approaching wheelchair with a well-
manicured hand. "This gentleman is Mr. Paul Short."

"Hoping not to get any shorter," the guy said from the wheelchair.

The quip broke the tension. Everybody chuckled. Warren
went on. "Mr. Short consults, on the matter of bombs, with Al-
cohol Tobacco and Firearms as well as the FBI and probably a
number of agencies with whose association he would be loath to
admit."

Paul Short held up the arm without a hand. The cuff of his
suit jacket had been folded once and pinned to the sleeve. "First-
hand experience," he said.

This time the laughs were paper thin, the smiles insincere.
Short caught the drift and motored away, over to a knot of ATF
personnel on the far side of the room. Warren followed him with
his eyes, then turned to Corso and Andriatta. "Don't be fooled
by the bad jokes. That there, folks, is a genuine American hero
of the first order."

"Really?" Andriatta said.

"The government found itself short of ordnance experts during the first Gulf War. Had personnel getting blown up left and
right. Put out a request to all government agencies for help." He
cocked his head Short's way. "Short was running the lab at Quantico. He'd already completed two full tours of duty. Won damn
near everything. Silver Star, Purple Heart, the whole shootin'
match." He let the words sink in. "But he volunteered anyway.

Said his country needed him. Took a leave from the Bureau and shipped out."

An unplanned moment of silence surrounded them until Warren regained his composure. "The ATF is charged with investigating all aspects of the bombs themselves. The FBI is working on the matter of the bank robberies. We believe these two separate lines of investigation are likely to bear the most fruit."

"I'll be glad to be help in any way I can," said Corso. "Ms. Andriatta here is just the hired help. Why don't you let her go on her way, so we can get started at whatever you've got in mind."

Warren was shaking his head before Corso finished talking. "Ms. Andriatta poked her nose into a number of sensitive areas and contacted a far greater number of people than you did, Mr. Corso. I'm afraid . . . despite your noble gesture . . . I'm afraid that, for the present, at least, we're going to require her assistance."

Corso got to his feet. Warren followed suit. A couple of the G-men in the back of the room started forward. When Corso merely stretched and rolled his neck, Warren held up a hand. The suits retreated.

Corso touched the screen. "Look . . ." he began. "I'll admit the bombs in the pictures looked a lot like the one Nathan Marino was wearing, but . . ."

"Made by the same hands," Warren said.

Corso collected his lower jaw. "You're sure?"

"Quantico says it's a match. Short agrees. One's a more sophisticated version of the other, but they say the signature is identical."

"That doesn't make any sense."

"No, it doesn't."

"How can that be?" Andriatta wanted to know.

"That's the sixty-four-thousand-dollar question, now isn't it?" said Warren. "How can crimes separated by over a year and twenty-five hundred miles be the work of the same person." The question settled over them like a pall.

"Excuse me for a second," Warren said. He turned and walked to the back of the room. Corso looked over at Chris Andriatta. She shrugged . . . as if to say she was at a loss for words. The whir of electronics picked up the slack in the conversation as Paul Short used the joystick to urge his wheelchair back in their direction. Freed of narrow confines, the chair was remarkably agile. Short rolled along the front of the screen, then spun the chair in a circle so that his good side was facing the others.

From his good side the wheelchair was neo space age. The joystick was surrounded by half a dozen color-coded buttons. An aerodynamic stainless-steel storage compartment covered the top half of the wheel.

Corso wondered if, in similar circumstances, he'd do that. If he'd always try to keep the undamaged side of his face pointing at strangers, or whether, after a time he'd cease to care, or maybe even come to find the discomfort of others amusing.

"That's some wheelchair you've got there," Corso said.

Short gave him a crooked smile. "That's kind of like praising a guy's wooden leg, isn't it?"

Corso laughed. "Yeah . . . I guess it is."

"It's an iBot," Short offered. "Guy namea Schenet invented it about five years ago. Stair climbing, four-wheel drive, telescoping seat, gyroscopes that can sense my center of gravity and make adjustments accordingly."

"Government issue?"

"Hell no," Short spit. "You must be thinking of some other government, or maybe back to the thrilling days of the GI Bill and all that shit. Those days are long over, man. Post-Reagan, the only kind of chair our government will provide you is one of those nifty collapsible models." He patted the arm of the chair. "Between this thing and my van, I had to sell everything I owned just so's I could be equipped to get around. It was either that or line up for breakfast with the droolers and the goners in some veterans' hospital."

Warren returned. He clapped a friendly hand on Corso's shoulder, took a look in Corso's eyes and removed it. He swallowed the smile. "Unless and until somebody shows me different, I'm going to have to assume something one of you did touched this thing off." He held up a restraining hand. "I'm not saying it was necessarily your fault or anything. Or that you had any idea what you were doing. But you gotta look at it from my end . . . we've got this Marino case sitting around for over a year. Nothing going on. All of a sudden Frank Corso's on the cover of *People* magazine saying how he's going to clear the matter up and . . . bingo . . . we start getting similar crimes all the way on the other side of the country." He spread his hands and tilted his head. "Coincidence?"

"You'd have a real hard time convincing me," Corso said.

"Me too," said Short.

Corso gestured toward Chris Andriatta. "I'll let her speak for herself, but as nearly as I can tell, we didn't come up with a damn thing back there."

"Me neither," she piped in. "Our line of inquiry was dry as a bone."

"The only thing I can think of that might be of interest was the amount of attention I seemed to be attracting," Corso said.

"Such as?"

Corso told the story of the two guys with the needle, then

segued into his near drowning. The story engendered several exchanged looks between Warren and Short.

"That's not how the local authorities tell the story," Warren said when Corso finished his recitation.

"I know." Warren looked to Andriatta, but got only the shake of her head.

"All that was before we met up," she said.

He turned his attention back to Corso. "So why do you suppose the local authorities would tell such a completely different tale?"

"I'm guessing they wanted me out of town as quickly as possible. The simpler the explanation for what happened, the faster they could send me on my way."

"Why did they want you gone?"

"That's a good question," Corso said. "If I'd hung around longer, that's exactly what I was going to find out."

"You seem to have touched a nerve."

Corso agreed. "Yeah . . . problem is I don't think it's the same nerve you guys are looking for. Their nerve has something to do with the response time the local PD managed after they got the call about Nathan Marino. There's a serious discrepancy as to how long it took the bomb squad to get under way."

"Places like that don't have bomb squads," Short scoffed. "They've got a couple guys who went to a seminar together. That's all."

"Whoever was supposed to show up . . . didn't," said Corso.

"Seemed like people were ashamed of the incident," Andriatta said. "Like somehow they all felt a little responsible for what happened to Nathan Marino."

"Why would that be?"

She thought it over. "Like maybe they felt like they could have done a better job of . . ." She searched for a phrase. ". . . of embracing him maybe. Of making him part of the community. Like they've all been too busy with their lives to notice one of their own had fallen by the wayside until it was too late."

Warren and Short exchanged another set of glances. A question hung in the air.

Warren checked his watch. "Might as well tell them," he said.

Short hesitated and then said, "We have reason to believe the incidents of the past two days will not be the last of it."

"What reason?" Andriatta asked.

"Good reason," Warren added.

Another brief silence ensued. After a moment, Warren broke the spell.

"Thus far we've managed to keep Monday's episode out of the media glare. They've been reporting it as a gas leak and we haven't bothered to correct them." He made a rueful face. "That's all over when the morning papers hit the stands in about forty-five minutes."

"The media will put it together for sure," Short said. "Bank bombings are pretty rare. Two in as many days is gonna raise antennaes."

"Three is going to cause a panic," Warren added.

"What are you guys doing about it?" Corso wanted to know.

Warren spread his hands in resignation. "We've done what we can. We've notified every bank in a hundred-mile radius. Told them to just do as they're told. Not to give the perps any excuse to blow anybody up. Other than that . . ." He paused for effect. ". . . there's not a whole heck of a lot we can do except try to trace the bomb material and wait to see what happens next."

"Let's wait somewhere else," Corso said through a yawn.

Warren nodded his agreement. "It's late," he said. "We've got some rooms over at the Glasgow . . ."

Corso waved him off. "Glasgow's a dump," he said. "You guys can stay wherever you want." He looked from one to the other. "We're over by Westwood Village, right?" He didn't wait for an answer. "Take us to the Beverly Wilshire."

"I'm afraid the government doesn't . . ."

"I've got an account there. It's on me," Corso said.

Andriatta got to her feet and slipped an arm through Corso's.

"I'm with him," she said.

19

"We can kick this thing around forever and it's still gonna be a mystery," she said around a mouthful of dinner roll. "But I *will* say this for you, Corso, you've got great taste in hotels."

Corso swallowed a bite of steak. Looked around the room. Very nice. Very chic. "Yeah . . . this place is right in line with my new approach to just about everything,"

"What's that?"

"When in doubt, throw money at it."

"It seems to be working," she said before biting another roll in half.

Corso sat back in his chair. "Yeah. That's the problem. It works every time. It's the curse of our society, isn't it? We spend our whole lives collecting things that turn out not to matter to us. So we go out and buy something else, as if bigger houses and cars and boats are going to cure the malaise of the soul."

"'The malaise of the soul'? Oooow," she teased. "You always wax this prosaic after a near-death experience?"

"I don't generally wax at all."

"Somebody I know once described you as an 'artist in reticence.'"

Corso followed another bite of steak with a mouthful of wine. "That's as close as anything, I guess," he said. "I've certainly been called worse."

"Yep."

Corso stopped chewing. Swallowed. "What's that supposed to mean?"

She batted her eyes and smiled at him. "I was just agreeing with you."

"Yeah . . . well don't be too agreeable."

"I mean . . ." She waved her fork at him. "It's not news to you is it that people mostly think you're a pain in the ass?"

"They can think whatever they want."

"They say you're arrogant, opinionated, reckless . . ." She stopped talking and leaned across the table. "First time Greg asked me to fly out to God's country and work with you, I turned him down flat."

"What changed your mind?"

"Turned out my condo needed a bunch of plumbing work. I figured I might as well make some money as sit around and listen to a bunch of fat-ass plumbers making noise."

"Now there's a vote of confidence if I ever heard one."

"Awww . . . don't worry about it, Corso. You're not nearly as bad as they say you are. Hell . . . you've actually got a little streak of chivalry in you somewhere. It's childish as hell, but you know . . . kinda touching."

Corso used his napkin to hide the sneer on his lips. "You got any ideas?" he wanted to know.

"About you?"

"About this whole bank robbery thing," he snapped. "About how Nathan Marino and what happened back East last year could be connected to the things happened around here today."

"It's a great idea."

"What's a great idea?"

"Robbing banks with a hostage. Puts the bankers at an enormous disadvantage. I mean, what in hell are they gonna do . . . let the perps . . ."

"You've been watching way too many police videos," he interrupted.

". . . let the *perps* blow up a perfectly innocent citizen so's they can hang onto some money that's insured by the Feds anyway."

"We just watched one who did."

She dismissed the idea with a wave. "He was Vietnamese. No way a Vietnamese banker is going to give anybody anything. Not a Cambodian either. Or a Laotian. It's just not part of Southeast Asian culture to become separated from folding money.

"Also . . . I fail to see how anything we might have done back on the East Coast could possibly have been the catalyst for what happened here in the past couple of days." She used the second half of the roll to wipe up the remaining béarnaise sauce in her plate. "You gottta admit . . . the timing's a bit suspect."

"More than a bit," he admitted.

"You said it yourself. It's been over a year . . . right? The case is colder than the proverbial well digger's ass. Nobody's paying the least attention to this loser chicken delivery guy who got blown to pieces in a bank parking lot way the hell out in the middle of nowhere, then all of a sudden your cherubic countenance is all over the media claiming you're gonna solve this thing . . . and next thing you know, the local *federales* are trying to force you out of town and persons unknown are trying to force you into the grave." She spread her hands in wonder. "Gotta be a connection somewhere."

Corso finished his wine, reached for the bottle and found it empty. "You want another," he asked. "I could call . . ."

She shook her head. "I'm gonna toddle off to bed here real soon."

"And . . . you know . . ." Corso began. ". . . if this whole bank-robbing thing had started up again back East . . . well maybe I could believe that we'd inadvertently stepped on somebody's grave . . . but, you know . . . what in hell does any of *that* have to do with any of *this*?"

"Beats me."

"And I'm still not sure what we're doing here," Corso groused.

"It's simple. They think we know something we don't."

Corso ran a hand through his hair. "This whole thing is straight out of some Franz Kafka novel."

"Story of my life." She said it wistfully, but a sadness appeared behind her eyes. She felt its presence and looked away.

Corso leaned in closer. "Tell me about your life," he said in a low voice.

"Which one?" she asked with a laugh.

"You choose."

Silence settled in. The sound of a distant car horn reached their ears, rhythmically bleating its one-note song, over and over before finally stopping.

"I never wanted any of this," she said after a moment. "All I ever wanted was a husband, a couple of kids, a house in the 'burbs, summers down the shore . . ."

"You're from New Jersey."

She cocked her head and narrowed her eyes. "How'd you know?" she asked. "I don't sound like Jersey anymore. I know I don't."

Corso put on an accent. "Summers *down the shore*," he mocked. "Only in Jersey do they call it that. Over to the ocean. Over to the coast. Maybe even traipsing to the seashore." He wave a hand. "But only in Jersey do they refer to it as *down the shore*."

She looked around the room and then over at Corso. "This is a long way from New Jersey," she said.

"Where in Jersey?"

"Freehold. It's . . ."

"I know where it is."

"Funny thing is . . . I've got no idea how I got from there to here. Not only didn't I see it coming, but . . . you know . . . I don't see any trail behind me either. It's like I've been about ten different people in my life and, every time, all I did was blink my eyes, and I turned up someplace else doing something new."

"You complaining?"

She mulled it over. "Yeah, I guess I am."

"What about?"

"Loss," she said. A sudden stiffness in her shoulder told Corso she regretted having said it, so he tried to lighten things up.

"What'd you lose?' he asked. The minute it passed his lips he knew it was the wrong thing to say. And suddenly it was as if her eyes were floating in space. No face, no boundaries, just a pair of angry eyes, intense and damaged beyond repair.

But she wasn't listening.

Corso tried to move closer, but she wasn't having it. She cringed as their shoulders met and got to her feet. "It's been a long day. I'm about ready to avail myself of that fancy room next door." She clapped a strong hand on his shoulder. "Thanks for dinner," she said. "We get a chance, I'll take you to Pink's for a couple chili dogs . . . on me." She made a circle with her thumb and index finger. "Best in L.A.," she said. "Hands down."

Corso got to his feet. He watched in silence as she crossed the room and disappeared out into the hall. After a time, he pushed himself back from the room service table, grabbed it by the edges and rolled it along in her wake, hoping to catch her scent as he pushed the table across the carpet to the door, which he held open with his foot as he eased the table out. Leaving the cart in the hall, he triple-locked the door, snapped off the overhead lights and then, in the darkness, mimed his way over to the bed.

When he bent to take off his shoes, his head began to spin. He sat up slowly, waited a moment and then tried again. Same result. For a second, he felt nauseous. He took several deep breaths, then crawled up onto the bed . . . one shoe on, one shoe off. The darkness began to fold itself around him just as he heard his mother's voice say something about . . .

20

Brown suit turned out to be Warren's FBI equivalent. Special Agent in Charge Jerry Morales of Zone Nine. L.A. County, and environs. Forty minutes after the victim and the money disappeared, Mr. Morales had pretty much lost his sense of humor.

His face was the color of the stoplight on the corner. He wanted to yell into the handheld radio but didn't want to be heard, so he had the plastic pressed hard against his lips as he sent admonitions and instructions out over the airways in a raspy whisper.

A brigade of cops and federal agents swarmed the area, emptying the entire ground floor of the Union Bank of California building, clearing the Westin's lobby and parking garages of civilians, as teams of law enforcement officers went through the hotel's nearly fourteen hundred rooms one by one, shuffling bewildered guests to the safety of waiting Metro buses, where they were whisked to god-knows-where in a cloud of diesel smoke. ATF had called in a pair of bomb disposal units, yet another enormous van and a lowboy trailer upon whose back a thick-walled detonation chamber rested uneasily. LAPD had cordoned off the cross streets a couple of blocks back from the scene, leaving the intersection black and bare of civilians like the deserted streets of an old science-fiction movie.

"I'm hungry," Chris Andriatta said for the third time.

"You just had breakfast," said Corso without looking her way.

"I had *half* a breakfast two hours ago," she corrected.

"Here comes Warren," Corso said.

Warren and Special Agent Morales had spent the better part of forty minutes nose to nose, arguing in a professionally bureaucratic manner common to organization men for whom passive-aggressive behavior has become second nature. Morales had repeatedly reiterated his position that the FBI had no intention of standing idly by while banks were being robbed in broad daylight. He believed that the best way to ensure the safety of the citizenry was to bring these miscreants to justice. Warren, on the other hand, had been more humanely oriented, arguing instead in favor of a hands-off policy, citing the safe return of Constance Valparaiso as witness to the sanity of this approach. Morales had been unmoved, insisting that his army of agents would get the job done and thus save the nation from bankruptcy.

Half an hour ago, they began passing a cell phone back and forth. By the time they'd finished, Morales looked smug. For his part, Warren tried to look calm as he made his way over to the car. From the corner of his eye, he caught Corso's quizzical expression. "He's got a lot of clout," Warren said. "Lots of people . . .

people in the know, think he's gonna be the next director." He folded his arms tightly across his chest. "Whatever he wants, he gets."

Warren heaved an exasperated sigh, bumped himself off the car and headed into the hotel. Corso turned his attention to the unfolding evacuation of the hotel. They came out in ones and twos. Dressed and undressed. Dazed and angry and scared.

It took the better part of an hour before Warren reappeared, hurried across the circular drive, took Morales by the elbow and pulled him across the pavement and out onto the sky bridge, where he began to whisper in his ear.

The sound of an electric motor pulled Corso's attention from the cops in the bushes back out into the porticoed driveway. Corso held his breath and winced as Paul Short's wheelchair bounced down over the curb, teetering dangerously for a moment before righting itself and rolling over to where Corso and Andriatta stood at the rear of the unmarked Chevy. He swung the chair in a quarter circle, keeping the unmarked side of his face toward Corso and Andriatta. He watched the whispering cops passing the cell phone back and forth for a few moments, then shook his head in disgust.

"They found her," he announced. "Handcuffed, hand and foot, up on the twenty-fifth floor." He anticipated the next question. "No bomb. No note. No nothing." He spread what used to be a pair of hands in resignation.

"Is she . . ." Andriatta began.

"She's scared shitless is what she is."

"Any idea how much they got?"

"It's not official . . . but the preliminary figure is about 2.3 mil."

Andriatta whistled. "Serious money."

"All in hundred-dollar bills. She says the note was specific about it."

"Same MO?"

"Mostly. They got her as she left the office last night. Two of them, this time. Ski masks. Stuck a gun in her ear and a needle in her arm. She woke up this morning with a bomb wired around her neck and a radio receiver in her ear. Most everything right out of the Valparaiso incident. Same description of the device. Same complicated instructions. She gets back to the room, finds a black bag on the bed. The voice tells her to put it over her head. She does as she's told. They stuff a ball gag in her mouth, hand-cuff her hands and feet simultaneously and leave with the bomb, the radio and the money. No muss, no fuss, no bother."

"Any word on the Malibu robbery?"

"Not that I've heard."

"This is quite a little growth industry these guys have got going on here," Andriatta said. "Working on three million in three days. Nice work if you can get it."

"These guys know what they're doing," Short said. "It may be quite a while before they make a mistake."

"Then the Bureau may be right," Corso said. "Maybe its time to 'just say no.' Let them blow up a few innocent folk without getting any money and hope that puts an end to it."

"Depends on what you think is more valuable . . . people or money."

"There's no sanctity of life," Andriatta said. "Never was, never will be."

Short barked a short, dry laugh. "Aren't *we* just 'cynics anonymous,'" he said with a sardonic smile. "Nary a romantic in the house."

"Realists, not cynics," Andriatta corrected.

"Same people who oppose abortion favor the death penalty," Corso said.

"I was in Rwanda," Andriatta offered. "The Hutus cut the hands off Tutsi men and the breasts off the women. They left them lying in the dirt, bleeding to death over nothing more important than tribal affiliation." She threw an angry hand into the air. "Something like eight hundred thousand people slaughtered while the rest of the so-called *civilized* world turned its back." She slapped her side and shook her head. "Don't talk to me about the sanctity of life."

"Dying there in the dirt might have been better," Short said.

"Better than what?" Corso asked.

Short opened his mouth to speak but changed his mind. Instead, he twirled the joystick, sending the chair in a tight arc until the mangled side of his face was visible.

"Better than some of the alternatives," he said.

Corso folded his arms across his chest. "Nietzsche said the only thing the dead know for sure is that it was better being alive."

"Nietzsche was wrong," Short said. "There are worse things than being dead." He fixed Corso and Andriatta with his single blue eye. "Trust me," he said.

"You seem to be doing okay," Corso commented.

"For a freak."

For a while, the great outdoors seemed to be devoid of oxygen. Andriatta finally broke the spell. "There's a lot of people worse off than you are."

The working half of Short's upper lip curled into a sneer. "So I should be grateful," he said. He nodded a couple of times. "That's what they tell you over and over in the hospital. How lucky you are to be alive. How grateful you should be."

"What happened?" Corso asked. "I mean, how did you lose your . . ."

Short cut him off. "First Bush war. Kuwait. I ran an ordnance-removal company. Coupla weeks after the war ended, we were checking the royal palace at Rabat for booby traps." He ran his glistening eye over them again. "I found one."

The moment was rescued when Morales and Warren started their way. Morales directed his attention to Corso and Andriatta. "Soon as I get a couple of debriefing specialists free, I want you two to sit down and tell us everything you can remember about what happened back East." He looked from one to the other. "There's got to be something. I don't believe in coincidence."

"We don't disagree . . ." Corso said, ". . . but we'll be damned if we can figure out what it is."

"Something you don't even know you know," Warren said. "Something obscure and seemingly meaningless."

Warren must have had his cell phone on vibrate. He reached into his pants pocket and pulled out a phone. Flipped it open and held it tightly against the side of his head.

"Warren," he said. He listened and then closed the phone.

"We've got a silent alarm from a U.S. Bank on the corner of Wilshire Boulevard and Dayton Way."

21

"Male. Thirty-five or so. Wearing a bulky red sweater and blue jeans. She says he looks like an Arab of some sort." The cop looked around, saw the faces of confusion on Warren, Corso and Andriatta. "We got a teller on the other end of the line. She was in the break room when it started. She's peeping out through the door."

They were crowded together in the front window of the El Torito Grille, diagonally across Dayton Way from the Wilshire Boulevard branch of the U.S. Bank. According to the officers on the scene, the suspect had been inside for nearly eleven minutes, nearly all of which had been chronicled by a teller, whose call to 911 had been transferred to the scene by LAPD Emergency Services.

El Torito's crew of chefs and waiters had been rounded up and banished to the bar. Morales was seated at a table in the rear corner of the dining room working his cell phone like a telemarketer. Warren and Corso had shouldered their way up to the window. Warren had shoved the café curtains aside and now had his nose pressed to the glass like a waif at a bakery window. Chris Andriatta was standing on a chair looking out over their heads.

The restaurant was two blocks east of Rodeo Drive. No more than five minutes from the scene at Fifth and Figueroa. On one side of the bank, Louis Vuitton offered a colorful line of upscale luggage and women's accessories; on the other side, Barneys of New York sought to set the style, then a Burberry and a café and Saks Fifth Avenue and a bistro and Niketown. You name it and it was here at the very epicenter of West Coast retail grazing. You had some money burning a hole in your pocket, this was just the neighborhood to help you put out the fire.

The streets teemed with tricked-out shoppers, the beautiful people seeing and being seen, focused inward, oblivious to the drama unfolding inside the bank, as the ripples of well-heeled humanity flowed this way and that, eddying here and there to gaze at the wares in the windows before moving on to deeper water, to one of those little salons and boutiques dotting the streets at regular intervals, places that played odd electronic music, places with trendy French names like Mal Maison, where a haircut or a sweatshirt would likely cost you five hundred bucks. Probably the last place in this part of the country where any politically savvy cop wanted a bomb going off.

"He's on his way out," the officer announced.

Morales left the table and hustled up to the front of the room just in time to see the victim shrug himself into the red backpack, negotiate the two steps down to sidewalk level, turn right and melt into the unsuspecting crowd on the sidewalk. Morales whispered into the phone.

"Moving west on Wilshire."

Soon as he was out of sight, Morales hurried over to the front door and let himself out. As he jogged across the street, Corso looked over at Warren, who shrugged. "The protocol is that the Bureau takes the lead." He looked away in embarrassment. "LAPD provides backup as necessary."

"What do you guys do?" Corso asked.

Warren ran a hand through his hair. "We wait."

Andriatta climbed down from the chair. She hooked a thumb at the bar. "I'm going to see if I can't rustle up something to eat," she said.

Corso grinned and shook his head. She dismissed him with a wave of her hand. "Sheeeesh . . . it's a restaurant, isn't it?" She peeled off from the crowd at the window and picked her way through the closely arranged tables toward the buzz of conversation coming from the lounge area.

"Any idea what's going on in Malibu?" Corso asked as they stared out into the street. "It's over," Warren said. "Vic was an older guy named Louis Erbach. Lives in the Colony. They took him out of his home about two hours before the robbery. Wired him up and sent him on his way. He walked out of the bank with $450,000 . . . give or take." He paused to swallow. "A guy named Prichert, calls himself a professional astrologer, found Erbach lying in the middle of a dirt road way up in Topanga State Park. The techs think he had a heart attack. Took him back to Santa Monica to the hospital. Bureau's got a team on hand, in case he wakes up."

They stood and watched the passing parade in silence. A sign reading CLOSED appeared in the bank window. A swirling breeze rippled the café umbrellas along the sidewalk.

"Much as I hate to belabor the obvious . . ." Corso started, ". . . whoever's doing this . . . there's sure as hell more than one of them."

"That's a whole new paradigm."

"Hey," a voice called. Corso and Warren turned toward the sound. Andriatta was holding something on rye in both hands. She tilted her head toward the doorway behind her. "I think you boys better come in here," she said.

They slalomed their way through the tables over to where she stood. She held up the sandwich. "Want a bite?" she asked Corso. "Pastrami and provolone."

Corso smiled and shook his head.

"The newshounds are on it," she said. Again she motioned with her head. She led them into the cool darkness of the bar. Half a dozen waiters and half as many cooks lounged around the bar area. Above the bar a new flat-screen plasma TV was tuned to the news. Aerial shot. No narration at the moment, only the whop, whop, whop of the chopper's rotor blades slapping the dirty air just above the rooftops.

The center of the screen was filled with a white Toyota Tundra. Over in the right lane, driving like an old lady. As the camera zoomed out to a wide-angle shot of downtown Beverly Hills, the truck put on its blinker and turned right onto Santa Monica Boulevard, heading west toward the San Diego Freeway and the ocean.

"This is Barry Logan in the Action News chopper high above an unfolding bank robbery in Beverly Hills."

"It was inevitable," Warren said.

". . . the same type of robbery we've reported for the past three days. The victim enters the bank . . ."

Two blocks down Santa Monica, a nondescript van pulled into the line of traffic behind the Toyota. Warren pointed. "The Bureau," he said.

"They don't get rid of that news jockey, the guy in the Toyota's gonna be in a world of hurt," Corso said.

As if on cue, another helicopter swooped into the picture. "*Whoa, baby . . .*" the newsman said. "*Looks like we've attracted some official attention.*" The passenger in the second copter could clearly be seen motioning for the news chopper to leave the area . . . to go down. The bright yellow FBI letters were visible on the sleeve of his dark blue jacket.

The newshound, however, was having none of it. "*This is unrestricted airspace,*" he shouted above the slap of the rotors. "*We've got every bit as much right to be here as you do,*" he shouted, as if the cops in the other chopper could somehow hear him. The station's logo flashed on the screen. "*This is Barry Logan, Action News Four. Once again safeguarding the public's right to know.*"

The news copter peeled off to the west, moving lower and slower, hovering just to the rear of the fleeing pickup truck. The camera jiggled slightly as it refocused on the white Toyota, which had stopped at a traffic light at the corner of Santa Monica Boulevard and Manning Avenue. The Toyota was in the center lane, third in line behind a flatbed truck carrying lumber and a bright blue PT Cruiser.

"I don't believe this," Warren said.

And then it happened. A bright yellow flash and, in an instant, the busy intersection disappeared. The News Four helicopter shook so violently it seemed about to join the pile of smoking rubble on the ground. By the time the camera was repositioned and steady, most of the torrent of flaming metal and broken glass had found its way back to earth; the smoke had cleared, leaving

the carnage on the street visible to the camera's unblinking eye.
Both the cab and the bed of the Toyota pickup had been vaporized.
Nothing but a twisted frame and four blown-out tires remained.
From the sky, the remains looked more like the unearthed skeleton of some ancient beast than anything vaguely mechanical.
The adjacent vehicles and their occupants had been left in various stages of destruction. Those nearest the victim's vehicle, even
from a distance, revealed little hope of survival. Those farther
removed from ground zero were without windows and pocked by
falling debris but seemed otherwise intact. As the camera rolled,
the bleeding and the uninjured poured out of their cars and trucks
and SUVs, stepping around and over twisted, smoking chunks of
debris as they made their way forward, hoping to help those less
fortunate than themselves. "See dat?" Somebody asked from the
back of the bar. "Look at dem people comin' out to help. We got
spirit here, man." A couple of other somebodies agreed.

"*What we have just witnessed . . .*" Barry Logan panted. "*What
we have . . .*" And then he did the smart thing. He shut up and let
the picture tell the story.

Took Chris Andriatta three tries to swallow a mouthful of
sandwich.

"Oh my God," she said.

22

Morales tapped the microphone three times. The conversational buzz in the room slowly subsided. "Ladies and gentlemen . . ." he began. ". . . I'd like to take this opportunity to introduce the other members of the team."

Corso laughed out loud. Andriatta elbowed him sharply in the ribs. He bent at the waist and whispered in her ear. "If this is a team . . ." She pulled her head away and elbowed him upright again. He leaned against the wall and smirked.

On the dais, Morales had introduced his way through the assembled law enforcement dignitaries and was ready to begin. He stepped up to a bank of microphones worthy of a presidential press conference. "I'm going to read a short statement, after which, I will field as many questions as time permits." He unfolded a small sheet of white paper, flattened it on the rostrum and began to read about how the Bureau was but one arm of the investigatory task force you saw before you this afternoon. About how the task force was dedicated to solving the series of bank robberies plaguing the Los Angeles area in recent days and how they felt certain the cowardly perpetrators of these heinous crimes would be brought to justice in a timely manner. And finally how all of those involved in the case would like to express their heartfelt sympathy for the victims of this morning's tragedy and for their families. At which point, he refolded the paper and slipped it into his suit jacket pocket.

The rush of shouted questions overwhelmed the acoustics. Morales pointed at the CNN reporter in the front row. The roar gradually subsided. "Can you give us an exact figure on the number of dead and wounded from this morning's explosion?" he wanted to know. Morales took a deep breath. "The last figures I heard were that we had four dead, thirteen others injured seriously enough to require hospitalization and another thirty or so treated at the scene and released."

"The victim," shouted another reporter. "Do we have an ID on the original victim?"

Morales produced a three by five card from his pants pocket. "The victim's name was Fazir Ben-Iman. Mr. Iman was a Lebanese immigrant who had been in the country for twenty-three years. He was a clinical psychologist, trained at UCLA, and worked at an outpatient clinic in the San Fernando Valley."

"What about the La Crescenta victim?"

"The victim's name is being withheld pending notification of next of kin."

"Has the investigation turned up any connection among the victims?"

"That's not something we can comment on at this time," he deadpanned.

"Are we to assume that all of these robberies were committed by the same . . ." She groped for a word. ". . . person or persons?" A grandmotherly woman in the front row asked.

"As this is an ongoing investigation . . ." The crowd wasn't in the mood for disclaimers. The second half of his answer was swept away by a rush of shouted questions. "Which is it?" someone yelled. "Person or persons?"

Morales could see he needed to throw them a bone or they were going to eat him alive. "We believe that today's incidents were the work of more than one person," he said.

"A group representing itself as 'America First' has taken credit for the bombings. They are demanding the release of abortion clinic bomber Eric Rudolph. They claim the bombings will continue until their demands are met."

The press jumped all over it. How seriously did the Bureau take this claim? Quite seriously but by no means exclusively. Prior to this, was this group known to the Bureau. Yes, it was. The United States does not negotiate with terrorists. It went on and on. The assembled media gnawed the news like a bone.

For his part, Morales hedged for all he was worth. "At this stage of the investigation . . . " became his much-repeated disclaimer.

"The usual suspects." Corso turned his head to the right. Paul Short wore a pair of blue coveralls. A prosthetic stainless-steel hook had been fitted over the stump of his right arm and a fake foot and shoe at the end of his right leg. A smudge of what looked like oil or grease adorned his right cheek.

"You just come from the scene?" Andriatta asked.

He nodded.

"Anything?"

He shook his head. "They've upped the ante," he said. "This last one had enough C-4 to stop a Bradley, let alone a Toyota." He paused to let his words sink in, "We found pieces of the victim's vehicle seven hundred feet away from ground zero."

Corso whistled. "Same type of bomb?" he asked.

He shrugged. "According to the people in the bank," he said. "Same handcuff arrangement around the neck. Same keypad on the front of the device." He stirred the air with the hook. "Could be one of the Bureau's techies is going to pry something useful out of one of the palm trees or one of the building facades, but I wouldn't count on it."

He smiled as much as the scar tissue would permit. "Only in L.A.," he said. "We got a multiple murder crime scene and all LAPD is worried about is traffic. Tell me they need to reopen the intersection as soon as they get the mess cleaned up." He shook his head in disgust. "They say . . . 'Hey, man, this is Santa Monica Boulevard' and that's supposed to cover the destruction of a crime scene."

Corso turned his attention to the dais, where Morales, without actually saying the words, was blaming the deaths on the interference of the media, on poor intelligence information regarding the size of the explosive device, which meant Warren and the ATF, sliding the blame toward everyone not connected to the FBI.

Short fiddled with the joystick, sending the chair in an angry circle. "Bullshit," he said. "There was no way to know they were going to increase the size of the charge. How were we supposed to know that? It was random. Or maybe even unintentional. Hell, if they'd put that much in the Vietnamese device, they'd have brought down the whole damn shopping center.

"If anybody's to blame, it's those idiots in the Bureau who don't seem to realize they're in over their heads here."

"So what do they do?" Corso asked. "Just stand around and let these people rob all the banks their little hearts desire?"

A flush of red appeared in Paul Short's cheek. "Until somebody comes up with a better idea . . . yeah . . . that's exactly what you do. You don't risk innocent lives. You play it safe and wait for these guys to make a mistake."

"You and I both know the Bureau isn't going to stand around while somebody blows up things and robs banks right under their noses. Not gonna happen."

Short wasn't listening. His attention was riveted to the ongoing press conference.

"Repeat the question," someone shouted.

The question, whatever it was, had drained the color from Morales' face, leaving him the color of leftover oatmeal. "The gentleman from MSNBC inquires as to the specifics of the instructions . . ." He was choosing his words carefully. ". . . the specifics of the instructions given the victims by the perpetrators."

Not satisfied with Morales' translation, the MSNBC reporter raised his voice. "Is it true that law enforcement agencies were warned not to interfere? Not to attempt to follow the victims after they left the banks? Not to attempt any type of tracking devices?" He went on to enumerate the exact thou-shalt-nots listed in the holdup notes. Obviously he'd seen a copy. Morales tried to say something, but the guy kept talking. "And isn't it the case that when the instructions have been followed to the letter, the victims have been returned unharmed?"

"As this is an ongoing investigation . . ." Morales began. The buzz in the room swallowed the usual disclaimer. He tried to excuse himself. The buzz got louder.

"I smell lawsuits hatching all over the L.A. basin," said Andriatta.

"By the score," Corso added.

"You can't sue the government anymore," Short said. "Award limits make it impossible to come out of it with any money. Only the attorneys end up with their pockets lined."

"Well then there's going to be a bunch of happy lawyers in town tonight."

"Bunch of bloodsucking scum," Short said.

Morales and the others were filing off the dais in the opposite direction. The crowd of media types was nipping at their heels like terriers, preventing them from escaping into the elevators.

"Let's get out of here." Corso took Chris Andriatta by the elbow and steered her toward the door. "Warren's looking for us, we'll be at the hotel," he said to Paul Short.

"Kill all the lawyers," Short responded with a smile.

Corso skirted along the black curtains, holding Andriatta by the hand and keeping as far from the shuffling crowd at the end of the room as possible. They reached the alcove beneath the green-and-white EXIT sign. Corso turned and surveyed the media event taking place over by the elevators. After a moment, he straight-armed the long safety handle and shouldered the door open. Before either he or Chris Andriatta could move, however, a Japanese guy with a wireless microphone stepped into the doorway . . . then a second later, another guy, African-American, this time, with a digital video camera up on his shoulder. "You're Frank Corso, right?"

The red light on the front of the camera began to blink. Corso felt Andriatta's hand slip from his grasp. As he turned her way, the reporter stepped between them, holding the microphone up to Corso's lips. "I'm Gordon Nakamura . . ." the guy began.

Corso slapped the microphone aside and stepped around the guy. Andriatta had vanished into the throng.

23

Corso dropped his room key onto the nightstand and picked up the remote. He stretched out on the bed, snapped on the TV and checked the bedside clock: 6:05 P.M. Pacific Standard Time. World News. Earthquake in Pakistan. Thousands dead. He turned off the sound, closed his eyes and drifted into dreamless sleep.

Seemed like seconds later, a loud rapping brought him to his feet. It was 7:16 P.M. He walked to the door, started to jerk it open, then thought better of it and peeked out through the peephole. Nobody in the hall. Then the rapping started again. This time long enough for him to realize it was coming from the adjoining door to the room next door.

He ran a hand over his face, crossed to the side of the room, pulled back the dead bolt and opened the door. Chris Andriatta stood in the doorway wearing one of the hotel bathrobes, white terry cloth, Beverly Wilshire embroidered on the right breast.

"You eat yet?" she wanted to know.

Corso shook his head and motioned her into the room. "You certainly got lost in a hurry," he said.

"I told you. I don't like having my picture taken." She settled a towel across her shoulders and shook her wet hair. "Besides, I needed to do a little laundry. I feel like I've been wearing the same clothes for a week."

Corso nodded his understanding. "You should have called the valet," Corso said. "They'd have had the stuff back to you in an hour or so."

She made a face. "You'll have to excuse me if hotel valets are usually out of my price range."

Corso held up a hand. "Sorry," he said. "There I go throwing money at it again."

"What about dinner? I'm famished."

"You want to walk over to Westwood Village?"

She pulled at the sleeve of the bathrobe. "Can I wear this?" she asked. " 'Cause everything else I own is drying in the bathroom."

"You could," he offered. "I, for one, think you look great in it, but my guess would be that it might be a bit, how shall we say, libertine . . . even for L.A."

"Room service then?"

"If you were hungry, you should have ordered something."

"I tried. They wouldn't let me use my own money. Everything had to be charged to the room."

"So?"

"So? . . . So I don't know you well enough to be spending your money."

"Neither do I, but I never let it stop me."

She laughed. "It's bad enough I'm standing around in your hotel room in a bathrobe."

"What's bad about that?"

"You know what I mean."

"You look fine. You smell great. What could be bad?"

She wagged a finger at Corso on her way across the room. "Don't start. Just because you're filthy rich and impossibly handsome doesn't cut any slack with me."

"Me neither," he assured her.

"The part of the world I just came from, I'd be stoned to death for being here with you"—she picked at the robe again—"like this."

Corso reached down and pulled at the hem of the robe. A crude tattoo adorned her right ankle. At first he thought it was a flower, but when his eyes adjusted to looking at it upside down, he could see that it was a parachute with some numbers along the bottom. She didn't wait for the question. "I had a lover once. He was in the airborne." She turned a palm toward the ceiling. "What can I say. It seemed like a good idea at the time."

Corso dropped the hem. "Major portions of my life fall under that category."

Her mouth took a downward turn. "It's like what we were talking about last night." She stopped, listening to herself but looking at Corso. "Was that just last night?" she wondered aloud. "With all that's happened . . . seems like some other century or something." She made a wry face. "Anyway . . . like somebody said the other night, 'life just seems to happen.'"

"Even if it is something you planned, by the time you get there, it doesn't look anything like you imagined it would."

"And nothing's as good as it used to be."

Corso smiled. "Listen to us. What a pair of geezers."

"Geezerdom doesn't scare me a bit," she snapped. "What scares me is the prospect of living to be a hundred. The way medical science is advancing, we're all going to have a half-life of twelve thousand years."

The line sounded rehearsed, but Corso played along anyway. "And you don't want to live to be a hundred?"

"Hell no," she said. "I don't have that much goodwill left in me. I don't think I can smile for that long. The sooner I get out of here, the better."

Corso kept his mouth shut. She sensed his discomfort and lightened up.

"Not like that," she said. "I didn't mean like . . . you know . . ." She put a hand on his shoulder. "What I meant was . . . the sooner I eat, the better."

She didn't wait for the laugh track. Instead, she bounced off the bed, walked over, seated herself at the desk and flipped open the room service menu.

Corso watched with amusement as she studied the menu as if a test was in the offing, before deciding on a chateaubriand for two . . . for one . . . baked potato, creamed spinach and a piece of macadamia nut cheesecake for dessert. Corso opted for pasta carbonara and two bottles of Heitz Brothers 1998 Cabernet. "The *Martha's Vineyard* vintage," she repeated into the phone before hanging up.

"What's so special about the Martha's Vineyard vintage?" she asked.

"The price," Corso said.

"You have no respect for money."

Corso laughed. "That's exactly what my mother says about me."

"She's right."

"I'm just a conduit through which money passes."

She crossed the room again and climbed onto the bed, where she sat cross-legged.

"Then give it away. The world's full of people who could use it."

"For some reason, I can't do that either."

"There you have it."

She picked up the remote and turned up the volume. Local news. This morning's explosion. The big bang was less than a minute away. The news copter had the white Toyota centered in the frame. *"This is Barry Logan in the Action News chopper high above an unfolding bank robbery in Beverly Hills."*

And then the FBI helicopter swooped into the picture. *"Whoa, baby . . ."* the newsman said. *"Looks like we've attracted some official attention."*

They'd edited out about thirty seconds of helicopter hijinx, then switched back to the studio, where the anchorman's solemn voice warned that what was to follow was perhaps not suitable for the young or the infirm, followed by the obligatory pause and a cut to the moment when the entire intersection seemed to disappear in a cloud of smoke.

Cut to the grim visage of L.A. mayor Antonio Villaraigosa calling for an independent investigation of today's debacle. He wants to know who saw fit to endanger the lives of his citizens. Who is to be held responsible for the death and destruction on Santa Monica Boulevard this afternoon. Who cared so little for Angelenos as to ignore the robber's instructions, especially after what happened in La Crescenta earlier in the week. He notes that, thus far, death has been visited only upon immigrants to our country and wonders out loud if the authorities don't somehow value such lives substantially less than they do others. Villaraigosa wants somebody's feet held to the fire. As long as they aren't his feet, of course.

Corso grabbed the remote and worked his way through the stations, looking for more footage of the helicopters. Ten minutes and twice around the dial and nothing. He started around for a third time when a knock on the door announced the arrival of room service. Corso pushed the mute button and threw the remote onto the bed.

Andriatta bounced up and opened the door. A brace of liveried waiters rolled a pair of pink-draped carts into the room. She followed the carts across the carpet like a hound dog on a trail, pulling metal covers from the plates as the caravan moved along.

By the time Corso had the wine decanted to his satisfaction, had tipped the waiters and sent them on their way, she was already halfway through her potato and making a serious dent in the chateaubriand for two.

Corso poured her a glass of wine, then watched with amusement as she put it down in a single swallow. He gave her a refill and started in on his own dinner.

They ate in silence, watching the muted television cycle from the local news to the world news and back. By the time Corso pushed himself back from the table, they'd made a serious dent in the second bottle of wine and a game show had replaced the news.

Chris Andriatta pointed across the table at Corso's unfinished pasta. "You going to finish that?" she asked. Corso shook his head and watched as the remains of his dinner found its way onto her fork and down her throat.

Having consumed everything except the napkin rings, Andriatta wiped her lips with the starched napkin and dropped it into her plate with a flourish. "That was great," she pronounced.

"It's amazing you can eat all of that and stay . . ." He searched for the right word. ". . . you know and stay relatively svelte."

She furrowed her brow. "Wadda you mean *relatively*?" she demanded. The wine had added slur to her speech. "I'll have you know I'm the same weight I was when I graduated from high school."

"Me too," said Corso. "It's just not all in the same place."

She looked down at herself. "Are you suggesting . . . "

Corso held up a moderating hand. "I was merely commenting that it's a wonder how you maintain your girlish figure while eating like a marine division."

She looked him up and down, searching for signs of irony. Satisfied, she crossed the room to the adjoining door. "I'm going to bed," she announced.

Corso checked the clock. "It's only seven-thirty," he said.

"I've had too much to drink," she said with a lopsided grin. "I'm going to bed before I make a fool of myself."

"You're among friends."

The grin turned licentious. "That's what I'm afraid of," she said with a wave of her fingers and a toss of her hair. Corso watched as she crossed the carpet and disappeared through the doorway. After a moment the light came on in the adjoining room. From where he stood, Corso could see her reflection in the big wall mirror. He watched as she turned down the bed. Her back was to him as she shrugged herself out of the bathrobe. Corso held his breath and tried to turn away but found himself unable. The reflected curve of her back and hips held his gaze in a stony grip. Mercifully, she snapped off the light, leaving Corso breathless, staring into the darkness, listening to the rustle of sheets as she made herself comfortable. He thought about closing the adjoining door but couldn't force himself to move. He turned away.

24

C orso wiped the hair from his eyes and tried, once again, to peer through the peephole in the door. No go. Either he'd developed glaucoma overnight or some unknown trick was required to screen one's visitors through this particular aperture. He glanced over toward the rumpled bed, found the digital clock on the far bedside table. Six-fifteen. Figuring the hour was a bit early for bad guys, Corso shot the bolts and jerked open the door. Warren and another burly ATF agent stood on the carpet. Warren smiled in that folksy way of his.

"Howdy," he said.

"Little early," Corso growled.

"Crime waits for no man."

The sound of Andriatta's voice in the hall told Corso he

wasn't the only one being dragged out of bed. "What's up?" he asked.

"Last evening . . . around eleven-thirty or so. We had a botched kidnapping attempt out in Thousand Oaks." Warren gave Corso a moment to process and then jumped back in. "Same MO. Woman comes out to her car on her way to work and there's a guy hiding inside with a gun. Except she's a veterinarian, works graveyard at an all-night veterinary hospital out on Roweena Boulevard."

"Yeah?" Corso ran a hand over his face.

"She always brings her dog with her. Seems Bozo tears up the furniture if you leave him alone in the house, you know, what the heck, she works in a vet's office, so it's no big . . ." Warren realized he was getting far afield and waved himself off. "Anyway, seems a 140 pounds of Rottweiler takes a serious exception to the guy in the car. Bites him all over hill and dale, according to the lady victim. Guy shoots the dog and gets away. She calls the local cops. They get a decent roadblock cordon around that whole part of the county in less than a half hour."

"And?"

"They get the usual kind of thing we pick up with roadblocks. People driving on suspended licenses, no licenses, no insurance, folks with warrants . . . you name it, they get it. An hour later they've come up with two dozen people who they're hanging on to for a variety of reasons." Warren anticipated the next question. "They didn't put two and two together. Wasn't until the day shift came on this morning that anybody wondered if maybe it might be connected to what we've had going on."

"So?"

"We want the two of you to have a look at them."

Corso winced and scratched his head.

Warren made an apologetic face. "This is the first real break we've had. We want to make sure we've got our bases covered."

"What bases are those?"

"We're hoping maybe one of the detainees is somebody one of you ran into back East."

Corso stepped halfway out into the hall. Another pair of carpet crushers held court at Andriatta's door. "Hey," he called.

Andriatta poked her head out.

"We go?" he asked.

"Son of a bitch shot a dog," she said.

Corso nodded in resignation. "Gimme ten minutes," he said to Warren.

Around L.A., nobody ever mentions the actual distance between places. The fact that one place is forty miles from another is utterly irrelevant. Ask how far it is from downtown L.A. to Thousand Oaks and an Angeleno will squint at his watch, allow for windage and the time of day and declare, "Just under two hours."

What would have required ninety minutes was, with judicious aid of a siren, covered in just over an hour. The Thousand Oaks Police Department building could as easily have been a shopping center. All flowers and Mission architecture on a nice tree-lined street, an Officer Friendly sort of place if ever a wiz there was.

Warren handled the introductions, describing Corso and Andriatta merely as witnesses. Thousand Oaks officials had been gracious in the manner of those burdened with a visit from a dowager aunt, all stiff necks, tight lips and crow's-feet.

Of those twenty-seven citizens detained in the minutes following the bundled kidnapping, eleven had been women. As was custom, TOPD had separated the suspects according to gender. The women were being held in what was normally a staging area for prisoners on their way to district court. Only reason they were using it today was because the males had filled up the general holding cells. Because surveillance was usually supplied by COs down on the floor with the prisoners, the need for one-way viewing windows had never before been called in question.

A pair of female officers escorted Warren, Corso and Andriatta into the room with the women suspects. "Line up against the back wall," one of the officers shouted above the protestations and shuffling of feet. Four more shouted orders finally accomplished the organizational mission.

When they got everybody quiet and settled in a ragged row, life's rich pageant found itself spread out along artificially distressed bricks. Coupla poor souls whose lives had been heisted by one drug or another. Hiding behind hollow eyes, hoping like hell this was going away before the rush wore off. Couple or three who were probably not going to be able to come up with the requisite green card. Short vacation in warm climate to ensue. Two scared-looking housewives and a huffy-looking Hollywood honey from whose attorney the TOPD would most assuredly be hearing forthwith.

Point was though, no member of the assembly caused so much as a glimmer in either Corso or Andriatta. Never seen any of them before. End of story.

In the men's end of the jail, things were no more civilized. They were led into a narrow hallway, dimly lit, smelling of stale coffee and staler breath. On the left, three empty interrogation rooms ran the length of the corridor. On the right, a single large holding area occupied the space. The men weren't as diverse as the women. All in all, it was a pretty seedy-looking group, ranging on the social scale from about Biker to Bum and back. Nobody you'd be asking home to lunch. The correctional officer nearest to Corso pushed the intercom button. "Line up against the back wall," his amplified voice directed. "Move in close; it's gonna be tight," she advised.

About a quarter of them did as bidden, another quarter began to shout one thing and another at the window, their inaudible protestations accompanied by a range of familiar hand gestures. Everybody else stood still and pretended not to have heard. The CO repeated the directions three or four more times before anything resembling a line began to form.

On the silent side of the glass, Corso worked his way down the row of sullen suspects, moving slowly, focusing on each man. Fourth guy down had one of those big square heads like the one he remembered from his rearview mirror in the moments before the SUV splashed into the lake. Corso was focused on the guy, trying to pull something . . . anything . . . out of his memory, when a movement from the far end of the line captured his attention.

Little Mexican guy. Freshly pressed shirt, buttoned all the way to the top. Baggy khaki pants and a pair of sneakers. Corso and everybody around him began to move that way. The guy was tearing at his clothes. Trying, it looked like, to tear the collar from his shirt. And then, no. He wasn't trying to tear the collar off the shirt, he was trying to get at something that seemed to be *sewn* inside the collar itself.

And then he had it in his hand. Small and white. He popped it into his mouth and swallowed, his Adam's apple bobbing up and down like a Ping-Pong ball, as the CO bringing up the rear called for assistance.

"Hey," shouted the officer next to Corso.

The effect of whatever the guy swallowed was violent and immediate. Looked like he'd been tasered. His spine snapped to rigid. His limbs went spastic. He convulsed once and fell to the floor, where he flopped around like a fish on a riverbank. And then, as quickly as it began, it was over. A pair of male correctional officers appeared at his side, turning him over and checking for a pulse.

Andriatta's fingers threatened to break the skin of Corso's arm. They didn't relax until the officer with his finger against the guy's throat looked up and shook his head. Warren's twang broke the silence. "What in Sam Hill was that?" he said.

25

"Cyanide? You gotta be shittin' me," Warren said. He caught himself and apologized for his language. "But I mean . . . isn't that just a bit excessive?"

"For what amounts to a traffic violation . . ." Corso said. "Yeah, I think you'd have to say suicide was a bit over the top."

Warren turned back to the medic. "You sure?"

The medic jerked a thumb over into the room, where his partner and another CO were zipping the deceased into a black rubber bag. "Look at him," the EMT said. "Look at his face. It's textbook."

What it was was cherry red. Fire engine red. The red that rhymes with dead.

"Guy smells like bitter almonds," the medic said. "Gotta be cyanide."

"Sounds like a James Bond movie," Andriatta said.

"Sounds ridiculous," Corso threw in.

"Got some kind of animal bites all over his torso and a serious-looking brace on his knee."

Warren and Corso exchanged knowing glances before Warren turned the other way, toward the TOPD sergeant who was running the local end. "What do we know about this guy?" Warren said.

"*Nada*. Nothing," the cop said. "No ID on him. Wouldn't give his name to the officer. We patted him down and put him with the others."

"What did he have on him?"

The cop opened the flap on a small manila envelope. He turned it over. A set of keys dropped out into Warren's upturned palm. Warren pushed the button on the intercom. "Get a set of prints before you take him anywhere."

"What was he driving?"

The sergeant looked embarrassed. "We don't know," he said. "Nobody bothered to keep track." He shrugged. "This was way more people than we generally process at one time. They figured, you know . . . as long as we had the keys . . ."

Warren separated the keys. Held up a worn car key. "This is the only ignition key on the ring and it's too darn worn to tell what it fits." He turned it this way and that in front of his face. "Foreign, if I had to guess," he said finally. He handed it to the sergeant. "Where are their cars?" he asked.

"Impound lot around the corner."

"Let's find out which vehicle was his." Warren jiggled the ring of keys. "Find out what everybody else was driving and we'll go from there."

The cop nodded his approval, stepped around Andriatta and

walked quickly toward the door at the far end of the corridor and disappeared.

Warren pushed the button again. "Hey . . ." he said. "I hate to do this to you, fellas, I surely do," he said in his best good ol' boy accent, "but I need you to take him back out of the bag for me. Sorry."

They didn't like it a bit, but did as they were told.

Corso and Andriatta followed Warren down the corridor around the corner and into the room where the body lay. Warren dropped to one knee beside the body.

The guy was somewhere in his fifties. Skinny, with bad skin tone. Tattoo of a skeleton ran down the inside of his right arm. Half a dozen dog bites on his legs and torso, blue around the edges and rimmed with blood. Tattoo on his chest said, "Death or Glory."

Warren looked up at Corso. "Whatta you think?"

"Could be one of the guys from the hotel room. He's the right size and the brace is on the right knee."

Warren looked at Andriatta. She shook her head. She allowed how she'd, "Never seen him before." Her tone suggested she was a little rattled. Warren put a reassuring hand on her shoulder. "Cyanide traps oxygen in the blood," he told her. "Won't let it get to the cells. That's how come his face looks like that."

A lab technician arrived. Everybody stood aside as he broke out his kit and took the guy's fingerprints. He was still packing up his gear when the sergeant reappeared.

"White Mazda pickup truck." He read the license plate number. "It's two blocks over in the overflow impound yard."

"You run the plate?"

"Truck's registered to a Zuelma Santana. Address in Oxnard. Oxnard PD talked to the woman. She claims she loaned the truck to one of her neighbors so he could make it to a job interview. Guy name o' Paco Reyes. Description matches the deceased, right down to the tattoo on the forearm."

"Clear the area," Warren said. "Establish a perimeter around the vehicle. I've got a team on the way. When they . . ."

"They're already here," the sergeant said.

A familiar voice chimed in. "The gang's *all* here."

The sergeant sensed the tension in the air and headed upstairs. Morales and another FBI agent stood in the doorway. Warren couldn't prevent a wry smile from crossing his lips. "Look what the wind blew in," he joked.

"We'd have blown in sooner if we'd been notified," Morales assured him.

"We've got it covered," Warren assured him back.

Morales dropped to one knee and examined the body, going so far as to roll the stiff up onto its side so he could look at the back. Warren stood over in the corner whispering instructions into his cell phone.

A coroner's team arrived on the scene. Bright yellow coveralls with black lettering on the back. Unlike the correctional officers, these guys were pros. They had the late Paco Reyes zipped into a bag, slung up onto the stainless-steel gurney and rolling out the door in three minutes flat. Warren used the interval to give Morales the short version of what had happened. "And you were here?" Morales asked incredulously.

Warren pointed at the one-way window. "Not ten feet away."

"Never seen a cyanide vic before," Morales said as the coroner's team left.

"Only in the movies," Warren said. The door clanked to a close.

"What now?" Morales asked. It was half question, half challenge, as if to say, "Okay, big fella, you've got the bit in your teeth here, let's see what you're worth."

Before Warren could respond, his phone rang. He listened for a moment and hung up without saying a word. "The dog likes the truck in a big way," he announced.

The air in the room changed from "maybe" to "probably." They passed a worried look around in a circle. "Let's go," said Warren.

The morning dew had burned off. It was going to be a scorcher. They left the car in the parking lot and headed diagonally across the street on foot. Warren and Morales walking fast, Corso and Andriatta trailing along behind. Two blocks over, they slipped between buildings and entered the parking lot of a cute little strip mall. Overhead, eucalyptus trees hissed and groaned under the weight of the wind, seeming to shimmer, their leaves changed from light to dark and back again as they quivered in the suddenly insistent breeze.

The ATF Emergency Response van was backed into an alley, directly across the street from the impound yard. The dented tailgate of the white Mazda pickup was clearly visible in the yard, a wire enclosure, separated from their present position by two sidewalks and four lanes of what would have been traffic had the police not blocked off the street at both ends and all points between.

An unmarked police cruiser had been parked across the mouth of the alley itself. Corso and Andriatta bent this way and that as they peered across the seventy yards separating their position from the Mazda pickup.

"They don't know for sure it's got a bomb in it though," Andriatta said.

Corso kept his head down. "Those bomb dogs are pretty damn good," he said. He nodded at the collection of bomb disposal equipment filling the strip mall parking lot behind their position. "They wouldn't have dragged all that crap out here if they weren't pretty certain."

Behind them, a pair of ATF bomb technicians struggled into their protective suits. By the time the pair had donned their equipment, Andriatta had found herself a seat along the curb and was refusing to move until somebody fed her.

Corso followed Warren and Morales into the ATF Emergency Response van, where another trio of technicians manned an entire wall of electronic gear. In the center three monitors relayed the action from across the street. Each of the men at the truck had a camera rolling. The third view was a fly-on-the-wall picture coming from a remote camera they'd set up in an FBI car on the east side of the alley.

Inside the bulky, steel belted, Kevlar suits, the ATF technicians looked a lot like a pair of Sta-Puff marshmallow men walking side by side across the intervening street. They flanked the Mazda, using the key the cops had taken from the suspect to unlock doors and peer inside. As their blunt hands rummaged around inside the truck, everyone involved held their collective breath, then let it out in a whoosh when, "Nothing in the cab," came cracking over Warren's handheld radio. Warren responded with something Corso couldn't hear, sending the technicians to the rear of the truck, where they again used the key on the back window.

Again the van seemed devoid of oxygen as the pair let down the tailgate and poked around inside the bed of the truck. This time the wait was shorter.

"Got a live device here," one of them said.

"Back off," was Warren's immediate command. They didn't need to hear it twice. The pair lumbered back out of the alley, made a quick left and moved far enough up the street so that the inside wall of a cinder-block building housing a flower shop was between them and the bomb. In unison they pulled off their visored helmets. Both were soaked with sweat. Each used a gloved hand to wipe the water from his eyes. And then again as they leaned back against the building sucking air with open mouths . . . everyone at the scene mouth breathing right along with them. In, out. In, out. That's when Short showed up.

Wearing nothing more than a pair of blue coveralls, he wheeled his chair at warp speed, cutting across the street and rolling up the alley, before bouncing to a halt at the yawning rear end of the Mazda.

26

The heavy breathing was over, the silence inside the van now deafening. Short's back was to the camera, so it was impossible to see what he was doing. Three or four times he reached into one or more of the compartments contained within his chair and came out with tools. He'd lean into the rear of the truck, fiddle around with something, lean back out, replace one tool with another and begin again. The longer he worked, the higher the tension level rose.

"I hope to God he's as good as you say," Morales muttered. "I don't want to be explaining to a subcommittee how it was we let a civilian blow himself all over suburban California."

"He signed a waiver," Warren said.

"Like that's gonna matter."

Warren lowered his voice. "We agreed," he whispered. "If we got the chance, we'd try to take a device intact. That's what you wanted, wasn't it?"

"I don't know," Morales said, hunching his shoulders, folding his arms across his chest. "Maybe we ought to follow protocol and detonate it."

Warren's face reddened. "You said we needed one intact."

Morales hugged himself tighter. "I'm having second thoughts . . ."

"Calm down."

". . . big time."

"You said the lab was getting nothing from the detonated devices."

Morales unwrapped his arms long enough to point at the TV screen. "We're breaking . . ." He paused long enough to shudder. ". . . God knows how many regulations here." He dropped his arms to his side with a slap.

"This is what I hired him for."

"Maybe . . ." Morales began, then he scowled and walked closer to the monitor. He tapped on the screen. "Is that smoke?" he asked.

Warren moved closer. No doubt about it. A plume of smoke was rising from the area above Short's head. "Looks like it," Warren said through clenched teeth.

The smoke continued to rise. Short continued to work.

"Get him out of there," Morales said.

"It's too late," Warren said.

"I won't be responsible for . . ."

"You already are."

They stood silent now, shoulder to shoulder, noses pressed to the TV screen. Several agonizing minutes passed before Short finally turned the chair in a slow circle and started back down the alley. The smoke seemed to be following him. Wasn't until the camera zoomed in again that they could see the cheroot clamped in his teeth and the ominous device resting in his lap.

"Is that the . . . ?" Morales began.

"I think so . . . yes," Warren answered.

"Where in hell is he . . ."

"Damned if I know."

As he breached the mouth of the alley and rolled across the sidewalk, the sight of the device in his lap sent the pair of ATF technicians hustling up the block as quickly as their bulky suits would allow. Inside the van, everyone squirmed as Short rolled out into the street. He paused long enough for them to grab a breath before heading straight toward the van. "He's not bringing that damn thing over here, is he?" somebody asked.

Warren's mouth hung open, but he did not answer.

"Doesn't he know the drill?" Morales hissed. "He's supposed to . . ."

"I don't think he much gives a shit," Corso said.

And then Short and his wheelchair disappeared from the cameras' view. An anxious minute passed. Hearts stopped. Nobody moved.

"Maybe he's . . ." Morales began.

Someone pounded on the side of the van. Internal organs contracted like dying stars. Nobody so much as twitched.

The pounding started again. Louder this time. One of the ATF men began emitting a low, keening sound. The guy next to him elbowed him in the ribs. The noise subsided. Corso broke the spell, pushed the door and peered outside. He smiled and shook his head. Warren and Morales moved to his side.

Short sat in his chair, his head encircled by a cloud of dirty smoke. A shiny steel device covered his lap. He ran his good hand over the surface as if he were petting a kitty. He grinned through the smoke.

"What's the matter with you people?" he wanted to know. "None of you ever see a bomb before?"

Seemed like everybody's throat was too dry to speak. "Gimme a few minutes and we'll see what we can find out about this thing," Short said cheerfully.

They watched in silence as he wheeled over by Andriatta to a weathered redwood picnic table set among the trees, where he put the device on a tabletop and began to pull tools from various compartments in the chair.

A young female ATF arrived at the van.

"What?" asked Warren impatiently.

"IAFIS got a match on the prints."

"Do tell," Warren said.

She swallowed her apprehension and began. "Fernando Reyes. American citizen. Fifty years old. Parents immigrated from Jalisco in 1947. Joined the Army right out of Glendale High School in '71. His unit was among the last to leave Vietnam. Did his twenty. Tried to re-up but failed the physical."

"Why?" Morales asked.

"Why what, sir?"

"Why'd he fail the physical?"

She was green. Fresh out of school. She rifled through the legal pad in her hand. "Doesn't say, sir."

"Find out."

She made a note. "Yes, sir."

"Go on," Morales prompted.

She paged back to where she'd left off. "After that he bounced around. Worked for an uncle as a landscaper for a while. Spent time selling recreational vehicles up in Fillmore. Applied to the state for permanent disability in '98. Was refused."

"What kind of disability?" Warren asked.

"Doesn't say."

"Find out."

"Yes, sir."

She gathered herself and continued. "After that, he pretty much disappears from the radar until 2001, when he gets arrested as part of a demonstration at the California Department of Veterans Affairs in Sacramento. Detained and released. No charges."

"Demonstrating for or against what?"

"I'll find out, sir." She flipped a page. "He's been living in Oxnard, in a mobile home he inherited from an aunt. Neighbors say he gets by on some kind of government check and by doing odd jobs around the neighborhood." She flipped another page. "As far as they've been able to ascertain, he's pretty much just a regular Joe."

"Let's get his complete military record," Warren suggested.

Morales agreed. "If he's got some kind of beef going with the vets, I want everything we can get on that, too. You get any resistance, use the Patriot Act to get whatever you need."

She nodded and started for the door.

"Did he speak Vietnamese?" Corso asked.

She paused and looked to Morales.

"Find out," he said.

"Vietnamese?" Morales asked.

"Just something I've been wondering about."

"You want to enlighten us?"

"Let's see what she gets."

Andriatta ambled over from her perch on the curb. "Short says he's ready for you guys," she said. She tapped the side of her head. "That guy's crazy," she offered.

"Sometimes it takes a crazy to catch a crazy," Warren said as they filed out of the van and headed across the lot.

"The stunt he just pulled—" Morales began.

"Like I said—" Warren interrupted.

"—could have killed us all," Morales finished.

"He didn't. And now we've got something to work with."

Morales shrugged as if to say he wasn't sure the risk was worth the reward.

Short had completely dismantled the device and had it laid out on the picnic table like the skeleton of some long-extinct monster.

"Looks harmless enough," Andriatta said. "Kinda pretty, actually."

Both Morales and Warren looked at her like she'd gone mad.

"You know . . . with all the different-color wire and all."

Morales grunted his disbelief. Short wheeled a one-eighty. "Ah . . . the brain trust," he said with a smirk.

"What have we got here?" Morales asked.

Short turned back to the pieces he'd arranged on the table. "What we have here is a very nice piece of work," he said. "The stainless-steel work is machine-shop quality. This wasn't manufactured in somebody's basement with a hacksaw and two pairs of pliers." He looked around to make sure he had everyone's attention. "This thing was very lovingly and professionally constructed." He pointed down at the collar apparatus. "Notice the flat two strands fixed inside the collar. Creates a circuit. Any attempt to cut through the collar breaks the circuit and sets it off. The rest of the thing is Teflon-insulated. The kind of stuff NASA uses in its rockets. The stuff isn't all that easy to come by, at least not without attracting some attention. I'm betting it's part of a burglary."

"What else?"

"The electronics are digital and completely up to the minute. Stuff you can buy in any Radio Shack store."

"What about the explosive?"

Short reached over and picked up what appeared to be an unbaked loaf of bread. He tossed it to Morales, who caught it with great care. "Military grade C-4—120 percent the equivalent of TNT. Very pure, very high velocity. Comes as a powder in fifty-five-gallon drums. The minute you begin to handle it, it plasticizes into something you can manipulate into any shape you've got in mind. It's got excellent mechanical and adhesive qualities. Hell . . . a block that size . . . you could stretch it from here to the roof without it breaking."

"Stolen from Twenty-Nine Palms?"

"Gotta be. This stuff is very tightly controlled. You'd need both an explosive authorization and an end user certificate." He threw his good hand into the air. "We were in Beirut or someplace like that, I'd say maybe we could fake the paperwork. Here . . . I don't think so. Gotta be stolen."

"It have a shelf life?" Morales asked.

"Ten years, at least."

Morales took a deep breath. "So, what do we do?"

Short thought it over. The wind slashed through the trees. "Long term, you try to trace the wire. Then you work the Secret Service to see what they know about the break-in at Twenty-Nine Palms. Short term, you follow whatever directions these people give you. That way, maybe you keep the carnage to a minimum."

27

Corso pressed his face against the window and looked west. The glass was warm against his cheek as he watched the sun ease into the Pacific Ocean and disappear. He peeled his face from the glass and checked his watch—9:20 P.M. Were it not for the palm trees outside the window, the conference room could have been anywhere in the world.

"Diminished respiratory capacity," Warren read. "Reyes failed the re-up physical because his lungs didn't meet Army minimums." He moved his finger down the page. "At the time of the physical, he only had an estimated 40 percent of healthy lung function."

"A smoker maybe," Morales said.

"That's what the Army claimed."

"What did *he* claim."

"Reyes claimed it was exposure to Agent Orange. Claimed to have been sprayed with the stuff in '74 while on patrol in the Mekong Delta. Told the Army doctors his lungs had never been right since 'Nam."

"Same thing with his disability claims." Andriatta read from a thick green folder with CONFIDENTIAL stamped across the side in red letters. "Claimed he was unable to hold down a steady job because he couldn't breathe properly. Between . . ." She paused while she moved her eyes to the bottom of the page. ". . . between August of '98 and earlier this year, he applied for state and military disability a total of sixtee—no eighteen times. Rejected on every occasion."

"On what grounds?" Morales asked.

"The state rejected the claim because his military records showed no evidence of exposure to Agent Orange."

"And the military?"

"The military blamed his condition on smoking and degenerative lung disease. Claimed it was not responsible for self-inflicted or genetically predisposed conditions. Referred him to the Veteran's Hospital in Pomona for treatment."

Morales straightened up in his chair. "Wait just a minute," he said.

"Constance Valparaiso," Corso chimed in. "Didn't she work as a nurse at a hospital in Pomona?"

"Pomona Veterans Wellness Center," Warren piped in. "Constance Valparaiso has worked there since June of '96."

"What's a wellness center?" Andriatta asked.

"An outpatient clinic," Warren answered. "Back at the end of the nineties the Veterans Administration shut down a whole host of hospitals all over the country. Consolidation, they called it. Supposedly getting rid of duplication of services." He waved a hand in the air. "Caused a hell of a stink at the time. People's wounded loved ones were getting shipped three states away. Demonstrations all over the country. Instead of big old hospitals, they opened a bunch of outpatient clinics to service the population who didn't need full-time care." He looked around the room, picked up the unspoken question. "My wife's got a nephew. Lost half a leg in the first Gulf War."

"I'm telling you, I don't believe in coincidences," Morales said.

"We don't even know if Reyes ever went to the Pomona clinic," Warren said.

Andriatta said, "Reyes wasn't looking for treatment; he was looking for money."

"Still . . ." Warren said.

Morales was already on the phone. He wanted everything available on Constance Valparaiso. Everything on the wellness clinic. Wanted all victims checked for any connection to either and wanted it right now.

Warren dropped Reyes's military record onto the table with a thump. "You all want the good news or the bad news?" he asked.

"Bad news first," Andriatta suggested.

"Reyes used his platoon leader as a reference with the VA. Guy named Paris Mamon. We got ahold of Mamon, who assures us Mr. Reyes had no military training whatsoever in the area of explosives. Strictly a grunt with a rifle."

"And the good news?"

"According to his platoon leader, he spoke pretty good Vietnamese."

All eyes turned Corso's way. "The video from the Vietnamese bank got me to wondering," he said. "We know he had the victims wired for sound so he could keep track of what was going on during the robbery, right?" Everybody nodded. "What I wondered was how the perp knew what was being said. How he knew things were going wrong and he wasn't going to get any money." He looked over at Morales. "What was the victim's name?"

"Anthony Huynh."

"How'd the perp know what was being said inside the bank unless he understood Vietnamese?"

Everyone began to talk at once. Warren's voice rose above the din. "What about Fazir Ben-Iman. Our clinical psychologist from the Rodeo Drive robbery . . ."

"Any connection to this Anthony Huynh?" Corso asked when things calmed down.

Morales hung up the phone and checked his laptop. "Nothing," he said.

"What about the other two?"

"What other two?"

"The other two guys who died in the bank."

"What have they got to do with it?"

Corso made a pained face. "Something Andriatta said the other day." She looked up, a quizzical expression on her face. "Something about how anybody who knew anything about Southeast Asian culture would know a Vietnamese bank manager wasn't going to fork over his depositor's money without a fight."

"Okay . . ." Morales' voice dripped with doubt.

"So . . . what if . . . just a supposition here, but . . . what if the La Crescenta robbery wasn't really a robbery at all. What if it was intended more as an object lesson for the authorities than as a bank robbery."

Morales leaned back in his chair. "You're suggesting what?"

"I'm suggesting that maybe the plan was to blow up the bank."

"Why would they want to do that?" Warren asked.

"So that we'd be damn sure they weren't kidding."

Morales was dubious. "You kill three people just to make a point?"

"What if you don't much see them as people."

"What else would anybody in his right mind see them as?"

"Gooks," Corso said. "Slopes. Slants. Rice burners."

"And Mr. Ben-Iman?" Morales asked.

"Camel jockeys. Sand niggers. Towel heads."

"You're suggesting these were hate crimes?" Warren asked.

Corso shook his head. "Not the way you guys use the term. I'm not talking about a bunch of well-intentioned antiabortion maniacs or some skinhead, neo-Nazi morons who hate everybody on the planet. Nothing like that."

"What then?"

Corso turned his palms toward the ceiling. "I don't know," he said. "It's just a feeling I've got." He waved a hand. "The bombs are too good for that. The whole idea of victims as bank robbers . . ." He trailed off.

"What about Rodeo Drive? Was that an object lesson too?"

"I don't think so," Corso said. "I think that incident happened because we didn't follow the directions in the note."

"We?" Warren wondered out loud.

"*We* have no idea what the note said," Morales protested. "Or even if there *was* a note."

Warren rolled his eyes in disbelief. "Of course we . . ."

"We have a confession."

"Free Eric Rudolph." Warren twirled a finger in mock excitement.

Corso jumped in quickly, heading the "blame game" off at the pass.

"Presuming it wasn't our prolife friends, and I'm telling you, the idea of committing murder over the sanctity of life makes about as much sense to me as screwing for virginity. Presuming that this was something more malevolent and less politically motivated . . . If it was somebody else . . ." He paused. ". . . it didn't take much to pull it off. All they needed was somebody on a rooftop. The minute they saw the choppers, they push the button and disappear. I'm betting the media helicopter alone would've eventually been enough to set them off."

Morales turned away, looking back over his shoulder. Corso eyed him closely.

"You guys by chance come up with any photo reconnaissance?" he asked.

Morales raised his eyebrows and poked a finger at his chest. Corso ignored the silent question and waited.

Morales thought hard before opening his mouth. "We've got satellite images of a guy on a rooftop a block and a half from ground zero. At full enhancement they're not nearly good enough for any sort of identification. Quantico's working on it."

Warren shook his head in disgust. "I don't believe you guys."

"Triangulation suggests the image is over six feet tall."

"How good is that?" Corso asked.

"Within an inch or so."

"Which eliminates Reyes," Andriatta said.

Warren boiled over. "I thought we had interagency cooperation on this one. I thought, *for once* . . ."

Morales was at a boil too. "Have you worked out the ramifications?" he waited for Warren to answer. "Have you?"

Before the situation could escalate, the door opened. A nondescript FBI agent stepped into the room, handed something to Morales and just as quickly disappeared.

Morales welcomed the diversion. For a moment . . . and then he blanched and crumpled the piece of paper into a tight ball. "The Army is refusing to provide Reyes's medical records." His hand shook and he tightened his grip on the wadded-up ball of paper. "They're citing privacy concerns." He held a hand as if to say "hold on." "The Twenty-Nine Palms theft is in the hands of the Secret Service. They refuse to provide us with anything there either." He made a face. "National security."

"That's all we've got," Andriatta said.

"And what's that?" Morales demanded. When nobody spoke, he answered his own question. "A guy with a beef against the Veterans Administration and the Army, but without the skills necessary to build the device. A bomb, parts of which may or may not have come from a theft of ordnance at the Twenty-Nine Palms Combat Center, back in February." He looked around the room. "Excuse me folks, but that's not a hell of a lot to go on. Not only is it darn slim, but we're poking our canoe into some very unpopular waters here. Anything that makes the Army look bad or makes the Vets look bad is going to be a political hot potato. Trust me on this."

"We need those records," Corso said. "The Army connection . . ." he began.

"Bite your tongue," Warren said.

Corso leaned back against the wall. He nearly smiled. "I didn't think of that," he said. "Nobody's going to want to hear about anything that makes the Army look bad, are they? Especially not with all the controversy surrounding the war in Iraq. Not with recruiting quotas so far down. Not with White House indictments. No sir, none of this is going to please the spin doctors in the least."

"Politics notwithstanding, the bottom line is that any sort of verifiable information is just not there. We've got one loser with a grudge. There's a million of these guys out there, none of whom is robbing banks with bombs."

"I've got a feeling," Corso said.

"Don't I feel better now?" Morales quipped.

Warren fixed Morales with a steady gaze. "We gotta have those records."

"What're you looking at me for?" Morales asked.

"You're the Bureau's fair-haired boy," Warren said. When Morales opened his mouth to deny it, Warren cut him off. "You're Dailey's handpicked successor. Everybody knows it. If anybody's got the clout to pull this off, it's you."

Morales made a disbelieving face. "Long as I don't mind relocating to Iowa about this time next week."

"It's tomorrow I'm worried about," Corso said. "About nine o'clock in the morning when the banks open."

"The Bureau is committed to another line of inquiry," Morales insisted.

"What if the Bureau's wrong?" Corso asked.

Morales sighed, then looked from one to another of them, taking his time before reaching out and plucking the phone from the cradle. "Get me the deputy director," he said.

28

Andriatta hugged heself. "It's way past my bedtime," she said. As if to prove her point, she yawned. "Excuse me."

Outside the windows, L.A. looked hopeful. Almost pristine. The palm trees swayed slightly in an onshore breeze, lending the city an exotic, tropical feel it didn't otherwise possess. An unexpected rain had washed the disappointment from the streets, leaving the city twinkling in the early-morning air.

Corso checked his watch: 5:36 A.M. They were alone in a fourth-floor conference room in L.A.'s version of a federal building. Warren and Morales had excused themselves and disappeared. In the interim they'd been offered and had accepted two more styrofoam cups of wretched coffee, as well as an offer of Krispy

Kreme doughnuts, which they had both seen fit to decline. Chris Andriatta got to her feet.

"I'm leaving," she said, patting her clothes into place.

Corso looked her over. "You mean . . . like the room?"

"I mean here. L.A. I'm going back home. I've had enough of this."

"Things are just getting interesting."

She stretched and groaned. "Same old, same old," she corrected. "Paper on paper."

Corso shook his head. "This is what they're good at," he said.

"They who?" She looked around the room.

"The ATF. The FBI." He pointed down at the floor. "Where we are right now is what they do best. They find things. They've got a huge database of information they've begged and bullied and borrowed from everywhere. There's no privacy. It's like something out of George Orwell. They know everything about everybody. They put their computers to work on lists and connections to lists and lists of connections to lists. Sooner or later, they find what they're looking for. They found Ted Kaczynski in that shack in the woods. If this Reyes character is connected to anybody capable of making that bomb, they'll find out about it."

She laughed. "I hope you're right," she said. "Send me a postcard. Lemme know how it turns out."

"Come on," Corso coaxed. "They may get a little crazy about jurisdiction and might even be a bit paranoid about shouldering the blame for anything"—he shook a finger in the air—"but these guys know what they're doing. They've been doing it for a long while and they've been taking notes the whole time."

She walked over and stood in front of him. She reached up and grabbed the back of his neck and bent him forward at the waist. She put her cheek next to his, held it there for a long moment and then kissed him gently on the cheek before letting him go. She gave him a wistful smile. "Another time. Another place maybe," she said.

"I'd like to think so," he said.

She turned and walked back toward her chair. She gathered her purse from the darkness beneath the table and headed for the door.

"It's been swell, Corso," she said, reaching for the door handle.

Corso started her way. "Okay . . . okay . . . if you're sure that's what you want to do." He reached for his wallet. She waved him off.

"I'll bill your publisher," she said. "Don't worry about it."

Corso stopped about a pace away. He took her in, as if for the first time. "First class," he said. "Make sure it's first class."

She laughed. "There you go spending other people's money again."

"I insist," Corso said with a smile.

"What would your mother say?"

Corso never got a chance to answer. Warren poked his head into the room.

"Come on," he said.

Corso inclined his head toward Chris Andriatta. "It seems Ms. Andriatta has had enough federal hospitality. She's headed home."

Warren worried the idea for ten seconds. "I don't think so," he said.

The color began to rise in her cheeks. "Am I under arrest?"

"Not unless you want to be."

"Then I'm leaving." She tried to bluster her way past Warren, but he held his ground. Her cheeks were flaming. "You can't . . ." she sputtered.

Warren held up a moderating hand. "Look," he soothed. "Let's not make this any more difficult than it already is. I apologize for the fact that neither of you was a particularly willing participant in this matter. Dragging people from their hotel beds and flying them across the country is not exactly according to protocol." He scratched his head and tried to look boyish. "But, you know . . . for better or worse, you've been privy to a great deal of confidential information regarding an ongoing investigation." He raised his hands and let them slap back to his sides. "I appreciate all the help both of you have given us." He looked from Corso to Andriatta and back. "I really do, but I can't take the chance that something you say or do might compromise an investigation of this nature . . . not at this point . . . not with so much at stake."

"This is bullshit," she screamed, launching a stiff arm at his breastbone, trying to drive Warren from the doorway. He rocked back onto his heels but otherwise didn't budge. When she gathered herself and threw a fist at his face, he caught her hand in his and in a single practiced motion, twisted it behind her back, where he moved it upward until the pain squeezed her eyes shut. She endured the pain in silence. He lowered his voice and spoke into her hair.

"You can wait in a holding cell while we finish this up, or we can all just keep on keepin' on, until we find out whether this line of inquiry is going to pan out or not." He released her hand and gave her a little shove back into the room. Her outrage was like a storm cloud in the air.

"Goddamn you," she screamed. And then again. "Goddamn you." Warren looked wistful. Like some cracker-barrel philosopher dispensing wisdom on a sultry Saturday afternoon. "We'll see, missy," he said. "We surely will."

Problem was, Andriatta was at full boil and not about to listen to homilies. Instead, she dropped her shoulder and went at him full speed, like a linebacker homing in on an unsuspecting quarterback.

He fended her off, using both hands, pulling his head in close to her body, where she couldn't get at him, then spinning her around by the shoulders before pushing hard, sending her staggering backward, directly at Corso, as if to say, "Here . . . take this . . . it's yours."

Corso wrapped his long arms around her and pulled her tight against his chest. She struggled, emitting high-pitched noises of exertion and frustration as she sought to free herself from his encumbrance. Corso could feel a tremor running through her body. Feel the animal within her trying to impose its will on a perverse and ambiguous universe. It took three or four minutes and half a dozen kicks to Corso's shins for her fury to subside. When the noises stopped and her body had ceased to tremble, Corso unwrapped his arms and prepared to defend himself.

Turned out not to be necessary. Her fury had passed. She mustered her dignity, wiped a lock of sweaty hair back from her face and took a deep breath. Her eyes met Corso's. Something had transpired. Something to do with her anger and the way he'd held her in his arms. Both of them knew it. They stood waiting for one or the other to say the right thing. Didn't happen.

"Seems I haven't got a lot of choice here," she said.

"Very temporarily," Warren assured her. "If it's any consolation to ya, I was supposed to start my vacation this week. Delia . . . that's my wife . . . we were gonna have our first vacation in nine years. Coupla weeks down in Antigua. Sand, sun, surf, the whole nine yards." He shook his head sadly. "Next thing you know people start blowing one another up . . ." Andriatta sneered at him and walked over to the corner of the room.

He shrugged and threw a glance Corso's way. Corso returned the shrug.

Warren started for the elevators. Andriatta stood still. Corso gestured "after you" and followed Andriatta down the long corridor.

The sign on the door read: DATA CENTER. Nothing more. What used to consist of entire walls of mainframe computers, lights blinking, reel-to-reel tapes whirling away, had, in recent years, been reduced to nothing more dramatic than half a dozen HP desktops scattered around a cramped space in the basement of the Morris Mayfield Federal Building.

Morales was already on hand when they arrived. "Past ten years," he was saying. "Pomona Veterans Wellness Center." The technician started typing. "Let's get us a list of every patient who used that clinic."

Morales introduced everybody. The techie's name was Plummer. No first name. No title. Just Plummer.

Andriatta gave Plummer a curt nod and sat down at one of the empty computer stations. She folded her arms and swiveled her back to the proceedings. On her right, the laser printer began to spit paper at an ungodly rate. "Nineteen hundred and forty-three names," the tech droned.

"Get me the names of every person who worked there during the same time period," Morales said. More typing.

Corso crossed the room to the printer. He pulled a handful of pages from the tray and spread them out on the desk in front of him. Sorted through them.

"Francisco Reyes," Corso said. "Used the clinic"—he traced

across the page with his finger—"looks like once a week, between . . . August of '98 and about eighteen months ago."

Morales looked Corso's way. "Used the clinic for what?"

"The service code is . . ." He read a ten-digit number.

Plummer typed it in as Corso read. "Outpatient support therapy," he said after a moment.

"Support for what?" Corso asked.

"Doesn't say."

"Can we sort out everybody with the same service code?"

"Easy." Plummer typed some more. "Three hundred sixty-three names."

"What about the employee list?" Morales asked.

"A hundred sixty-nine direct employees."

"How many contractors?" Warren asked.

"No way of telling. Contractors get paid by the General Accounting Office. We'd have to check with GAO when they open in the morning."

It went on for two hours. Every reference and cross-reference imaginable. Andriatta never moved. Just sat there staring at the wall in a futile act of defiance. By the time they finished the second pot of coffee, Morales was beginning to sweat. With the exception of Constance Valparaiso, none of the victims were linked to the clinic in any way. "We may be barking up the wrong tree," Warren said finally. "This whole veterans angle just might be a wild-goose chase."

"Don't even think that," Morales said. "We come up empty here . . ."

He let the end of the sentence slide away.

The door opened. A young agent stood in the doorway beckoning Morales to come to him. "What is it, son?" Morales asked.

The agent started to speak. Looked from Corso to Andriatta, then back to Morales. "You're among friends," Morales assured him.

The guy swallowed hard. "There's been a shooting," he said.

Everyone in the room stiffened. Andriatta spun her chair in a half circle.

"Who?"

The guy pulled a hand out from behind his back. He had something written on a small blue piece of paper. "Raymond G. Fritchey."

"And why would the shooting of Mr. Fritchey be of interest to me?"

"Mr. Fritchey is married to the former Patricia Hildreth."

Warren stopped what he was doing. "Hildreth . . . where do I know that name from?" he asked.

"Her father is Brian Hildreth. State director of veterans affairs."

Morales sat up straight. "Go on."

"She's pregnant."

Impatience crept into his voice. "And?"

"Apparently she's been kidnapped."

29

At 180 miles an hour the sound of the engine was little more than an insistent whine. The morning sun caused Corso to shade his eyes with his hand as he watched the identical Sikorsky helicopter carrying Short and the others disappear into the bank of puffy clouds to the east.

Morales pulled the headphones off and turned his body in the seat. "Here's what we've got so far," he said. "Sacramento PD got a 911 call at 7:02 this morning. Shots fired. First response team finds this Raymond Fritchey lying facedown in his driveway. Car doors flung open. Two bullet holes in his chest. They call for a tac squad to go through the house, which comes up empty. Neighbors identify Fritchey as the occupant. He and

his pregnant wife Patty live there. Both cars are on the premises. Other than hearing gunshots, nobody saw anything."

"No note? No demand?" Warren asked.

"Not yet."

The pilot eased the stick forward. The helicopter began to
drop.

"Anyway," Morales continued, "SPD managed to interview
the husband before they took him into the operating room." He
checked his notes. "According to Fritchey he's getting ready for
work when he hears a commotion out in the driveway. He runs
out and finds two guys dragging his wife across the lawn. One
of the guys pulls a gun and shoots him. That's all he remembers
until he wakes up in the hospital."

"Description?"

"Two males. Both white. Medium height. Medium build."

"No ski masks? No gloves?"

"He thinks he might be able to identify them."

"Doesn't sound like the same crew at all," Andriatta offered.

"Unless they've thrown caution to the winds," Corso said.

"Why would they do that?" she asked.

"Maybe they see Reyes getting caught as the beginning of the
end."

Morales nodded in agreement. "What else could it be? Another coincidence?" he asked. "We leak the Reyes story. We name
him as a suspect in the bombings, hoping it'll give this bunch
pause to wonder. Maybe buy us a little time. We turn the screws
a little and neglect to tell the press he's dead, so maybe we get the
perps wondering if maybe he's running his mouth. And what . . .
somebody else just happens to snatch the California VA director's
daughter the next morning? Just like that? Out of the blue?" He
looked around the cockpit. "I'm not buying it for a minute."

"You didn't find a single thing in those files that suggested Reyes was anything but a loner and a malcontent," Andriatta argued.

"Then we must have missed something," Morales retorted.

Warren changed the subject. "What was she doing outside at that time of the morning?"

"She was on her way to her mother's place. Hubby says he doesn't like leaving her alone during the day. Pregnancy's been a bit dicey. She's supposed to stay off her feet as much as possible."

"How far along is she?" Andriatta asked.

"Seven and a half months," Morales said.

Everybody winced in the short seconds before the radio crackled out a pack of static. The pilot said, "Copy," and banked to the right. "You copy that fifty-one," he said into his microphone.

"Copy," came the answer.

The sensation of falling returned as the helicopter broke through the layer of clouds and the ground suddenly came into view. Twelve hundred feet above the ground, the whine of the turbine engine was replaced by the familiar slap of rotors as the pair of helicopters eased themselves downward through the last wisps of cloud, until the park surrounding the state capitol building came into view, and then, off to the right, the capitol building itself, all gold and white and gleaming in the clean morning air.

A thousand feet up. You could make out the color of the cars in the parking lot.

"They've diverted us to the park across the street," the pilot announced.

"Any reason?" Morales asked.

"Just said they had a problem."

The pilot pulled the microphone away from his lips and pointed. "You seeing what I'm seeing?" he asked everyone in the cockpit.

Eight hundred feet. Corso leaned forward. He swept his eyes over the ground below. The capitol. The gardens, with great splotches of color here and there. The palm trees. The gold ball on top of the dome. The . . . And then, just like that, he picked up on the lack of movement. For two blocks in every direction, nothing moved. Wasn't until they dropped some more that he could make out the roadblocks, the squad cars strewn this way and that, blocking off the surrounding roadways to traffic. The moderate size of the backups said the blockade hadn't been in place for long. The solid line of people leaving the capitol building via the back door suggested something dire was afoot.

"Looks like ants," Warren commented as they settled onto the ground.

No doubt about it. Either they were staging a fire drill or an evacuation of the state capitol building was in full swing. A hundred feet above the grass and falling like a leaf. The pads hit the grass with a lurch. The engine began to wind down. The pilot flipped switches and turned knobs. A cloud of loose dirt and debris surrounded the helicopter. As the rotors slowed, the swirling dust sank back to earth, leaving a beige haze floating in the thick morning air as everyone stretched their cramped legs and struggled out of seat belts.

A moment later they were out of their seats and onto the grass, bent at the waist as they duck walked out from beneath the final lazy turns of the rotors. Andriatta followed along at a sullen trot as they traversed the grass and then the wide boulevard separating the capitol grounds from the park.

Minute they got onto the capitol grounds, the place was packed with people and abuzz with speculation. The capitol building's displaced workers had spread themselves out along the central walkway and around the circular garden, where they'd broken up into conversational groups of five or six, the better to speculate on the cause of this morning's unwelcome interruption.

Warren and Morales used their badges to clear the way. As they exited the rear of the crowd and approached the state capitol building, a pair of California state troopers trotted up to bar the way.

"FBI," Morales shouted.

"What's the story?" Warren demanded.

They shrugged in unison. "Nobody tells us anything," said the nearest cop. "Just told us to get the building emptied as quick as possible."

The other cop gestured toward the back door of the capitol building. "Whatever it is, the brass is all huddled up inside trying to decide what to do next."

At that moment, the buzz of an electric motor announced Short's arrival. He dropped the chair into low gear, bounced up the first set of stairs, whizzed over the wide stone landing and started up the second tier, his chair rocking from side to side as the powerful hydraulic mechanism lifted him over step after step.

The state troopers looked on dumbfounded.

"He's with us," Morales said.

"Yeah," said one of the cops. "The bomb guy."

"From TV," said the other cop.

Short's ATF crew jogged along in his wake, lugging equipment boxes, taking the stairs two at a time as they struggled to keep up. Without further ado, Morales and Warren followed suit.

Corso started to follow, but instead glanced back over his shoulder, intending to beckon Andriatta forward. 'Cept there was nobody there. Somewhere along the line, Andriatta had melted into the crowd and disappeared. He paused, considered trying to

find her among the hundreds of milling bodies, then headed up
the stairs after the others, who had disappeared from view.

By the time Corso jerked open one of the big brass doors, the
others had already crossed the foyer and were standing out in the
middle of the rotunda, directly beneath the ornate capitol dome.
Raised voices rolled around the curved interior as Corso crossed
the great seal of the state of California and joined the others.

"I'm not leaving." The guy was in his fifties. Lithe and fit, he
looked like a surfer in middle age. Except for his face. His face
was filled with blood and anguish. A vein in the side of his neck
looked dangerous to his health. What had once been a head full
of blond hair, age had turned the color of unpolished brass. A pair
of state troopers stood sentinel at his elbows. The deep wrinkles
in his sleeves suggested they'd recently been restraining him by
the arms.

A cop in a gray pin-striped suit held up a moderating hand.
"Let us handle this," he said soothingly to the blond guy. "There's
no point in you . . ."

The sound of approaching footsteps pulled his head around.
The sight caused his entire bald head to furrow in wonder. "Who
in hell called you guys?" he asked.

"What's going on?" Morales asked.

"My daughter . . ." blondie began.

"You'd be Mr. Hildreth," Warren said.

The cop's forehead furrows were so deep they looked like
louvers. He opened his jutting jaw to demand an explanation, but
Morales beat him to the punch.

Morales stepped in close to Hildreth. "Have you heard from
your daughter?"

The guy bobbed his head up and down. "She called"—he
checked his watch—"twenty-five minutes ago. She said she was

coming here." He pointed down at the floor. "Said I had to be here to meet her."

"Was that it? That's all she said?" Morales asked.

Hildreth took a deep breath. Swallowed hard. "She said they'd kill her if either of us failed to follow directions."

"She mention a bomb?" Corso asked.

Hildreth looked even more stricken. His eyes were wide as he shook his head.

The bald cop stepped between Corso and Hildreth. Put his hands on his hips. "Who's this?" he wanted to know.

Warren took over. "Mr. Corso is consulting with us on another case," he said.

"What's this about bombs?" Hildreth asked.

Warren threw an arm around the bald cop's shoulders and pulled him aside. Corso watched as Warren brought the other man up to speed. The cop nodded several times before stepping back. "But you don't know for sure," he said.

"No," Warren answered.

"What bomb?" Hildreth demanded. "I've got a right to know what's going on around here, damnit. This is my daughter and her unborn son we're talking about here. If there's something about a bomb . . ."

Warren leaned in close to Corso. "Where's our friend Ms. Andriatta?"

"No idea," Corso said, staring straight ahead.

Warren gave Corso the once-over, looking for signs of duplicity, then turned and hustled off toward the nearest wall, pulling out his cell phone as he walked. His face was animated as he whispered instructions into the mouthpiece.

The tic tac of another set of heels echoed through the rotunda. A uniformed trooper crossed the inlaid floor and handed a note to baldy, who read it once and again before passing it on to Morales. His lips moved slightly as he read.

"Let her through," Morales said.

"What if . . ." the cop began.

"There's no 'what if?'" Morales assured him. "It's a proven fact. If we don't follow directions . . ." He shot a glance at Hildreth, caught himself and swallowed the rest of the sentence. He turned to face Warren and Corso and the rest of the team. He gestured them closer. "We've got a blue Dodge van at the north roadblock," he said in a low voice. "A young woman who has identified herself as Patricia Hildreth says she has orders to drive right up to the capitol steps and wait for her father to come out of the building and join her." He paused and looked around the room. ". . . at which point she says she's supposed to receive further instructions."

Hildreth swam his way past the cops and confronted Morales.

"My daughter . . . you've heard from my daughter?"

"In a manner of speaking," Morales said.

"Captain." Another voice ricocheted through the dome.

Hildreth stepped away from the others and peered over toward the front entrance, where a guy in a blue suit was waving his hands around. A moment passed. Captain whoever translated the hand signals. He turned and faced the others.

"She's on the way," he said.

30

By the time the van rolled to a halt at the bottom of the stairs, each of the eight fluted columns holding the Roman portico aloft had at least one frightened soul cowering behind it. As the crow flew, they were no more than forty yards from the blue Dodge van, which was, at that moment, nosed up to one of the huge concrete planter boxes surrounding the building.

Overflowing with purples and reds and yellows, the massive containers unified style and substance as they simultaneously gladdened the eye and served as a security barrier, preventing anything short of a tank from driving closer to the building.

As they'd awaited the van's arrival, Hildreth had started for the door, hoping to meet his daughter and her unborn child at the moment of their arrival. A wave of Morales' hand had quashed any such notion.

And so, behind the cowering collection of federal agents, just inside the first set of brass doors, Hildreth was being held at bay by the same pair of burly troopers who had, a moment ago, found themselves hard-pressed to stop a loving father from carrying out what seemed little more than a father's duty. When they finally had his writhing body pinned to the floor, he'd looked up at Morales and screamed, "It's my daughter, for Christ sake. Wouldn't you go to your daughter?" he bellowed.

Morales had signaled the cops to help Hildreth up. They'd maintained their hold on his elbows as they tilted him into an upright position and set him carefully on his feet. Morales walked over and looked the other man in the eye. "Yes, I would," he said. "I'd be doing the same things you're trying to do if I were in your position."

Hildreth jerked his arms free, ran a hand through his hair and began straightening out his suit. "If you think"—he gulped greath mouthfuls of air—"if you think I'm going to stand idly by while my daughter . . ." His voice began to break. "While my daughter . . ." He was unable to finish. Overcome by emotion, he'd turned away, a series of disappointed sobs shook his body as he paced out into the middle of the rotunda where he dropped his face into his hands and cried.

He had finished crying and was blowing his nose for the third time when the van rolled to a stop out front. Whatever emotional reserves he'd mustered in the prior minutes went straight out the window. He bolted for the front of the building; the soles of his shoes slapped the floor like tentative applause as he made for the front doors and his endangered daughter beyond.

Five seconds later, he found himself surrounded by half a

dozen cops, ATF types and FBI agents whose collective weight and unified resolve proved sufficent to bring him to a halt. He'd gotten far enough to be able to see the van idling at the bottom of the stairs. Everyone held their breath. Waited. Grabbed another quick gasp of air and waited again. Nothing happened. Normal breathing resumed.

Short motored over. He jerked his head, indicating he wanted to chat. Corso and Morales followed him out into the middle of the room. He didn't bother to turn his best side toward the others this time, just leaned forward in the chair and dropped his voice to a rough whisper. "No matter what . . ." he growled. ". . . no way we can let this guy and his daughter get anywhere near one another." He looked from one man to the other until he was satisfied they'd gotten the message. His face was pinched and sweaty; he was obviously distraught. No vestige of his usual jocularity was present. "The minute the perp hears Daddy's voice, that girl's going off like a Roman candle."

The image caused Corso and Morales to suck air. The trio was silent as they made their way back to the top of the stairs.

The van's windows were tinted dark enough to make the occupant of the driver's seat little more than an occasional sense of movement behind the glass.

On the left, Hildreth groaned. "What's . . ."

Corso stepped around Morales, getting shoulder to shoulder with Hildreth. He bent at the waist and spoke directly into the man's ear. "I can only imagine how hard this must be for you. But you've got to understand . . . if we're right about who's responsible for this . . . then the very worst thing you could do is to run down those stairs to your daughter's side."

Hildreth turned his head and looked at Corso for the first time. Corso put a reassuring hand on his arm. "You saw what

happened in L.A. the other day." The other man nodded in horror. "Then you know these people aren't kidding. They don't
give a damn about collateral damage and they don't give a damn
about you and your daughter."

"You think . . . these people are the same ones who . . ."

"There's a good chance," Corso said. "And if we're right, it
means they'll have her wired for sound. They'll know the minute
you get to her side."

Corso threw a look at Morales who picked up the vibe and
walked to Hildreth's other side. "We've got an army of agents and
police officers checking rooftops, hilltops . . . anything high," he
assured Hildreth. "We're looking for any place that might provide the perpetrators with a line of sight. The longer this takes,
the better our chances of coming up with something, so just hang
in there."

"I don't understand," Hildreth said. "Do they want money?
I can . . ."

Corso cut him off. "If this were about money, they'd have sent
her to a bank."

Corso closed his eyes for a moment, for long enough to
imagine what it would be like to have a loved one in this kind of
peril . . . in a situation where nothing in his previous existence
mattered . . . a moment in time where neither intention nor
means mattered a whit to the people holding the cards. He imagined . . .

"Coming," somebody yelled from over by the door.

They hurried over in time to see the driver's door taking the
last rhythmic bounces on its hinges before coming to rest. They
sorted themselves out among the columns and waited for her to
appear, but nothing happened—only the tic tic of the van's engine and the distant roar of traffic . . . until . . . the van rocked

slightly on its springs, causing those beneath the portico to press forward . . . to hold their collective breath until . . . until nothing—and then a woman's foot stepped out onto the ground, white tennis shoe, from the five red stripes it looked like K SWISS, baggy baby blue sweatpants, and then a second shoe, until a pair of legs, visible only from the shins down, appeared beneath the bottom of the front door.

They watched as the toes turned back toward the van as she reached inside for something . . . something she was having difficulty getting past the steering wheel . . . something that caused her to raise up on her toes for a moment before settling back to the ground and shutting the driver's door with her hip.

She'd inherited her father's slim build and thick blond hair. She wore a baby blue sweat suit with letters UCLA emblazoned down each sleeve. The university logo was also printed on the front of the sweatshirt. Or at least it looked that way. Hard to tell with the explosive device hanging from her neck, the oversized steel handcuff reflecting the rays of the sun, the ominous black steel box hanging down over her chest, resting uneasily on the bulge of her distended middle. She stood for a moment with her left hand folded beneath her prodigious belly for support, as she swiveled her neck to take in her surroundings, looking this way and that as if committing the scene to memory.

Corso watched as she suddenly cocked her head, listening to the electronic voice in her ear. She hiccupped out an answer and began sidestepping away from the vehicle, one step, two steps, and then three before she raised a battery-operated megaphone to her lips. Her hand shook. Her finger had difficulty finding the trigger and then difficulty pulling it. She said something that didn't get amplified, checked her hand and then tried again. "Daddy," she croaked. "Help me."

It took three cops to keep Hildreth from rushing toward his daughter. "Patty," he bellowed, "Patty," as they dragged him back behind the big brass doors, back into the foyer, where his plaintive cries were barely audible to those outside.

Short motored out past the columns, until the front wheels of his chair were scant inches from the top step. She raised her megaphone again. "They say my father . . ."

Short waved her off. He brought his good hand to his lips, raised a single finger and made the "be quiet" sign. She began to sob. "Please," she pleaded. "If I don't do what they say . . ."

Warren peeked out from behind a granite column. "Let the Bureau handle it, Short," he growled. "This isn't our end."

"The longer this goes on, the less chance she's got," Short said without ever moving his eyes from the young woman at the bottom of the stairs.

Down below, Patricia Fritchey pulled the protective arm from beneath her belly and used her index finger to push the microphone deeper into her ear. "I'm trying," she wailed. "Can't you hear me, I'm trying."

She listened again. Everyone watched, horrified as her face dissolved into a puddle of fear. "Please," she begged. "I'm trying," she blubbered, bringing the bullhorn up to her mouth once again. "Daddy." She was screaming now, over and over, until the effort brought her to her knees. She sat on the bottom step, weeping and moaning, and calling for her daddy to come and rescue her.

Morales looked over at Warren. "Maybe we gotta let him go to her," he said.

"The minute that happens they're both dead," said Short.

"If we don't, she and that baby are dead."

"There's nothing . . ." Warren started.

His disclaimer was too late. By the time the words covered
the distance to where Short had been sitting, the wheelchair was
already over the edge, two steps down, rocking ungracefully from
side to side, as Short manipulated both the joystick and the brake
with great dexterity, maneuvering the chair down over each suc-
cessive riser without losing the constant battle with gravity.

The whine of the powerful engine pulled Patty Fritchey's eyes
upward. It took her several seconds to process what she found
herself looking at. She blinked twice at the gruesome figure moving her way, then opened her mouth and screamed.

Having no way to stop the chair's downward momentum in
the middle of a flight of stairs, Short kept coming, ignoring her
cries. Bouncing from side to side like a scarecrow in the wind, he
descended stair after stair after stair, until he was no more than a
dozen risers above the hysterical young woman who lay sprawled
and spent on the chiseled stones below.

The voice in her ear brought her head up in time for her to
see Paul Short bounce down onto her level. Her eyes opened
wide in terror. She screamed again. Over and over until her voice
began to give out.

"That motherfucker's crazy," somebody to Corso's right said.

"Either got real big balls or a real small brain," somebody else
countered.

"Or both," added a third.

On the flat now, Short wheeled the chair in a one-eighty. Patricia Fritchey was wailing and trying to inch away from the horror in
the wheelchair, pushing herself along on her hip, the steel fingers
surrounding her neck swinging back and forth as she moved, snail-
like, across the face of the stairway.

Short opened one of the several tool compartments built into
the side of his chair. Everyone held their breath and waited for

him to come out with a tool of some sort, wire cutters or a screwdriver, something like that. Instead he produced a small yellow pad and a tiny pencil. He wrote something on the pad and turned it her way.

Her mouth hung open as she read the message. She started to speak, but he cut her off with a slash of the steel hook. He flipped a page and wrote something else. Again she read the message. This time she nodded in silent understanding. She ran a hand over her face and then said something inaudible to whoever was listening.

Short was nodding his head now. Writing again. She read the note, cleared her throat and spoke. "They say he's coming. He's on his way."

"No. No. He's coming, I swear. He's . . ."

She looked down at the box covering the top of her belly. Short had a screwdriver in his good hand and was removing the numerical keypad from the front of the device. Moving with greater speed than would have seemed possible for a man with two hands, he removed the fasteners and dropped the screwdriver into his lap.

They watched as he spoke to her. As she shook her head and began to blubber.

"I can't," she said. "Oh really, I can't."

Short again signaled for her to be quiet. She began to weep again. After a moment, her spine seemed to stiffen. She sat up straight on the stair. Gave Paul Short a long resolute look and then took the box in both hands.

At the top of the stairs breathing was again suspended as Patricia Fritchey worked her nails between the face plate and the box and then slowly, ever so slowly, began to pull the inner mechanism out into the light of day, moving it upward and out of the box until a rainbow of wires became visible.

Short wasted no time. He leaned forward until his nose was very nearly in her lap. From a compartment on the right side of the chair, he produced a small pair of wire cutters. The sight of the tool flushed whatever resolve she might have mustered. She began to sob again, her breath a series of audible gasps. The voice in her ear said something. "He's coming," she said and then plastered a hand over her mouth.

As Paul Short poked the cutters among the maze of wires lying across the top of her stomach, he made eye contact with Patricia Fritchey. They gazed into each other's eyes for longer than was polite. Almost as if they formed some sort of pact, some sort of mutual recognition, in the elongated seconds before he lowered his ruined head and snipped a wire.

31

C orso pulled his head back behind the pillar, rested his cheek against the cool stone and counted to ten. When nothing exploded, he leaned out far enough to refocus one eye on the pair at the bottom of the stairs. Short was poking around inside the mechanism, using the steel hook to separate wires. Patricia Fritchey couldn't watch. She had her head turned to the side and, if the knots along her jawline were any indication, appeared to be grinding her molars to dust.

Corso watched in morbid fascination as Short reached into the maze of color-coded wires, hesitated briefly, then snipped something. And then again and again. Apparently satisfied, he wiped his brow with his sleeve and sat back in his chair, chest heaving from the emotional effort. Sensing a sudden lack of movement, Patricia opened one eye.

Short pressed his index finger to his lips and used the same finger to indicate he wanted her to turn her back to him. She did as bidden, scooting around on one hip until she faced in the other direction. The trembling in her shoulders was visible from the top of the stairs. Short reached out and put the hook on her shoulder.

He waited for her shaking to subside, then reached out and took hold of the steel fingers encircling her neck. For the third time in the past ten minutes, breathing became optional as Paul Short slowly . . . ever so slowly . . . pulled the metal locking mechanism apart. He spread the tines as far as they'd go, allowing her to bend forward and free herself of its metallic grip. She sat in stunned silence for a moment, then reached up and ran her hands around her unencumbered throat. Stifling a cry of joy, she struggled first to her knees, then to her feet.

Short placed the device gingerly on the landing. Before she could move away, he reached out with his good hand and pulled her down into his lap. A forward thrust of the joystick sent them rocketing across the walkway at warp speed. Patricia Fritchey locked her arms around Paul Short's neck and hung on for dear life as the speedy wheelchair put distance between themselves and the bomb.

The pair got half a dozen planters up the walkway when the control keys on the bomb began to blink red and green . . . red and green.

"Watch out," someone shouted.

And bang . . . first a small yellow flame, followed by a puff of white smoke. Then the bomb went off, the sharp sound tearing the fabric of the morning, the concussion rocking the blue van on its springs, sending the official assemblage cowering behind their columns once more, as bits of stone and metal rained back to earth in a rush.

Anguished cries rang out from within the capitol building and then, just as quickly, subsided. A moment later, the great brass door banged open and Brian Hildreth staggered out. His eyes followed the cloud of smoke and dust as it rose toward the heavens, then locked on the unlikely pair sharing a high-tech wheelchair.

"Oh God," Brian Hildreth cried. "Thank God."

He rushed down the stairs at a loose-jointed lope, shouting his daughter's name as he moved along. He was watching his own feet on the stairs, so he didn't see Paul Short stiffen in the wheelchair. Didn't see Short raise his good hand to the sky in alarm. Didn't hear the broken voice shout out the single hoarse syllable. "No."

In some nonverbal way, Corso immediately understood. Without willing it so, he dashed out from behind the pillar and began descending the stairs three at a time, closing the distance between him and Brian Hildreth with every maniacal stride.

The sound of Corso's boots slapping on the stone stairs brought Hildreth to a sudden stop. He turned his head in wonder, just in time for Corso to grab him in a bear hug, to lift him from his feet and then catapult both of them sideways, up and over the beautifully carved balustrade, four feet and four legs pointing straight up in the air, as the pair somersaulted off of the staircase, down into the flower bed below.

The collection of state and federal employees at the top of the stairs bolted forward, fanning down over the stairs with Warren at the forefront as they rushed toward the spot where Hildreth and Corso had disappeared. Security cameras covering the front of the capitol building recorded what happened next.

Experts who analyzed the tape would later agree that the van must surely have contained somewhere in the vicinity of one hundred pounds of plastic explosive in order for it to have caused the degree of damage and destruction visited upon the both the building and the brave law enforcement officers whose lives were forfeit.

Of those who survived, several were able to describe the moment of detonation with sufficient clarity as to create a consensus. They shared a general agreement that the blue Dodge Caravan levitated no less than four feet off the ground at the crack of the first explosion, the sound of which froze everyone in their respective tracks. Of the second explosion, even the survivors remained a bit fuzzy. Suffice it to say the van went off with sufficient force as to register a 3.7 on the University of California seismograph, nearly five miles distant.

Corso had pulled Brian Hildreth over onto his back and had just loosened his tie when the van went suborbital. Although the concrete frame of the stairway prevented the force of the blast from reaching them directly, the explosion sucked the air from Corso's lungs and filled his mouth with dust. Hildreth had landed on his back with Corso on top of him and had the wind driven from his lungs. He gagged and gasped for air that wasn't there, his mouth hanging open, his arms flailing. And then it began to rain bits of van, and they could both breathe again as the air was filled with the sound of broken glass, falling piece by shattered piece to the ground. Then the cacophony of calls and curses and cries coming from above.

Corso helped Hildreth to his feet. Through the smoke and dust they could see that the force of the blast had bowled Short's

wheelchair over backward. Patty Fritchey had regained her feet
and was helping Paul Short extricate himself from the chair. Her
father was panting like a miler as he went lumbering across the
littered grass to her side.

Corso went the other way. Through the flowers and the bushes,
where the height of the wall lessened with every step. Until he
could climb up onto the stairs . . . the whoop whoop of nearby
sirens ringing in his ears and the sight before his eyes wrenching
his innards into a knot.

Half a dozen men lay unmoving on the debris-covered stairway. Another dozen were still on their feet. From the look of it,
everybody was wounded to one degree or another. The nearest
victim . . . the one who'd been closest to the van when it went
off . . . he lay sprawled at Corso's feet, his head twisted at an impossible angle . . . one of his legs bent in a direction it had never
been intended to bend. What was left of him seemed afloat in a
pool of blood. Corso looked away for a moment and dropped to
one knee beside the body. He lifted a hand and felt for a pulse.
Nothing. David Warren was never going to see Antigua.

Where the van had been sitting was nothing more than an
eighteen-inch hole in the concrete. Bits and pieces of debris littered the ground for nearly as far as the eye could see. Sirens approached from all directions at once. Back over his shoulder Brian
Hildreth and his daughter were locked in an embrace. Short was
back on his wheels and moving Corso's way.

Corso sat down on the step next to David Warren. He was
still holding Warren's hand in his. Seemed silly, but he couldn't
bring himself to put it down.

32

Morales circled his former desk, slipping personal items into a cardboard box he held against his chest with one arm. Corso sat in a red leather chair beneath the window, his long legs stretched out before him, his fingers laced behind his head.

"It was the woman," Morales said as he moved. "I was so damned worried about the woman and her baby . . . I never . . ." He tried to stop himself before he could begin making excuses again. "Think it was probably because I've got two daughters of my own. You know . . . maybe I was extrasensitive or something. I . . ."

"How old?" Corso asked.

"Nine and eleven." Morales stopped, dug around in the bottom of the box until he found what he was looking for. A gold-hinged frame. He flipped it open. Two beautiful girls. The younger of the two was missing both front teeth. The older looked a lot like Morales. Same strong chin and wide-set eyes. "I kept picturing myself . . . you know in that guy Hildreth's position. Like it was my daughter out there with a bomb around her neck." He looked to Corso for understanding. "I don't know, man," he said finally.

"What now?"

Morales sighed. "The bottom line is we lost three federal officers this morning. Probably another ten who'll end up on restricted duty." He waved a disgusted hand. "We're all over the TV. CNN and everybody else is camped out down in the lobby." He threw a commemorative pen set into the box.

"What now for you?" Corso asked.

Morales emitted a dry bark of a laugh. "I was the officer in charge man. What do you think? You think the Bureau likes this kind of ink?" He laughed again. "The party's over for me. As of tomorrow I'm on paid administrative leave. The Bureau will keep me in limbo until everything gets sorted out, then they'll send me someplace where they don't have to look at me anymore."

"Sounds kinda harsh."

"SOP," Morales shot back. "The Bureau is an unforgiving mistress."

Corso watched as Morales went inside himself.

"Any word on the Hildreth woman and her baby?" he asked.

"Resting comfortably at home."

"What about Short?"

Morales smiled. "There's talk of a presidential medal."

Corso shook his head. "He sure as hell saved the day."

"Didn't he ever."

Morales stiffened for a moment and pulled the pager from his belt. "Plummer," he said under his breath. Corso watched as he pushed the button, then read the text message as it scrolled by. "Says he's got something interesting."

"Like what?"

"We'll never know."

"Why's that?"

He went back to rifling through the desk. "I'm off the case man. I'm persona non grata around here." He dropped the box on the desktop with a bang.

"Come on. Don't be like that."

Morales shot him an angry look. "You're a troublemaker, you know that?"

Corso sat up in the chair. "I prefer to think of myself as a provocateur."

"Yeah . . . well, you're going to have to provocateur somebody else. I'm in enough trouble already."

"Let's go down and see what Plummer's got. What have you got to lose?"

"Oh . . . let's see . . . my pension . . . my retirement . . ."

"Details . . . details."

He retrieved the box from the desktop. "Go home, Mr. Corso."

"Soon as we see what Plummer's got, I'm outta here." He held up two fingers. Scout's honor.

"All you want is another chapter for your book."

"I like to finish what I start."

"Well . . . I'm finished. How's that?"

Corso looked away. Morales was pulling open drawers. "Besides . . ." he said. "I've got no official standing anymore."

"Apparently Plummer doesn't know that."

"Yeah . . . well . . . he's the only one."

"Come on. Let's just go see what he's got."

Morales kept packing the box. "Hell, Corso, at this point, I don't even have enough authority to get you a plane ticket home. You're gonna have to . . ."

"I'll handle my own plane ticket," Corso said.

Morales looked up. "And you'll take Ms. Andriatta with you?"

Corso waved a dismissive hand. "She's long gone."

Morales made a rude noise with his lips. "She's in a holding cell in the basement. Warren had ATF pick her up at the Long Beach Airport about an hour after she ditched us. She's been down there all day bitching about the food."

"I'll take her with me," Corso offered. "On my dime."

Morales heaved another giant sigh. "Warren was a good man," he said.

"Yeah . . . he was."

A morbid silence settled over the room. Even the flags seemed to droop.

"Come on," Morales said finally. "Let's go."

Corso rocked himself to his feet. He followed Morales out of the office and down the hall to the elevators.

Plummer was exactly where they'd left him earlier in the day, sitting at the center console pecking away at he keyboard. A half-eaten ham sandwich on whole wheat lay moldering on the desk-top.

"Don't you ever go home?" Morales asked him.

Plummer grinned and shook his head. "I'm completely self-contained," he said. "They throw food in the door a couple times a week and I'm good to go."

"Whatcha got?" Morales asked.

"Actually, it was the GAO who got." Plummer fingered the keyboard for the better part of a minute before folding his arms across his chest. "It's been a lot of fun. I've never had access to the whole shebang before." Screens filled with names and numbers flashed across the bank of monitors. "I ran every access code in the state VA system. Everything that happened in Pomona between 1998 and early last year. Couldn't find a thing that connected to that Reyes character. Then I ran the other victims and except for the Valparaiso woman there wasn't anything there either."

Morales wasn't in the mood for banter. "Cut to the chase," he growled.

Plummer looked hurt. "No need to get snippy," he said.

"You really haven't left here, have you?" Corso asked.

Plummer shook his head. "Why?"

Corso filled him in on what had transpired at the state capitol building earlier in the day. By the time he'd finished talking, Plummer had collected his lower jaw and was feeling apologetic. "Jeez . . . I'm sorry . . . I didn't . . . I . . ."

"What's GAO got for us?" Morales asked again.

Plummer swiveled back around to face the monitors. He tapped on the screen with his index finger. "Right here," he said. "It's a list of GAO payments made for Pomona. Same time period. All the people who were issued checks and what services it was they got them for."

Corso bent at the waist and put his face close to the screen. "I'll be damned," he said. Plummer pushed another button. "No shit," Corso said.

Corso straightened up and crooked a finger at Morales. "You better see this," he said. "Might be you can avoid reassignment to Iowa."

Morales wore a dubious expression but wandered over anyway. Plummer pointed again. Morales frowned and leaned in closer. "For what?"

"Contractor services," Plummer said, typing again. By this time Morales very nearly had his nose pressed to the screen. He used his own finger on the screen.

"How many is that?"

"Fifty-seven," Plummer chimed in. "One a month for the better part of five years." He looked up at the scowling Morales and anticipated the next question. "Same thing," he said. "Contractor services."

"What services?"

"Group leader."

"And the other one."

"Guest lecturer." Plummer pushed another key and rolled himself out of the way. "Here's the fun part," he said. Both Corso and Morales stepped up to the machine. "Look at the service code," Plummer prompted.

"Same for both," Corso said.

"Same dates too," Plummer pointed out. He changed screens. "Look at this one," he said.

"So . . ." Corso said. ". . . whatever veterans' group Mr. Reyes attended in Pomona back in '98 was facilitated by our Mr. Ben-Iman?" He looked over at Morales and kept on talking. ". . . and our Mr. Nguyen, the bank manager, was a onetime guest lecturer at the same group in late 2002."

"That's not all," Plummer said. Another screen appeared. A picture of a man in uniform appeared on the screen at the far end of the bay. "Seems our Mr. Nguyen used to be a colonel in the North Vietnamese Army. Got into the country on a State Department visa exemption." Before they could respond, another picture appeared. Ben-Iman this time. "Mr. Ben-Iman, it turns out, wasn't Lebanese after all." He left a pause for effect. "He was Iranian. Just told people he was Lebanese."

"Lots of them do," Morales said. "What's the point?"

"Damned if I know," said Plummer.

"How many patients passed through that group during the time period we're looking at?" Corso asked.

"While Mr. Ben-Iman was the facilitator?"

"Yeah."

"A hundred ninety-seven."

"All with the same service code as Mr. Reyes?"

Plummer shook his head. "I'm guessing it depended on the diagnosis."

"How many with the same service code as Reyes?"

More typing. "Looks like nineteen."

"Print me a list," Morales said. "Names, addresses, phone numbers. The whole thing."

Corso raised an eyebrow. Morales met his gaze.

"It's not tomorrow yet," he said, picking up the telephone. He waited. A voice squeaked on the line. "Get me the ATF," he said.

Morales turned his back and began whispering into the phone. Corso leaned closer to Plummer. "Reyes own a credit card?" he asked.

"Most everybody does."

"Could you run it for me?"

"Sure."

33

"Of the original nineteen, two are dead and another two are incarcerated."

"Dead how?" Morales asked.

The ATF supervisor checked his notes. "One of throat cancer. The other one, a guy named Boyd Sylvain, was killed just about eighteen months ago. They found him shot to death in a Wal-Mart parking lot down in Encino. The PD are handling it as a mugging gone wrong."

"And the two in jail?"

"Both for drugs. Both have been inside for over a year."

"And the others?"

"We've eliminated six, for one reason or another."

"That leaves nine."

"Three have moved out of state." He held up a hand, as if to forestall another question. "We're following them up," he said. "Should have something in the next couple of hours."

"And the others?"

"We've got three in custody and a very nasty standoff situation developing with a fourth."

"Nasty how?" Corso asked.

The ATF guy looked Corso over.

"He's with me," Morales said.

"So was David Warren."

Morales turned red. "Yeah," was all he said.

"The only reason I agreed to do the Bureau's dirty work was to maybe get some sense of closure for the Warren family."

"I understand," Morales said.

ATF checked his notes again. "Got a guy named Larry Kelly out in the Dry Lake area. Another vet with a grievance. He's taken the VA to court a dozen times. He put three shots through the door when we demanded entry. Says he's got a wife and three kids in there with him."

"Ugly," Morales said.

"Worse. He's got a garage out back of the house. First, the dogs hit all over the place. Then we did a wipe test on the workbench and got a chemical positive for C-4. God only knows what he's got in the house with him. We've got a negotiator on the scene. Last I heard Kelly was refusing to talk to him. Says he's not coming out."

"You said you've got three in custody?"

ATF consulted his notes again. "Martin Wellsley, Gordon Jones and Mike Sanford. We found identical explosive devices at the homes of Wellsley and Jones. All wrapped up and ready to go. Sanford had the better part of thirty pounds of military-grade

C-4 in his toolshed. Happens he's still in the Army Reserve. You wanna guess where he does his reserve duty?"

"Twenty-Nine Palms," Corso said. "In the armory."

"Touchdown."

"Any of them got anything useful to say?" Morales asked.

"Not a peep. Five seconds in, they all lawyered up."

Morales nodded knowingly. "You guys did a hell of a job," he said.

"You didn't let me finish" the guy groused. "After they lawyered up, I sent an Assistant U.S. Attorney in to have a few words with each of them. You know, see if maybe we couldn't find somebody who wanted to do less time than everybody else for co-operating with the investigation." He made a face. "The AUSA was in the building anyway on another matter and I figured, you know . . . what the hell, why not?"

This time Morales kept his mouth shut and waited. ATF milked the pause for all it was worth. "Lo and behold if Mr. Wellsley and his mouthpiece didn't decide that seven to fifteen sounded a hell of a lot better than twenty-five to life."

"I'll be damned," Morales said.

"There's a problem."

"What's that?"

"You know the standard deal we cut with them. You give us everything you know. You cop to it in open court. You're a major player in the arrest and conviction of everyone else involved in the crime. And then and only then will we live up to our end of the bargain."

Corso spoke up. "You don't believe the guy?" he asked.

"Problem is, we *do*." He waved his notes in the air. "Everything he says is well and good. The hitch is that he hasn't got a hell of a lot to give us that we don't already have, and some of what he is giving us is guesswork."

"What's he saying?" Corso asked.

"Pretty much the way you guys had it drawn. There's this bunch of guys who wind up in the same support group in Pomona. All of them disabled to one degree or another. All of them feeling like the government owes them something. Like they've been big-time cheated by the system. To quote Mr. Wellsley, '. . . like they been used and thrown away.'"

"Just like that? By coincidence, they all wind up at Pomona?"

ATF threw a sly glance at Morales. "Your friend here is pretty sharp," he said, before shifting his hard blue eyes to Corso. "No coincidence about it. Mr. . . ."

"Corso."

"Friend of mine in the VA system tells me it's pretty much common knowledge . . . you get one of these group wreckers . . . somebody who's poisoning the whole system with his attitude . . . you send his ass up to Pomona. That way he can't claim you're not providing him with the service he's entitled to, but you don't have to put up with his rants and raves either."

"So they got all the real malcontents under one roof."

"Tried a different therapeutic approach too."

Corso and Morales waited for him to go on. "From what he tells me. This idea of 'tough love' was all the rage back in the nineties." When nobody disagreed, he went on. "So they try something a bit less supportive and a bit more confrontational. They hire this guy Ben-Iman to facilitate the group. He's not only got the credentials, but he's one of those self-made types who came to this country with a quarter in his pocket, not speaking the language . . ." He rolled a hand around his wrist. "You know . . . the whole immigrant Horatio Alger story."

"Which was the attitude got his butt sent to Pomona as well."

"Of course."

"A match made in heaven," Corso added.

"So Ben-Iman's a real Tartar. No-nonsense. Hold the whining. Bootstrap yourself back into society. Take responsibility for yourself. Stop blaming others for your problems."

"I've heard worse ideas," said Corso.

"Haven't we all," ATF agreed.

"And they can't just stop showing up for sessions, or the government will cut their benefits," Morales added.

"Or stop them altogether," ATF amended. "Our man Wellsley says that's exactly what happened to a couple of guys early on."

"So every Wednesday night for five years . . ." Corso began.

"These guys are sitting there hating every minute of it."

ATF looked over at Morales. "You check the VA records. You'll find a bunch of people come and gone over that time period." He waved a finger. "But you'll find this little nucleus of discontent who was there the whole time."

"So what happened?"

"So Ben-Iman is cutting them no slack. He keeps bringing in guest speakers who've had it harder, people who are physically worse off, people who started lower and still made something of themselves."

"Our Mr. Nguyen, the bank manager," Corso ventured.

"Bingo."

"The guy in Malibu?"

"Death camp inmate."

"The woman over on Figueroa . . ."

"Cancer survivor."

"All of them guest lecturers?"

"Yup."

The news had a sobering effect. Everyone took a minute to process the information. Corso broke the spell. "Whose idea was this thing?"

"According to Wellsley . . . he was approached by Larry Kelly about a year and a half ago."

"The guy who's barricaded in his house?" Morales asked.

"Yup. Wellsley says Kelly told it like it was. Said it was dangerous, illegal as hell and damn well might get them killed or sent away forever. But he also said it was a chance for them to get what was coming to them. Even up a few scores and all end up with enough cash to live out their lives somewhere else."

"Five years in the same group and you probably get a pretty good idea who might go along with a crazy-ass scheme like this," Morales said.

"Interesting point." ATF held up that finger again. "Wellsley says he doesn't know for sure, but he thinks Kelly might have asked somebody who turned him down. He says he heard Kelly say something about how they couldn't afford to have so and so walking around."

"Our friend from Wal-Mart maybe?" Corso asked.

34

She was asleep, curled up on the narrow metal cot, her legs drawn up to her chest, her face pressed to the wall. Corso stood for a moment looking down at her, feeling the rhythm of her steady breathing. After a moment, he reached down and gave her shoulder a gentle shake.

"Go away," she said.

"You sure?" he asked.

The sound of his voice brought her upright, rubbing her eyes as she rolled over and looked around. "It's about damn time," she said.

"Things have been a bit hectic."

She was on her feet now, smoothing her clothes, trying to shake her hair back into place. "What time is it?" she demanded.

Corso checked his watch. "Nine-fifteen."

She kicked the cot in anger. "Do you have any idea how long I've been here?" She didn't wait for an answer. Instead she stomped out of the cell and looked up and down the hall in both directions. "Where's that goddamned Warren," she wanted to know. "I'm gonna . . ." Corso threw an arm around her shoulder and began to whisper in her ear.

By the time he'd finished, her anger had morphed into a wan and weary silence. She leaned back against the wall with tears in her eyes. "That's not right," she said. "That's just not right."

"We got 'em," Corso said. "At least most of 'em anyway."

Her eyes turned to stones. "What's that supposed to mean?"

He gave her the specifics. One dead, three in custody, another barricaded in his house. "If I had to guess, I'd say there's probably still two or three running around somewhere."

"Are they . . ."

"Don't worry about it. This is where the Bureau gets to do what it does best and we finally get to go home."

"I can't go home," she argued. "I have to go back to that damn hotel and pick up my belongings. Among other things, my passport is back there."

"Mine too," Corso said. "We'll get out of here first thing in the morning."

The news allowed her feet to move. She began to amble down the corridor with Corso. When he strolled on past the elevators, she stopped walking, shaking her head as she locked her knees and refused to move. She pointed toward the door at the end of the hall. DATA ROOM. "No way," she insisted. "That's it. I'm not . . ."

"Just want to say my good-byes," he said. "You can wait here if you want."

She pretended not to hear.

"You can wait out here if you want," he said. When she folded her arms across her chest and turned away, he started down the hall. Halfway to the door, he heard her footsteps trotting along in his wake.

He smiled and pulled the door open wide, bowing at the waist in a courtly manner, standing aside and ushering her into the room, before stepping inside and closing the door.

Plummer was still at his post. In the past four hours, somebody'd emptied the wastebaskets. Everything else was precisely as it was before. Morales was on the phone. The expression on his face said he wasn't ordering Chinese takeout.

"Brief me in an hour," Morales said into the receiver before hanging up.

"Nice to see you're still with us," Corso said with a smile.

"Amazing what having a few suspects in jail will do for a guy's popularity," Morales quipped.

"Anything new?"

"Kelly," he said to Corso.

"Yeah?"

"Offed himself before the tac squad could get inside the house." He threw a disgusted hand into the air. "Looked like we had something going too. Short talked his way inside the house. Thought maybe he had the guy turned around."

"That Short's sure got a knack for putting himself in the middle of things, doesn't he?"

Morales agreed. "Kelly musta figured he didn't have much to worry about from a guy in a wheelchair. From what I hear, Short gets the guy halfway to the front door when the guy pulls out a gun and blows himself away."

"That's gonna make things dicey," Corso said.

Morales waggled a hand. "Both Sanford's and Jones's attorneys are fishing for deals in exchange for cooperation." He allowed himself a smirk. "This time we're not making any promises until we hear what they've got to say."

"It's always amazing what people suddenly remember when they're looking at twenty-five to life."

"Life's hell," Morales scoffed. "The AG's insisting on the death penalty for whoever did the capitol building."

Corso gave a low whistle. "Can't have folks offing federal agents."

"No, we can't."

Morales walked around Corso, over to where Andriatta stood.

"I feel like we may owe you an apology," he said.

"You didn't kidnap me and drag me out here," she snarled. "You've got nothing to apologize for."

"Anyway . . ." he said with a small smile. ". . . let me apologize for any inconvenience this whole thing may have caused you. I'm certain that Mr. Warren would never have gotten you involved in something of this nature had he known . . ." He searched for the rest of the sentence. ". . . if he'd . . ."

"I just want to go home."

"I don't blame you," he said. "So do I." He lowered his voice. "I'm sure Mr. Warren . . ."

Corso wandered over and stood next to Plummer. "Nice work on pulling those guest lecturer names out of the GAO list," he said.

"It was your idea," Plummer said, still typing away. "All I did was compile the data."

"What if somebody was already on the GAO payroll?"

"Full-time?"

"As a consultant."

"*And* as a lecturer?"

"Yeah."

He thought it over. "I don't know," he said finally. He laced his fingers and cracked his knuckles. "You got somebody specific in mind?"

Corso nodded his head. "Can you run the name for me?"

"Sure."

Corso picked up a thoroughly chewed pencil from the desktop and printed the name. Plummer brought it close to his face.

"Isn't that the . . ."

Corso put a finger to his lips. "Just between you and me," he whispered.

Plummer changed screens and typed in the name.

"Three times," Plummer said. "July '97 . . ."

Corso cut him off. "Thanks," he said.

Plummer got the message. He poked the keyboard twice and the names and dates disappeared. "You think he . . ." Plummer began.

"Wait fifteen minutes, then show Special Agent Morales," Corso said. "Can you do that for me?"

Plummer said he could.

A hand on his shoulder brought Corso to his full height. Morales had his amiable face on. "I owe both of you a round of thanks."

Corso tried demure, but Morales wasn't having any of it. "Don't quote me on this, but we wouldn't be where we are in this investigation were it not for the pair of you." He ran a gaze over both of them. "You guys have a knack for asking the right question at the right time."

"Even a blind pig will occasionally root up an acorn," Corso said.

"Even if the pig *has* been wearing the same clothes for a week," Andriatta added without the slightest trace of humor.

"I can probably get you aboard a military transport . . ."

Corso cut him off. "We've got reservations back to Pennsylvania first thing in the morning," he said.

Morales nodded knowingly. "What *can* I do for you two?"

"A ride back to the hotel maybe," Corso said.

Morales walked over and picked up the phone.

"One more room service dinner?" Corso asked Andriatta.

"Actually, I was hoping for another cardboard sandwich," she said.

"I'll call the concierge, see what they can do," Corso said.

Morales appeared at Corso's shoulder. He stuck out his hand.

"Take the elevator down to parking level three. There's a car and a driver waiting for you there." Corso shook his hand.

For a mad moment, Morales considered wrapping Andriatta in a hug. By the time he made up his mind, she was out the door and gone.

"Later," Corso said as he followed her back down the hall to the elevators.

They made the short ride in silence.

Parking level three smelled as if exhaust fumes had been mixed into the concrete at the time of construction. This far beneath ground, the weight above their heads was palpable, almost as if it rested partly on their shoulders. Illuminated EXIT signs seemed to point in all directions at once. An assortment of FBI vehicles filled the space. The elevator bonged once and disappeared. Corso looked in both directions.

"We must have beat the car," he said.

Andriatta only grunted and turned away. She walked in a tight circle, the sounds of her heels echoing through the concrete cavern like pistol shots. The squeal of tires and the sound of a car engine pulled Corso's head around.

"Here it comes," he said.

But he was wrong. Instead of the omnipresent unmarked Chevy, a Ford conversion van whipped around the corner, rolled right at them before making a hard left and screeching to a halt in one of the handicapped parking spaces adjacent to the elevators.

The driver killed the engine. The van rocked slightly on its springs, then the sounds of a sliding door filled the air. Corso and Andriatta listened as the whine of a hydraulic lift filled the air. They passed a knowing look as the lift folded itself back into the van and the door slid closed.

Five seconds later, Paul Short and his wheelchair appeared. The sight of Corso and Andriatta brought him to an abrupt halt. "Hey," he said.

"You just getting back from Dry Lake?" Corso asked.

Short nodded. "You guys coming or going?" he asked.

"Going," Andriatta answered.

"I hear you nearly got the guy out of the house."

Short lifted his good hand from the control panel. He held his thumb and forefinger about a half inch apart. "This close," he said. "He was right there."

"What happened?"

Short shrugged. "Who knows what's going through the mind of a guy like that?"

"Another guy like that maybe," Corso said.

"Birds of a feather."

"Something like that."

"Or maybe somebody he knew."

Short leaned his head back. "You got some sort of itch you're looking to scratch?"

"I just thought you might have known the guy," Corso said.

"Now how would I know a dude like that?"

"Maybe from when you guest lectured at his veterans' support group."

Short's face thought about a denial but changed its mind.

"They're just faces to me, Corso. Gigs I take on for the money."

"Must get tiresome," Corso said. "Parading yourself all over like some circus animal. Appearing here and there. Come and see the freak." Short began to push himself out of the chair. "Especially with all you've done for your country. All the risks you've taken. What you've sacrificed."

"You don't know the meaning of sacrifice."

Behind Paul Short the black FBI sedan had rounded the corner and was rolling their way. Short heard the sound of the tires and threw a glance back over his shoulder.

He smiled and opened the wheelchair's control panel. The car stopped. The driver got out.

Andriatta didn't need an invitation. She walked away, hurrying over to the car and throwing herself into the backseat. The driver looked at Corso. "You coming" he asked.

"Just a second," Corso said.

The driver walked back and climbed into the driver's seat.

Corso waited until the driver closed the door. Corso looked around. "Just us here, Short, and between you and me and the lamppost, the one thing I know for sure is that *you're* the one who put this thing together. *You're* the one who constructed those bombs and talked Kelly into putting together a crew. It's the only way any of it makes any sense, and eventually they're going to figure it out upstairs."

"You're crazy."

"Not crazy enough to get involved with something like this mess."

It was all Short could do not to smile. "There isn't a shred of evidence to connect me with anything."

"Especially since Mr. Kelly so conveniently offed himself." When Paul Short remained silent, Corso continued. "It's gonna come out, man. That's why conspiracies never work. They rely on people keeping their mouths shut, which of course we all know is something human beings are incapable of. Somebody tells somebody. It's human nature. The only way to keep a secret is never to tell a living soul."

"You lead a rich fantasy life, Mr. Corso."

"Everywhere you go these days, you leave a paper trail. There's just no helping it. You guest lecture at veterans' groups, you show up on the GAO payroll."

"You're dreaming."

"I hear Kelly shot himself through the heart."

"So?"

"Risky business, man. Lots of things could go wrong with a heart shot. That's why nine out of ten guys . . . they decide to commit suicide . . . they stick the gun in their mouths and blow their brains all over the ceiling. The head's a sure thing."

"He was a tortured soul. Probably wasn't thinking clearly."

"I wonder what would happen if a coroner bothered to check the angle of entry. I wonder if he'd find that Kelly held the gun like this"—He clasped his hands in front of his chest—"or whether he'd find the slug came from considerably lower than that." He gestured at Paul Short. "Say something like down where you are."

"You're starting to piss me off, Mr. Corso."

"You're the tortured soul, Short. Not poor Kelly. He was just an asshole who blamed his failure on others. He had the great misfortune to grow up in our present-day 'blameless society,' a shitty little world where even the most atrocious actions can be attributed to poor potty training or absentee parents." Corso dismissed Short with a wave of his hand. "The party's over, man. You're going down for this."

The smile he'd been keeping under wraps found its way to his face. "Maybe I'll make a run for it." The grin got bigger. "They'll never find me."

"Gonna just blend into the crowd, huh?"

Short pointed at Corso with his hook. "You know something asshole, you really ought to wipe that self-satisfied expression off your face. You really should." His facial expression looked as if he'd suddenly detected a vile odor in the air. "About the time those assholes stopped following the plan and started freelancing, my dog could have figured it out. You hear me? This wasn't about threatening to kill unborn babies, man. This was about getting people's attention. About somebody finally giving a shit about what's going on with veterans." He shrugged. "You were right about conspiracies. Even if they'd stuck to the plan, sooner or later the whole thing was going to come apart. Hell, I never had any illusions about walking away."

"Well then I guess you won't be disappointed."

"I'm fresh out of disappointed, Corso."

"You were a hero."

He shook his head. "I was a fool. Just another dope who believed in a bunch of romantic bullshit that didn't exist."

Another crooked smile crossed his ruined face. He pulled open the control panel and flipped a switch. "I'm not going to prison." He looked up at Corso.

"Ten," he said.

Corso went cold. His mouth tasted of dirty metal.

"Nine."

Corso turned and ran toward the car. "Go! Go!" he screamed at the driver, using his hands in a frantic gesture of retreat.

"Eight," he heard just as the engine began to roar and the car screech backward in a cloud of tire smoke. Corso threw himself onto the hood, grabbing the windshield wipers with both hands, face-to-face with the driver, screaming, "Go! Go!" at the top of his lungs.

"Six," Corso counted in his head as the driver got off the gas and whipped the car around the corner in reverse. Centrifugal force nearly tore Corso from the hood of the car, only the windshield wipers kept him in place.

"Five," as the FBI car dragged its front fender along the block wall, sending a shower of sparks into the subterranean air.

"Four," as they rear-ended a parked car and ground to a halt. Corso lost count as he was thrown up and over the windshield, the wipers still clutched in his hands as he bounced once on the roof before sliding down onto the trunk of the car.

Inside the FBI car, Andriatta was up on her knees, her face no more than a foot from Corso's when, from the far side of the garage, Corso heard Short's voice say the magic word. "Zero."

And then the crack and the awful sucking of air in the second before the explosion battered his eardrums and set the building to shaking.

35

"LAX always makes me feel like the circus must be in town," she said.

Corso looked around and smiled. "Now that you mention it."

"Place is a zoo," she groused.

When he didn't respond, she slackened her gait, looked up. "You ever listen to anybody other than yourself for more than ten seconds at a time?"

Corso thought it over. "You ever do anything but bitch?" he asked.

She stopped in the middle of the concourse and looked around in disbelief. The flow of bodies broke ranks and split, separating the squeaks of shoes and the whirs of wheels into separate streams, leaving the pair marooned on a narrow atoll of floor.

"Did you just call me a bitch?"

"No. I just asked if you ever stopped bitching about things."

"You'll have to excuse me if I fail to see the difference."

"One's a noun. The other's a verb."

She stammered in mock disbelief. "I didn't volunteer for this, you know."

"Yes you did. You signed on for pay . . . signed on to help out on an investigative piece. *You're* the embittered international correspondent, remember? You're little Miss 'been there and seen that.' Nothing that's happened with us lately should have been much of a surprise to you. Nothing's a given. You just roll with the flow and wait to see what happens next. You know that at least as well as I do. So what's the big deal?"

"The big deal is that I've had enough. I want to go home." She shook a finger in his face. "Nobody has the right to . . ."

"Is that what you told the Taliban? You tell them you'd had enough of them and their little turbans and that you demanded to go home this instant?"

She stalked off. Corso followed along in her wake. "I didn't think so," he said to her back. " 'Cause if you'd started this kind of shit with them, they'd have taken you out back of the tent and put one in your ear."

Corso watched as she tossed her hair and stiffened her spine in resolution. After a moment, she melted into the throng at the end of the concourse. Corso watched, trying to pick her out from among the multitude of heads waiting for their flights to be called. Unable to make her out, he made his way across the concourse to the newsstand, found an *L.A. Times* and took it over to Mickey D's, where he bought himself a number two with a Diet Coke, found a table and proceeded to eat and read at the same time.

Only took Corso a minute to realize two things. First off, he realized how long it'd been since he'd read a newspaper. Secondly, he immediately knew he'd best keep it that way. Better stay away from the TV too. The bombing story was everywhere. His picture was plastered all over the front section of the *L.A. Times*. Complete bio and current photo on page four. News-wise, two names had been added to the list of those in custody. Horace L. Danbury and Jeffrey M. Byrne. Short's death was mentioned only peripherally. He was described as a "former FBI consultant."

A picture of a capitol building maintenance worker standing knee deep in broken glass occupied the front page. The rear axle of the van was visible in the background, lying twisted and broken on the lawn, its shredded tires hanging from the rims like steel-belted vines. Worth a thousand words for sure.

The Feds were playing it close to the vest. Victims remained anonymous. They'd released only the names of those in jail and those in pieces. Other than that, all they'd say was that the investigation was ongoing and that they anticipated further arrests.

Corso took his time. Worked through the world news, the metro section and finally the sports before trashing the paper and making his way into the American Airlines waiting area. A quick scan of the area revealed Andriatta wedged into a seat near the center. Corso ambled over and stood in front of her.

She took her time looking up.

"Long as we've got some time on our hands, why don't we get you a ticket back to Newark," he said.

She shrugged and got to her feet. Together, they made their way over to the counter, where they stood in silence as a family of four tried in vain to arrange seats next to one another. "We're on our way to Edgewater, Pennsylvania, by way of Pittsburgh," Corso told the woman behind the counter. "How quickly can we turn it around and get back to Newark?" Corso watched as her long, square fingernails tapped the keys. "A 10:07 A.M. to Pittsburgh. A forty-minute layover, then an 11:59 to Newark."

"Nothing later today?" he inquired.

She shook her head. "Once a day to Newark."

"What about to Seattle?" Andriatta asked.

Before the woman could ask the computer, Corso waved her off. "Never mind," he said. "I'm not headed home just yet."

"Oh?" Andriatta said.

"I've got a few loose ends I want to look into."

"Such as?"

"How many to Newark?" the woman wanted to know.

"One," Corso said.

"None," Andriatta said.

The woman put her hands on her substantial hips and scowled from one to the other. "What's it gonna be?" she asked.

"One."

"None."

She looked at them sideways and smiled. "You're putting me on, right?"

"I thought you couldn't wait to get back home," Corso growled at Andriatta.

"I changed my mind," she said.

"I'm lost here."

"What else is new?"

Corso opened his mouth to speak but couldn't find the words. He ran a hand through his hair and looked at the ceiling. "You want to give me a hint?"

She stepped in close. The top of her head barely reached his chin. "It's like you said before. I signed on for this thing."

Corso shook his head in disbelief. The gate on the right was calling for first-class passengers to board. "That's us," Corso said.

Andriatta let her feet do the talking. Corso turned to the woman behind the counter. "Sorry," he said.

She was amused. "Maybe you ought to tell her that," she said.

36

The Hertz kid turned bright red. "There's a . . . a bit of a problem, I'm afraid."

"What kind of problem is that?" Corso asked.

"The balance on your Number One Club account."

"How much?"

"Forty-three thousand six hundred seven dollars and twelve cents."

Corso pulled his head back in awe. "Is this a joke?"

"No, sir."

"What for?"

"A Chevy Suburban." He traced the invoice with the tip of his finger. "Serial number . . ."

Corso cut him off. "The one that ended up in the lake?"

"Yes, sir."

"I took out the extra insurance."

"Yes, sir. I can see that?"

"Then how can I owe Hertz for the car?"

"It says here that the police are listing the incident as a suicide attempt. Our insurance doesn't cover anything like that, so the liability falls back on you."

"That's ridiculous."

"Yes, sir."

Corso leaned on the counter and pondered the situation. "Tell you what . . ." he said after a moment. ". . . What say we let the lawyers sort that one out for themselves."

The kid's eyes rolled in his head like a spooked horse. "Yes, sir," he said tentatively. "The lawyers."

"In the meantime you rent me something with four-wheel drive . . ."

The kid strove to speak, but Corso kept talking. ". . . Ms. Andriatta and I will drive it into town for the night. First thing in the morning, she'll be back with the car."

"I can't do that, sir."

"Look," Corso began. "This isn't the kind of thing that's going to get settled between you and me, here and now."

"No, sir."

"So . . . with that in mind . . . what say we let Hertz's attorneys and my attorneys do what they already get paid *way* too much for doing."

"I can't do that, sir."

Corso turned to Andriatta. "Rent us a car. I'll pay you later."

The kid managed a waxy grin. "All I need is a credit card and a valid driver's license," he said.

Andriatta shook her head. "Every piece of ID I own is back at the hotel," she said.

"Gotta have the plastic," said the kid.

Corso looked around the terminal. The Dollar and Enterprise desks were dark and empty. "You're the only rental car company open," Corso said.

"Yes, sir," the kid agreed. "Nasty night like this, folks tend to go home early."

"Walking is pretty much out of the question," Corso said.

"Yes, sir."

Outside, it seemed to be snowing in circles. Windblown flakes passed through the realm of the overhead lights, cascading out of the blustery darkness, swirling into view for just long enough to make a sense impression before falling to the earth like icy darts from the great beyond. The twenty-four-seater from Pittsburgh was already collecting snow on the wings. The tracks made by the baggage carts, only minutes old, were nearly obliterated.

Corso paced a quick lap around the area in front of the desk. He pulled his wallet out of his pocket, dug around inside for a moment and came out with a platinum VISA card. He threw it onto the desk with a flourish.

"Charge the balance to my card."

The kid's eyes opened wide. "You mean like the whole . . ."

Andriatta stepped up to the counter. "Stop it," she said to Corso.

Corso kept his gaze glued on the kid. "I'll buy the damn car," he said.

Andriatta picked the card off of the desk and handed it back to Corso. "Stop throwing your money around," she admonished. "Your mother wouldn't approve."

A tense moment passed. Corso snatched the card from her fingers and was about to return it to his wallet when something inside caught his eye. He slid the credit card back inside and then pulled out a business card. He looked over at the kid.

"Can I use your phone?"

"If it's local."

Corso held out his hand. The kid surrendered the receiver. The cord didn't reach over the desk, so Corso had to read him the number. The kid dialed. One ring. Two rings, then three, before a voice came on the line.

"Carl," Corso said. "This is Frank Corso. Yeah. Yeah. Hey . . . yeah, L.A. on the TV. Yeah. I'll tell you all about it. Yeah sure. Hey . . . I was wondering if maybe you could help me out with a problem. I'm at the airport. I need a ride into town." He briefly listened. "It's a long story, man. I'd really appreciate it. Yeah. Ms. Andriatta . . . my associate . . . yeah . . . no . . . no luggage. Thanks. Really . . . thanks. See you then."

Corso gave back the receiver and turned to Andriatta. "Twenty minutes," he said.

She nodded and crossed to the middle of the terminal and took a seat. Corso followed along like a stubborn puppy. He left a seat between them when he sat down.

They sat looking out at the gathering gloom. Another small jet sent plumes of windblown snow into the air as it taxied away from the terminal, out onto the runway, then disappeared out of sight. "Thanks," Corso said.

"For what?" Andriatta asked, looking straight ahead.

"For keeping me from making a fool of myself over there."

"I promised. Remember?"

"I'd have regretted it later."

"Your mother's voice."

"Big time."

Another silence ensued. "I'm sorry," Andriatta said.

"For what?"

"For being such a bitch back in L.A."

"Don't worry about it."

"No really . . . I mean it."

"Consider it forgotten."

"I'm amazed you put up with me for as long as you did."

Corso looked puzzled. "Put up with what?"

She reached across the empty seat and punched him in the arm. "Stop it."

"I'm the same way," Corso said. "There's something about somebody pulling rank on me that brings out the idiot in my soul."

"Especially when it's the government," she said. "When the people who are supposed to be on our side, when the people who are supposed to be helping us out turn out to have an agenda of their own."

"Everybody has an agenda."

"That's always been hard for me to accept." Corso watched as she went through some inner dialogue with herself. "I guess I've always been a bit naive," she said. "Maybe even a romantic."

"That's the same thing Short said."

She looked surprised. "What?"

"That he'd been a fool for believing people and institutions were better than they turned out to be."

"World needs more people like that."

Corso shot her a quick look. "Maybe."

By the time Carl Letzo arrived, they were out of small talk. Corso was stretched out, fingers laced behind his head, feet halfway over to the next row of seats. Andriatta, had tried the opposite approach, pulling her feet up into the seat with her, scrunching up, and was trying to use the armrest as a pillow.

Corso closed his eyes and began to dream. He could see the shipwreck. Just south of Mukilteo. Lying half-up on the beach like some dead animal washed ashore by winter's weather. And then the noise of shoes. Somebody cleared a throat.

Carl wore a long, tweed overcoat. The roughness of the fabric and the length of the sleeves made it look like it might have once belonged to his father. Corso gathered his feet beneath him and pushed himself upright. "Really appreciate you coming down here on a night like this," he said.

"No big deal," Carl assured him.

"How you doing?" Corso asked.

"Hargrove hasn't fired me yet," said Carl with a crooked grin.

"Let's see if we can't fix that," Corso said.

37

Clad in a white courtesy hotel robe, Andriatta stepped through the adjoining door and looked around Corso's room. She rubbed a towel around her head and neck. "Seems like weeks since we were here last."

"Yeah," Corso said. "Like some other life or something."

"Seems like weeks since I had a shower."

"First time I was ever glad to see my old clothes."

She used the flat of her hands to press her hair between the folds of the towel, then shook her head to get everything more or less in the right place.

"How come you insisted on the same rooms we had the last time?"

"I was hoping something would come to me." He waved a

hand in the air. "Something . . . you know . . . something that was right in front of my face when I was here the last time . . . something I failed to see."

"I don't for the life of me understand what you're looking for."

"I'm looking for a link. Something that connects what happened in L.A. to what happened here."

"It's over," she said. "The people responsible are either locked up or in the graveyard."

"Not all of them."

"Who appointed you the minister of justice?"

"I like things neat and tidy."

"In case you haven't noticed, the world's a mess."

"There's a connection."

"What if there's not?"

"Fernando Reyes was one of the guys who jumped me in my room."

"Because he had a bad knee?"

"Because his credit card history shows he bought an airline ticket from L.A. to Pittsburgh, then on to Edgewater. He flew in the day I arrived and flew back home the day after the attack."

"It could be . . ." she stammered. "I don't know . . . maybe . . ."

"There's no maybe," Corso said.

A knock sounded at the door. Corso tensed but didn't move. The banging came again, louder this time. Corso eased over in his stocking feet and peeked through the lens in the door. Satisfied, he pulled open the door. A hotel maid stepped into the room carrying a bundle in both hands. "Jour oder stoof," she said, offering the makeshift package to Corso, who took it, thanked her with a five-dollar bill from his pants pocket and quickly shepherded her back into the hall.

Andriatta followed along as Corso carried the bundle over to the desk. The package was a bedsheet, pulled tight in all directions and tied crosswise. Corso tugged at the knots until he got one to budge, then shook some of it out onto the desk.

Mostly it was paper. All the stuff they'd collected before being hijacked to L.A. by the government. Corso's research notes from Nathan Marino's parents and brother. The research from the newspaper archives. Andriatta's interviews with his schoolmates. Nathan's high school yearbook. The stuff they'd been going through when they'd answered the proverbial knock on the door.

Corso picked through it with his fingertips and folded the sheet back over the top like a diaper. "I'll go back through it in the morning," he announced.

"You hungry?" Andriatta asked.

Corso nodded and checked the clock. Seven-twenty in the evening.

"Where the hell did the day go?" he asked.

"We got a late start out of L.A. and lost three hours to time zones," Andriatta offered. She smiled. "Not to mention turning out to be the curse of Hertz Rent-A-Car." She snapped her fingers. "There goes the day."

Corso crossed back to the desk, slid the bundle of paperwork down onto the chair and found the room service menu. He handed the little leatherette binder to Andriatta.

Half an hour later they were stretched out, eating on the bed, finishing up a pair of mediocre steaks and mounds of garlic mashed potatoes. Corso reached over and poured the last of the wine into her glass. The first bottle had disappeared in a heartbeat. The second had taken a little longer. He stuffed the bottle neck down into the wine bucket.

"Sure you don't want to change your mind about dessert?" Corso asked. "We could always call room service again."

"No . . . no . . ." She waved him off. "I'm getting fat as a cow."

"You sure?"

"Positive."

Corso rolled off the bed onto his stocking feet. He bent and picked up his tray.

"Get the door will ya?" he asked.

Andriatta scrambled to her feet. She stood at the edge of the bed for a moment and brought a hand to her forehead. "Whooo," she said. "Had a little too much wine methinks."

"No such thing," Corso said. "You can't be too thin, too rich or drink too much good wine."

Corso followed her across the carpet. Her first try at opening the door was thwarted by the safety lock. Bang. "Oops," she giggled and tried again.

Corso placed his tray on the floor in the hall, then returned to the room and retrieved the other. "Nothing worse than old food in the room while I'm trying to sleep," he commented as he crossed the room. "I always feel like it's looking at me in the dark."

"Are you serious?"

"Swear to God," Corso said, stepping back inside, taking the door from her hands and securely locking it.

"Must be your rural background," she said. "Putting it outside must be the urban equivalent of hanging it up in a tree so's the bears don't get it."

"Something like that," Corso agreed.

Andriatta stifled a yawn with the back of her hand.

"We gotta stay up," Corso said.

"Why's that?" she asked around another yawn.

"Because . . . for us . . . it's only five-thirty at night, remember? We go to sleep now, we'll be up in the middle of the night."

"I feel like I haven't had a good night's sleep in a week."

"Why doncha see what's on the tube?" Corso suggested.

Chris Andriatta crossed to the bed stand, picked up the remote and snapped on the television. She propped a pair of pillows against the headboard and lay down.

"Here it is," she said.

Corso crossed the room to see what she was talking about. Sure enough, there was Morales mouthing silent words into a microphone. Corso watched as she tried to find the volume control. The picture switched to the debacle on Santa Monica Boulevard. Then to one of ambulances arriving at emergency rooms. Then back to Morales. "Something else. Anything else," Corso pleaded.

"Don't you want to hear what they're saying?" she teased

"I'd rather watch a spleen being removed," Corso said.

"Oh come on."

"My own."

Morales' voice suddenly filled the room. "We believe the group has effectively been put out of business," he was saying. "As of this morning . . ."

"Please," Corso begged. "Anything but . . ."

He moved to the side of the bed and tried to snatch the remote from her hand, but she saw it coming and rolled away laughing. Corso put one knee on the bed and tried to pry the remote from her grip. When it seemed for a moment that his superior strength would prevail, she used her free hand to reach up and grab him by the shirt, to pull him off-balance, sending him sprawling head-first across the bed.

"Oops," she said.

Their bodies lay crosswise. Corso could feel her beneath him, her belly heaving, straining for breath under his weight.

"Off, brute. I'm suffocating here." She shoved him, not hard.

Corso rotated his body. Still on top of her, only now his face was in her feet and his feet were in her face.

Andriatta said, "Lost your compass?"

Corso made a slow, deliberate revolution until their faces met, their bodies ran parallel, their feet touched, their legs touched.

"Oh my, what's that down there?"

"The remote," he said quickly.

Corso started to roll off her, but she jerked him back.

"Wait," she said, her voice husky and low. "I think I like this."

Her breath on his cheek felt warm and smelled like red wine. Her right arm now rested across his back. Try as he might to keep his head up and away from hers, his neck muscles gave out. He relaxed them and let his mouth meet hers.

For half a second the kiss seemed so pure and innocent, then their chemistries exploded. Beneath him, she let him know that she, too, had been drawn into the fireworks. He felt her hands reach beneath his shirt, move up and explore his chest, her fingers digging into his flesh as if she were clawing her way inside him. Her hands moved down and grasped his belt, struggled to open his pants. The hesitation he had felt earlier disintegrated, and instead of attempting to hide his arousal, he pressed it against her as he tore the bathrobe from her body. She dropped her hands to her sides, went limp and said in that husky voice of hers, "Fuck me, Corso."

He did. She writhed beneath him, crying out for mercy, and

for more. He kept it up. No words passed between them, only
their eyes spoke as she moved rhythmically, and though she didn't
speak of love, he could feel her excitment and that just made him
want to give her more of what she wanted.

When he finally let go, he realized that the primal roar that
filled the room was coming from his mouth. They lay in each
other's arms, panting, dripping sweat, their heartbeats and blood
pressure gradually seeking normal rates. The telephone rang, a
distant tinkling sound. Corso rolled over and picked it up. "Yes,"
he said. "Just fine, thanks. Yes. Okay." He hung up. She raised an
eyebrow.

"It was the desk. They wanted to know if everything was okay
in here."

They looked at each other and laughed.

38

Corso brushed the bundle of paperwork from the chair seat, sending the contents sprawling out over the floor. He sat down at the desk and picked at the mess on the floor with his foot. Nathan Marino's high school yearbook slid from the top of the pile, coming to rest against his ankle. Wilson High School's flaxen-haired Viking stared blankly back up at Corso, who used his big toe to open the cover. The inside page was blank.

On the far side of the room, the bed was a mess, sheets and blankets strewn this way and that, the duvet huddled on the floor at the foot of the bed like some flowered beast. He imagined he could still see her outline on the sheets. See where she had slid over and made her way across the carpet to the adjoining door sometime during the night.

He pulled the phone book from the center drawer, flipped through the yellow pages, found the number he was looking for and dialed. A young woman answered the phone. "Enterprise," she chirped.

Corso told her what he wanted, read her his credit card and driver's license numbers, then suffered on hold for the better part of ten minutes as she ran the numbers through the system.

Another round of twenty questions before they mutually agreed that whenever the Enterprise people arrived with the car, they'd have the desk ring his room, at which point he'd come downstairs and sign on the dotted line.

After replacing the receiver in the desk unit, he picked up the Wilson High School Yearbook and leafed back to Nathan Marino's picture. He sat and stared at the picture, as if expecting some sort of enlightenment to flow from the photograph to himself. When no such epiphany was forthcoming, he began to leaf through the yearbook, marveling at the freshness of the faces, of the almost palpable hopes and dreams emanating from the pages. He found himself staring at the faces, wondering what they looked like now. Wondering how many of them would like to start over. Maybe get another chance at their aspirations.

He turned another page and stopped. Turned back. Brought the page closer to his face. Read the name under the picture and smiled. "Well, well," he said out loud.

"That's a deep subject." She stood in the adjoining doorway, wrapped in a sheet, her hair sticking out in all directions. "This is what happens when you go to sleep with wet hair," she said.

"That's what hats are for," Corso said, crossing the room to her side, taking her in his arms and planting a small kiss on her cheek.

She looked up into his eyes. "About last night . . ." she began.

"Why don't we just let it be?" Corso suggested.

She thought it over. "Such a guy thing," she said after a moment. "Doing it is one thing. Talking about it"—she waved a hand in the air—"worst nightmare."

"I'll try to get in touch with my more sensitive side."

"No you won't."

"You're right. I won't."

She laughed that deep, rich laugh of hers. "How about a shower and we go out to breakfast somewhere?"

"Soon as they bring the car."

"What car?"

"Enterprise is bringing us a nice new SUV sometime in the next hour or so. I need to be here when they arrive."

She wriggled free of his grasp. "Let me know when you're ready, big fella," she said with a salacious wink, before sliding back through the adjoining door and rustling out of sight.

Corso hurried to the bathroom, undressed quickly and stepped into the shower. Took him twelve minutes to get showered, shampooed and into a fresh set of clothes. He was combing his wet hair straight back when the phone rang. The desk.

Another twelve minutes and he was back in the room with the keys to the new ride. He poked his head into Andriatta's room. The sound of a blow-dryer was coming from behind the bathroom door. He waited for a lull in the roar, then called her name. Nothing, so he called again. This time she stepped out. "That was fast," she said.

He twirled the keys around his finger. "We're mobile again," he said.

"They must have known how hungry I am."

"They heard about how cranky you get."

She laughed. "Let me grab my purse."

On the way out Corso removed the DO NOT DISTURB card from
the door handle. As they started for the elevators, she slipped her
arm through his. Half a dozen steps later she changed her mind
and took her arm back.

"Unprofessional," she said.

The lobby was nearly empty. Andriatta began to veer left toward the front doors, but Corso clapped a hand on her shoulder.
"Give me a minute," he said. "I've got something I need to do."

He walked quickly to the reception desk. Behind the counter
a dark haired girl in a blue blazer was shuffling registration cards.
"Mr. Shields here?" Corso asked.

"I'm afraid not," she said with a smile.

"When will he be in?"

"I'm afraid I don't know." Same toothy grin.

"You're afraid a lot."

"Excuse me?"

"I said it sounds like you're afraid a lot."

Her cheeks reddened. "Do I . . . do I say that all the time . . .
I'm sorry . . . I just don't know what else to say. It was all so sudden. Nobody . . . I mean not even Mary Anne . . . she's the assistant manager . . . not even Marys Anne knows for sure."

"Knows what?"

"Knows why Mr. Shields left so suddenly."

"When was this?"

"Yesterday."

"He quit?"

"I think he took a leave of absence. Corporate is sending
somebody to take his place while he's gone. At least that's what
people are saying."

"What people?"

"You know . . . like in the lunchroom."

"Do they say anything about why he left?"

"Something personal."

"Like?"

She shrugged in helpless resignation.

"No idea where he might be?"

Another shrug. This time accompanied by a sad shake of the head.

"Okay. Thanks," Corso said.

When he turned to leave, he found Andriatta close by his right shoulder.

"What was that all about?"

"Just trying to reconcile a couple of facts."

"What facts are those?"

He put a hand on her back and eased her away from the desk.

"A while back, I was making conversation with the hotel manager . . . guy named Randy Shields. I asked him if he knew Nathan Marino . . . you know, just sort of conversationally. He said he knew *of* him rather than knew him personally."

"And?"

"He volunteered the information that he wasn't in the same high school class as Nathan was which was why he didn't know him very well."

"And?"

"And this morning I was flipping though that yearbook you picked up and lo and behold there was Randy Shields in all his adolescent glory staring back at me."

"You must have misunderstood him."

"Possible."

"Why would anybody lie about a thing like that?"

He began to move her toward the brass doors. "That's the question now, isn't it?"

39

The frozen snow crunched under the SUV's tires; it sounded like they were driving on broken glass as Corso wheeled into the parking lot, bounced over the collection of frozen ruts and came to a stop as close to the building as he dared. He took several deep breaths before turning off the car and easing out of his seat belt. Andriatta had one leg out of the car when Corso put a restraining hand on her shoulder.

"Might be best if you stayed in the car," he said.

"I thought I was a full partner here?"

"I don't think this guy's going to talk to me if you're around."

"Place looks dead. What makes you think he's in there?"

Corso pointed to the old Jeep Wagoneer nosed up to the

sidewalk, its windows clear, its oxidized red paint dull but free of
snow.

"I'm betting that's him."

"They have food in there?"

"Pickled eggs and pigs feet," Corso said.

She thought it over. "Leave the keys," she said.

Corso climbed out of the driver's seat and closed the door.
He spread his arms for balance as he picked his way through the
frozen tire tracks and icy footprints to the side of the building, to
the narrow walkway protected by the eaves, where blessedly bare
pavement led to the front door.

Charlie's Bar was nearly empty. Nobody playing pool. Nobody sliding shuffleboard discs down the polished hardwood.
Only things moving were the neon signs around the perimeter
of the place and the rolling hips of the hula-doll lamp behind
the bar. Same bartender. Two guys down at the far end drinking whiskey at ten-thirty in the morning. Herm Marino on his
usual stool at the other end, half a beer resting on the bar in
front of him.

Corso ordered a Pabst and sat down one stool away from
Marino.

"I seen you on the TV," Marino said. "Sounded like you put
the whole damn thing to bed."

The bartender slid the draft beer onto the bar. Corso nodded
thanks.

"Still got a few loose ends," Corso said.

"About my Nathan?"

"Yeah. I think so."

"That what you doin' back here?"

"Yeah."

Marino downed the rest of his beer. He slid the empty glass

across the battered wooden bar just as a refill arrived. He took a sip, used his sleeve on his upper lip.

"We don't need none of our business on the TV. Already been enough of that. Don't need no more."

"Last time we talked, you told me Nathan was gullible. You said the only times he ever got in trouble was when somebody else talked him into doing something stupid."

"What about it?"

"Who?"

"Who?" Marino repeated.

"Who talked him into doing stupid things."

"You know, kids . . . classmates of his."

"Which classmates?"

Marino took another sip. "Kid named Andre Hollingquest. Got himself killed in the war." He pointed toward the south wall. "Him and that Randy Shields that runs the hotel downtown. They was forever getting my Nathan in trouble."

Corso picked up his beer and downed it in a single pull.

"Thanks," he said to the bartender, throwing a five-dollar bill on the bar. He moved one stool closer to Herm Marino and leaned in.

"Mr. Marino . . ." he began. The other man turned his bleary eyes Corso's way. "Your son was nothing more than the victim of this thing. He had nothing to do with planning any of this. He wasn't guilty of anything more serious than maybe being gullible."

"You sure?"

"Absolutely."

"Then what happened?"

"I don't know yet."

Marino picked up his beer, brought it up to his lips, then changed his mind and set it back on the bar. "You let me know . . . when you figure it out, you let me know."

"I will," Corso promised.

Marino ran his thumb and forefinger over the corners of his mouth. His red-filigreed eyes took Corso in, then turned away. "You were right," he said to the wall.

"Excuse me?"

"I said you . . . you and my old lady . . . you were both right. I was way too hard on the boy." He slid his beer over in front of him but made no move to raise it to his lips. "He *was* what he *was*. I shoulda let it go at that."

Corso wanted to ease the man's pain, but knew Marino's sorrow was beyond anything he could say.

"I feel like he's come and gone without me knowing who he really was."

He looked to Corso for understanding, got a silent nod. "Like I'd always been looking at him in the mirror or something." His voice broke. His eyes teared up.

The bartender turned his back and went sliding down to the far end of the bar.

"I hear he was the kind to forgive and forget," Corso offered.

"What about me? How do I forgive and forget?"

"I don't know," Corso said in a whisper.

Herm Marino turned the stool to face the wall. He took a long pull from his beer.

Corso got to his feet. "Take care now," he said.

Marino waved one of his big gnarled hands but kept his face averted.

Corso started for the door. Six paces from the bar Herm Marino called his name.

"Yeah," Corso said.

"You make sure you come and tell me what happened."

Corso said he would. The bartender's eyes followed him to the door.

Despite the slate-gray skies, the light reflecting from the snow and ice squeezed Corso's eyes to slits as he slipped and slid his way back to the rental car. Andriatta had started the engine. The interior was like a sauna. Corso got himself all the way belted in before closing the car door.

"You get what you wanted?" she asked.

"Yeah," Corso said.

"Which was?"

Corso leaned back in the seat and mulled it over. "I confirmed something I been thinking ever since this whole thing started." Corso turned the heat to low, rolled down the window. "I told the police at the time, but they didn't want to hear about it. Those guys jumping me in my hotel room had to be an inside job. Somebody with a working knowledge of the hotel and a set of keys had to have helped those guys out. There's no other way they could have been sure the floor was free of other hotel staff. No way they could have gotten into the room where they keep the laundry. Hell, no way to even know there was such a place. No way to know I was in my room unless they were listening to my phone calls. And all of that's not to mention the fact that they had a key to my room." He blew air out from between pursed lips and ran a hand through his hair. "It's all right there . . ." he said, ". . . except the locals don't want to hear about it."

She cocked her head and took him in all over again. "What's

the matter?" she asked. "You look like somebody shot your dog."

"Just a sad old man," Corso said.

"What now?"

"Breakfast."

"It's about damn time."

40

Ruth Hadley made him the minute he walked in the door. It was just before eleven and the breakfast crowd had pretty much cleared out. Outside, the Bullseye Diner sign was so caked with drifting snow and ice that the vivid display had been reduced to little more than a glowing memory.

Andriatta and Corso settled into a booth down at the far end, directly across from the register. Ruth finished cashing out the pair of Pennsylvania state troopers, wished them well by name, then squeaked her way over to where Corso and Andriatta sat. "Nice to see you come back," she said, turning over their coffee mugs and filling them with coffee. Corso allowed how he, too, was glad to have returned and introduced Andriatta as his friend and colleague.

"Concubine," Andriatta corrected with a smile.

"Well, that's a lot more fun now, isn't it?" Ruth said, matching her tooth for tooth. She pulled an order pad from the pocket in her apron. Patted herself down for a pen, found one, clicked the end and waited.

"What can I get for you folks?"

Corso ordered scrambled eggs and rye toast. Andriatta opted for a short stack of pancakes, a side of bacon, eggs up with hash browns and wheat toast.

"Y'all expecting somebody else?" Ruth asked with a wry smile.

"She's a woman of her appetites," Corso said.

"How nice for you," Ruth said before turning and heading back behind the counter. She tore the order from the book, clipped it to a little spinning contraption, then disappeared through the swinging kitchen doors.

"Was that aimed at you or me?" Andriatta asked.

"No idea," Corso said. "I guess it cuts both ways."

Andriatta sat back in the booth and thought it over.

"I think she's got a crush on you."

Corso was horrified. "She's a thousand."

"What's that got to do with anything? A woman's gonna think what a woman's gonna think. Age got nothing to do with it."

"Come on. Get real."

"I'm serious."

"So am I."

They were still tossing the idea back and forth when the squeaking of Ruth's shoes announced the arrival of breakfast. When Ruth had gone, Andriatta lowered her voice. "Did you see the way she looked at you?"

"You're crazy."

"You must be blind."

"She's a married woman."

"Oh . . . like that stops anybody these days."

Corso chewed a piece of toast as he watched Ruth make the rounds with the coffeepot. When she returned to the register, Corso slid to the end of the booth.

"I've got something I want to ask her," he said.

"I'll bet you do."

"Stop it."

She forked in another mouthful of hotcakes and laughed.

Corso got to his feet and moseyed over to the cash register. She was straightening money in the register drawers when he leaned his arms on the counter.

"Now what can I do for the famous author?" she asked.

Corso put on his best conspiratorial face. "You said something about getting a real steal of a deal on a piece of property down in Florida."

Her expression took on a sly quality. "Did I?"

Corso leaned in closer and lowered his voice. "Yes, ma'am, I believe you did."

She raised a painted eyebrow and looked at him from the corner of her eye.

"What if I did?"

"You mind if I ask how that happened."

"We knew somebody who knew somebody who was strapped for cash."

"Mind if I ask for a name?"

"Which one?"

"The one you knew."

She considered it. "I think I better ask my old man," she said finally.

Corso watched as, once again, she disappeared through the swinging doors. A minute passed, and then two, before she reappeared and crooked a beckoning finger at Corso, who ambled down to the break in the counter and followed her into the kitchen.

He was short, not much over five feet, a wiry specimen dressed all in white, except for the dabs of egg yolk adorning the front of his apron. Looked like he hadn't shaved in a week. The hair on his chest and the hair from his beard met just below his prominent Adam's apple. His expression said he wasn't all that happy to make Corso's acquaintance. "You got a problem with something?" he wanted to know.

"Nothing that's got anything to do with you," Corso assured him.

"So why all the questions?"

"I'm still working on what happened to Nathan Marino."

His scowl deepened. "He got blown to shit. That's what happened to Nathan."

"I hear he was a nice kid."

"Nice kids are a dime a dozen."

"His family has a right to know what happened to him." Before he could answer, Corso went on. "I hear you've got a couple of girls of your own. Something like that happened to one of them, I'm betting you'd want to know what happened."

He took a deep breath. "So what's that got to do with Florida?"

"All right . . . let me do this another way. Was Randy Shields the guy who knew somebody in a bind?"

Ruth and Myron exchanged meaningful glances. "What if he was?" Myron asked.

"Was he?"

A muted bong sent Ruth scurrying out to the front of the diner.

"Yeah," Myron said. "It was him." He cracked eggs two at a time, dumping the contents into a stainless-steel bowl, dropping the shells into a trash can beneath the counter. "He come in one time. Got to gabbing with Ruth." He shook his head in disgust. "My old woman got a bad habit of sharing her business with people she don't know." He pulled half a dozen pieces of bacon from a tray, slapped them on the back of the grill and weighted them down. "She tells him we been thinkin' about retiring down to Florida. He tells her he might know where we could get us a prime piece of real estate." He shrugged. "Just sorta happened from there."

"Seller was a guy named Short. Paul Short."

"If you already know all this shit, why you in here busting my balls?"

"I just needed to make sure."

"The sale was good," Myron said. "Went through title and escrow and everything. I don't wanna hear about how there's something wrong with the sale."

Corso held up a hand. Scout's honor. "Far as I know there's no problem."

Myron walked to the window, spun the little steel carousel and pulled down a couple of orders. "Randy Shields come into the diner often?" Corso asked.

Myron scrambled the half dozen eggs with a whisk. "You want gossip you better talk to my old woman," he said. "That's her end of the business."

Corso thanked him for his trouble and pushed his way through the doors just as the eggs hit the grill.

Andriatta was forking the last morsel of what looked like a

piece of lemon meringue pie into her mouth as he arrived. She looked up at Corso.

"Waiting makes me hungry," she explained.

"I'll settle up and we can get out of here," Corso said.

"I'm going to hit the loo. I'll meet you in the car."

Corso arrived at the cash register just as Ruth was ringing up the elderly couple at the far end of the counter. She favored him with a small smile. "I'm guessin' you'll be on your way back to Seattle here pretty soon," she said.

Corso handed her the bill. "Pretty soon," he said. "Just got a few loose ends I want to tie up."

She punched open the register and then leaned part way across the counter. "That Nathan Marino . . . he deserved way better than he got."

Corso nodded. "I believe he did."

"Can't say that about many of us, can you?"

"No, ma'am . . . I don't believe you can."

41

The hotel lobby was jammed. Suitcases, backpacks and garment bags overflowed brass luggage carts. The air was abuzz with a dozen conversations. Looked like a tour bus had dumped about sixty German tourists onto the registration desk in a pile.

One look told Corso the conversation he wanted to have with the assistant manager was going to have to wait. He turned and was headed for the elevator when a familiar voice called his name.

"Mr. Corso" rose above the din.

Corso looked around. Didn't see anybody he knew and once again started for the elevators. The voice sounded again. Corso stopped.

Carl Letzo spread the crowd enough to wedge his way through.

"I was just trying to leave you a message. I thought maybe you guys might need a ride."

Corso told him about the new rental. "Place is a madhouse," he commented.

"Where's Andriatta?" Carl asked.

"She headed upstairs to her room. I think maybe nature was calling."

"Till just the other day, I didn't even know for sure that ladies did such things," Carl deadpanned.

"So what changed your mind?"

Carl looked around the lobby as if the walls had ears. He gestured with his head over toward a little collection of furniture outside the door to the lounge. Corso followed him over. He waited as Carl unbuttoned his father's overcoat and draped it over the arm of the couch like a tweed vestment. They sat in a pair of overstuffed chairs separated by a marble-topped coffee table. "What's up?" Corso asked.

Carl looked around again. "I think maybe I've accounted for those lost nine minutes." He sensed Corso's confusion. "Remember . . . the cops said it took the bomb squad less than ten minutes from the time they got the call to get to the scene. Folks in the bank said it was more like twenty."

"I remember."

"I did a little digging around."

"And?"

Carl shook his head in disbelief. "It's just so typical of this place."

"Enlighten me."

"Seems . . . on the morning in question . . . the emergency dispatcher wasn't at her post."

"Where was she?"

"Out on the back porch of the police station smooching with her estranged boyfriend, who, it just so happens, is a city patrolman."

"Who was minding the store?"

"Seems they been feuding and needed to make up."

"No phone backup?"

"Nope."

"Was he on duty?"

"Yep."

"So you call 911 and nobody answers?"

"Yep."

"So . . . she's fired; he's fired. The city apologizes. It's over."

"She's not fired and neither is he."

"How can that be?"

"She's Hargrove's youngest daughter. Hargrove got her the job."

"And they can't fire him without firing her."

"Right on."

"And everybody and his brother's covering it up?"

"Right on down the line."

Corso spread his arms wide. "There's your breakout story, man. The cover-up. Nathan Marino blown to pieces when he might have been saved and everybody from the police chief on down is keeping his mouth shut. Front page. Above the fold."

"Like Hargrove's ever gonna let that story hit the streets."

"You got a local TV station? Take it to them."

"He owns that too."

"Wait till the next time he leaves town."

Carl's face hardened. "He's out of town right now."

"Write it today. Run it tomorrow."

Carl squirmed in the chair. "No way. God . . . I did that . . ."

"Time to stop telling yourself what you *can't* do, Carl. Time to start dwelling on what you *can*. Do it. Leave the house to the termites. Pack your ass up and get out of town. You've got a lot of talent, Carl. Go find someplace where you can use it like a real journalist."

Carl looked away and went silent. Corso could feel his profound discomfort and decided to change the subject.

"Whatta you know about the guy that manages the hotel?" he asked.

"Randy Shields?"

"Yeah."

"Just got back in town about a year ago."

"How long had he been gone?"

"Hell . . . since about five minutes after he graduated high school."

"Really?"

"Only difference was he came back."

"Know where he was all that time?"

"Somewhere out in California. Married young from what I hear. Came back from the paratroopers with a gimp leg. Had a son while he was in the service. Kid got killed in a car wreck. I guess Randy was driving the car. Tore the marriage to pieces from what I hear."

"You know the woman?

Carl shook his head. "Never brought her around here."

"How long ago was this?"

"Few years back."

"What else?"

Carl thought it over. "I hear he could pound them pretty good."

"Where'd he do his drinking?"

"VFW hall mostly."

"Bad habits?"

"None I've ever heard of." Corso watched Carl go though his memory bank. "I hear he had a hell of a grudge against the government."

Corso felt the hair on his arms begin to rise. "Over what?"

"I guess he didn't feel like they took care of him after his injury. Guy I know said he felt like the accident that killed his son would never have happened if they'd helped him out, helped him get a car . . . you know, a car equipped for somebody with a disability. I guess he sued 'em and everything."

"No shit," Corso said.

Carl eyed him. "I touch a nerve here?"

"You have no idea," Corso said, getting to his feet in a hurry. He reached down, offered Carl a hand and pulled him to his feet. He bent slightly at the waist, putting his nose very nearly on Carl's.

"Go back to the office, Carl. Write the damn story. Do whatever you have to do to get it on the front page. Pack your car. Leave this one-horse town and don't look back."

Corso strode quickly toward the elevators, breaking into a trot for the last few yards, stuffing his arm into the closing door and levering himself in, much to the chagrin of the half dozen or so people already inside the elevator car.

He jogged down the hallway to his room, unlocked the door and rushed inside. The door to Andriatta's room was closed and locked. He could hear her voice. On the phone maybe. He resisted the urge to eavesdrop and knocked instead. The talking stopped. A moment later he heard the bolt slip back into the door.

She threw her arms around his shoulders, got up on her tiptoes and gave him a kiss. "How'd it go?" she wanted to know.

"I think I got it," he said.

"Got what?"

"The connection."

42

The smile was smug, the desk immaculate. Everything geo-metrically aligned with everything else. Fancy pen set, desktop flags, federal, state, and some sort of local pennant. Coupla gold framed photos from another era. One gleaming wooden guest chair at each front corner. Gold nameplate exactly in the center. POLICE CHIEF A. J. CUMMINGS it read.

"I thought we'd seen the last of you," she said.

"I'm like the bad penny, Chief. I just keep turning up.

"To use another adage, you seem to have grown a little moss this time." Corso introduced Chris Andriatta. "We're working the case together."

"What case is that?"

"Nathan Marino."

The chief leaned forward in her chair and put her elbows on the desk. "I'm wondering if perhaps the fact that I agreed to see you hasn't muddied the water a bit, Mr. Corso. Or worse yet, I'm thinking somehow I failed to make myself clear to you." She laced her manicured fingers together and paused for effect. "The Marino case is still open. It's an ongoing investigation and as such is absolutely off-limits to amateurs such as yourself."

"It was amateurs like us . . ." Corso began.

She held up a hand. "I don't give a damn what you did out in California or what kind of role the Bureau may have permitted you to play. As long as you're within my jurisdiction, you're going to keep your nose out of ongoing investigations or I'm going to clap your famous butt in jail so fast it'll make your head swim." A pause and a glare this time. "Am I making myself clear here, or should I go on?"

Corso clamped his jaw shut.

"He can be a little hardheaded, but eventually he gets the message," Andriatta offered with a smile.

"I hope so," the chief replied. "Because if he doesn't, you're going to be bailing him out every day until he leaves town."

"I think I know what happened to Nathan Marino," Corso said.

The chief looked at Andriatta, who shrugged and offered an upturned palm.

"Mr. Corso," she began, "I'm going to listen to what you have to say here, not because I have the slightest hope that you're onto something, but merely because an officer in my position has an obligation to examine any and all potential evidence in an ongoing investigation." She folded her arms. "I'm all ears."

Corso took a deep breath, shot a glance over at Andriatta and then gave the chief the *Reader's Digest* version of what had happened in California. Took ten minutes. The chief never blinked.

"All of which has exactly *what* to do with the death of Nathan Marino?" she asked when he'd finished.

Corso gathered himself. "I could be wrong . . ."

"You have a documented *history* of being wrong," the chief corrected.

This time it was Corso who paused for drama. "Be that as it may . . ." he began, ". . . but I think what happened to Nathan Marino here last year was that somebody used him as the trial run for the same bank robbery scheme that played out in L.A. this week."

"Why Nathan Marino? Why Edgewater?"

"For pretty much the same reasons I think. They're both on the fringe of things. Nathan Marino lived his life on the fringe of society. He wasn't important, or indispensable or much missed by anyone other than his loved ones." Corso's eyes clouded over for a minute. "I think maybe he was perceived as somebody whose passing would be unremarkable."

The chief kept her face as bland and expressionless as a head of lettuce.

"Why Edgewater?"

"Same reason. 'Cause it's out there on the edge. Nowhere near the center of anything, and definitely not the kind of place to make the network news."

The chief smiled. "Well that certainly didn't work now, did it? Nathan Marino wound up in every paper in the country."

"That's what they failed to account for."

"What's that?"

"The fact that there's something about a victim with a bomb around his neck that captures the imagination. Something that people don't forget. Instead of keeping it low-key, the thing went national."

"And the national attention didn't deter them?"

"On the contrary, it's what pushed them over the edge. It added a touch of glamour to what was basically just a revenge crime."

"And they just picked Edgewater out of a hat."

"Not at all."

"Why then?"

"Because it just so happened that one of them moved back home to Edgewater. Gave them a place to try the idea out . . . about as far away from Southern California as they could get."

"And who might that be."

"A guy named Randy Shields."

"Are you serious? Randy Shields is a respected member of our community. He's in the Rotary. The Chamber of Commerce. He's . . ."

"He's gone is what he is," Corso said.

For the first time, the smug smile wavered. "Gone how?"

"Yesterday, he took an emergency leave of absence. Nobody seems to know where he went or what the problem was."

The chief unfolded her arms and sat back in her chair. "You know, Mr. Corso, your little recitation here is an object lesson on the kind of sloppy investigative work for which you have become . . ." She went looking for a word. ". . . let's, for the sake of charity, say . . . famous." She leaned back farther. The spring groaned. The thin smile got wider. "You remind me of those well-intentioned farmers who come out one morning and find crop circles tramped into their cornfields. First thing that comes to their minds is 'it musta been aliens.' They skip right over drunken college boys and weird professors . . . over *everything* terrestrial for that matter, in favor of something from outer space." She showed her palms in wonder. "Go figure."

"I'll admit it, Chief, the whole thing is pretty far out there. A bunch of wounded veterans get together in what's supposed to be a therapeutic setting and decide to heal themselves by robbing banks. Sounds more like Hollywood than history."

"It surely does," said the chief. The spring groaned again as the she pushed back the chair and got to her feet. "Thank you for sharing, Mr. Corso. I'll take your suspicions under advisement. You may consider your civic duty done."

Corso didn't budge. "Which means you've no intention of looking for Randy Shields. No intention of looking into any of it."

The chief was shaking her head. "What it means, Mr. Corso, is that whatever I'm going to do, I'm not going to share it with you. Now, if you'll excuse me."

Andriatta got to her feet. Corso stayed put. She reached down and put a hand on his shoulder. When he still didn't move, she tugged on his shirt.

"If there's nothing else, Mr. Corso," the chief prodded.

"There's the matter of how my car wreck managed to become listed as a suicide attempt."

The chief moved out from behind the desk and ambled toward the door. "Subsequent forensic examination revealed damage to the car which could not be accounted for in a suicide scenario."

"Somebody better tell Hertz Rent-A-Car."

The chief pulled open the office door and stood aside.

"I'll take care of it," she assured him.

Corso got to his feet. "So then you're admitting you think somebody purposely pushed me into the lake."

"Quite the contrary, Mr. Corso, we believe it was a hit-

and-run. Someone losing control on an icy road . . . someone scared . . . someone . . ."

Corso's patience was gone. He strode quickly out of the room. Chris Andriatta watched satisfaction flicker in the other woman's eyes, then followed Corso back into the hall.

43

Dirty gray clouds drifted overhead. The air was wet and cold, sending a shiver down Corso's spine as he and Andriatta crossed the police department parking lot. Out to the north, the horizon seemed to be drowning itself in the lake's black waters. Corso pulled out the keys and pushed the wrong button. The horn began to honk. Took him a full thirty seconds to get it to stop.

"At least you didn't get yourself arrested," Andriatta said.

Corso kicked at a pile of snow, found it frozen solid and came up limping.

"Son of a bitch," he muttered under his breath as he jerked open the car door and threw himself into the driver's seat.

"I guess that's pretty much the end of the party," Andriatta said. "Unless of course you're looking forward to a little jail time."

"Like hell," Corso countered.

He stuck both hands in his jacket pockets and came away empty.

"Shit," he said.

"Other than having no idea when to quit, what's the problem?"

"My cell phone."

"What about it?"

"I drowned the damn thing."

"You'll probably get in less trouble without one."

Corso ignored her admonition. "I'm going to that mall out on the highway. They're bound to have a place I can get a new phone."

"Give it a rest, Corso."

"You coming?"

She thought it over. "Malls don't work for me. Why don't you leave me at the hotel. I've got a few things I'd like to take care of anyway. Give me a call when you're on your way back. I'll meet you out front."

Corso started the engine. "Here we go," he said.

He dropped the car into gear, eased out of the parking lot and into the street.

"I can't convince you, can I?"

"Convince me of what?" Corso asked as he turned right at the first stop sign, drove two blocks and turned right again.

"To let this thing go."

He made a quick left on Lakeshore Drive. The hotel was four blocks down.

"Why would I do a thing like that?"

"Because it's better for your health and well-being."

"I've been threatened by a lot worse than Chief Cummings."

Corso pulled the car under the portico. A kid in a uniform hustled over and opened the door. Andriatta popped her seat belt. Corso leaned her way, perhaps for a parting word, perhaps even for a quick kiss, but she was off the seat and gone without a backward glance. The kid closed the door. Corso watched her walk inside, then drove off. Her disapproval hung in the air like the scent of dying flowers.

Took him the better part of an hour and a half and a 180 bucks to get a new phone. One with a charged battery and the same number he used to have, which took a bit of research, since he had no idea what his number was since he never called the damn thing.

Halfway back to the hotel, he called Andriatta. She was waiting outside when he pulled up. "You feeling better now," she asked as she got settled in.

"Howsabout some lunch?" he asked in reply.

"Sounds like a hell of an idea."

"First I'm gonna make a coupla calls, so I can eat my lunch in peace."

Corso pulled the car out of the way down to the far end of the half circle making up the hotel's driveway. He put the car into park and pulled the phone from his jacket pocket. Next he hoisted himself partway out of the seat and produced his wallet, from which he drew a business card. Andriatta fiddled with her purse as Corso dialed the phone. "Special Agent Morales please." He listened. "Can you tell me when he will be?" He listened again. "No. No. I'll call him back. Thank you."

"I hate that phrase," he said.

"What phrase is that?"

"Away from his desk. What the hell is that supposed to mean? Hell, the dead are away from their desks."

"Why Morales?"

"I want him to run Randy Shields's name through the computer. I'll bet dollars to doughnuts he comes up as being part of that Pomona veterans group."

"And if he does?"

"That makes me right."

"Is being right that important?"

"It is to me."

"Explains why you're single."

"So I'm told."

He dug around in his wallet again. Came out with another business card and dialed. She raised an eyebrow. "The boss," he said. After dialing the number, he used his thumb to raise the volume, then pushed the speaker button. He set the phone on the console. The sound of the ringing phone filled the inside of the car. A woman's voice answered the phone.

"Greg Wells's office."

"This is Frank Corso. Can I talk to Greg please."

"Oh . . . yes . . . ," she stammered. "Mr. Wells has been trying to reach you. I'm sure he'll . . . oh yes."

Two clicks and a buzz later.

"Frank . . . Jesus . . . where the hell have you been?"

"I fell into a rabbit hole," Corso answered.

"I've been trying to call you for days."

"I lost my phone."

"I'm so sorry."

He looked over at Andriatta. Her eyes were dark as asphalt. "No reason to be sorry," he said. "It was just a phone."

A moment of silence ensued.

"You haven't heard?"

"Heard what?"

"About Chris Andriatta."

Corso's brow furrowed. "What about her? She's . . ."

"Just this morning. Her building superintendent found her dead in her apartment. She'd been shot in the head. The cops say it was murder. Said she'd been dead about a week."

Corso stopped breathing. He looked down at the phone on the console just in time to see her finger break the connection. Something hard and insistent was pushing at his ribs. He looked down. A big-bore revolver was pressed hard against his side, midway between his hip and his armpit.

"Drive the car," she said. "Make a single move and you're dead."

The phone began to ring. She picked it up, found the power button and switched it off. "I'm not going to tell you again," she said, grinding the barrel into his side. "Next time I'll put one through your kidneys."

Corso did as he was told, wheeling the SUV out of the driveway and into the street. "Turn right," she directed. Corso complied.

They left town heading south, covering territory Corso had never seen before. Stunted forests and hardscrabble farmland. Land that, in better times and places, people might have ignored altogether.

Corso kept an eye on the odometer, making certain he knew how far they'd traveled. In 11.6 miles, she jammed the gun harder into his side and told him to slow down. She slid the window open, watching the mailboxes glide by.

"Turn here," she said.

Corso pointed the car down a snowy lane bordered on both sides by swaybacked wire fences. A pair of windblown ruts said somebody had broken the trail for them since the last serious snowfall. The big car negotiated ruts with little more than an occasional shake and rattle. Corso's knuckles were taut and white.

The house was set back in the trees. A snowy-roofed rambler with a Jeep Cherokee parked in the snow outside the double garage. "Pull up beside that one," she directed. Again Corso complied. "Hey, listen . . ." he began.

"Shut up," she said.

A pair of floodlights mounted up near the apex of the garage roof suddenly snapped on, bathing the area in weak yellow light, dividing the area into dark and light with nothing between. The woman reached over and turned off the car.

"Turn off the headlights, take the keys out and give them to me," she said in a voice he'd never heard before.

When Corso didn't move, she lifted the barrel of the gun until it was level with his ear. "This can end right here," she said.

Corso snapped off the lights and used both hand to remove the keys from the ignition. He dropped the key ring into her outstretched hand. A sense of movement at his shoulder brought his head to the left. Randy Shields stood in the driveway beside the car, holding what looked like some sort of assault rifle.

"Get out," the woman said.

Corso hesitated. She ground the gun barrel into his ear and repeated the order. He did as he was told.

He stepped out into the snow, where Shields motioned with the rifle, then followed Corso toward the side door of the house. Corso heard the car door slam, heard the crunch of the woman's boots on the frozen snow. A shaft of dim light formed a triangle at the base of the doorway. Corso hesitated. Shields butted him forward with the rifle. Corso staggered slightly as he lifted a foot into the doorway.

Inside the door, one either moved left into the kitchen or continued forward, down a steep flight of stairs. "Downstairs," Shields ordered.

Corso moved carefully, using a crude handrail attached to the wall. Three steps down, a well-lighted workbench came into view. He kept moving but slowed enough to force Shields to prod him onward with the rifle. As their bodies came together, Corso made his move.

He reached behind, grabbed a handful of Shields's plaid wool coat and pulled hard, bending at the waist, lifting his captor up and onto his back. And then the extra weight buckled his own knees, sending them both tumbling head over heels down the rickety wooden stairs.

Corso forced a final rotation and came out on top. He grabbed the rifle in both hands and tried to wrestle it from the other man's grasp. The sound of footsteps pulled his attention from the wrestling match; he looked up just in time to receive a blow behind the ear . . . and then another. His vision swam. The third blow turned out the light.

He drifted in blue water, with the sound of the gulls in his ears and the rolling of the deck beneath his feet, sunning himself until he heard voices and looked for another boat. Nothing. He tried to raise his arm to shield his eyes from the bright sun but couldn't.

Then he was awake. Rough cinder-block walls. Taped to a wooden chair. The voices were behind him. Anxious and full of doubt. "I told you this asshole was going to be a problem. I told all of them."

Her voice was bitter and impatient. "You were right. Does that make you happy? Our whole goddamn lives are in jeopardy, but at least you can take pride in being right."

"It wasn't my fault."

"Nothing's ever your fault, is it? Not Bobby being dead. Not botching your end of the operation. Nothing. Not ever. It's the government's fault. It's bad luck. It's . . ." She stopped. "He's awake," she said after a moment.

"Well he ain't gonna . . ."

"Shut up," she said. "We're not going to have one of those detective-story scenes where the chump finds out what's going on right at the end."

Corso heard a rustling, followed by two minutes of silence, then the sound of her shoes coming his way. He tried to throw himself over backward, but the chair wouldn't budge. From the corner of his eye he saw her arm and the needle in her hand. He watched in horror as it penetrated his coat and shirt and finally his skin. He bellowed through the tape covering his mouth, shaking himself from side to side until the warmth overcame and the shade came down.

44

He was ten years old when the soldier came to the house. He stood in the window and watched the khaki vision climb out of the dusty Ford sedan, his uniform pressed and starched, his chest a rainbow of ribbons, his sleeves awash in stripes and chevrons. His bearing was regal. To a ten-year-old who lived twelve miles from a town where the gas station, the post office and the grocery store were one and the same, he could have been just about anything wonderful . . . maybe a commodore or an admiral or maybe even a grand vizier. He carried his hat under his arm as he mounted the front steps and knocked on the sun-warped screen door.

It was late August. One of those years when the cicadas buzzed in the trees like Jew's harps. As always that time of year, it was oppressively hot. Mama had rigged a swamp cooler in the parlor window and she kept the shades drawn in vain hope she could keep the languid afternoon air at bay. Despite her efforts, the contraption managed to accomplish little other than to blow wet straw all over the room and raise the dripping humidity a few notches higher.

At the back of the clearing stood an arched grape arbor, built way back when the grassy patch of ground had first been claimed from the ancient forest. According to his mother, the land had never been suitable for the growing of grapes, the soil too heavy with clay, the climate too hot and the air too humid. After a few years, she said, even the withered bunches of fruit that appeared and quickly died every spring, disappeared altogether, leaving only the thick leathery leaves to cover the arbor in a veined blanket of green, within whose cool and tranquil shade his father spent his summer days, sitting on the bench with his back to the house, mumbling under his breath at whatever soul-eating demons he'd brought back home from that frozen foxhole in Korea.

His mother got halfway to the door, saw the stranger on the porch and returned to the kitchen to fetch her teeth. Other than for meals, infrequent trips to town and seasonal visits to church, she kept her teeth in a glass on the windowsill over the kitchen sink. She returned, wiping her hands with a dish towel as she walked.

She pushed open the screen door, forcing the soldier to retreat to the top step. "Help you?" she asked.

"Excuse me, ma'am," he said with a slight bow of the head. "I was given to understand this was the home of Mario Corso." She kept wiping her hands as she looked him up and down.

"That's right. You know my husband?" she asked.

"Yes, ma'am," he said.

"You was in the war together?"

"Yes, ma'am."

She considered his answers. "He's out back," she said finally. "Come on along. I'll show you." She draped the dish towel over the porch rail, skirted him on the stairs and strode quickly toward the side of the house. "Could I? Uh, ma'am . . . I need to get something . . ."

He held up a finger and then moved quickly to the Ford, where he reached under the front seat, pulled out a brown paper bag and hurried back to her side. The muscles on the side of her jaw quivered like they did when something was wrong and heads were about to roll. The boy held his breath. To his surprise, she merely turned and walked around the side of the house with the soldier in tow.

The second they were out of sight, the boy burst out the door and headed around the house in the opposite direction. He fended off limbs and bushes on his way around the back of the toolshed, where he peered around the corner directly into the near end of the arbor.

His mother was already on her way back to the house. The soldier stood in the shade at attention. Waiting for the boy's father to take notice of his arrival. After several minutes he said, "Gunny, it's me."

The boy's father stopped talking to himself and looked up. Half a minute passed. "That you, Aldo?" he asked.

"It's me, Gunny," he said. "How they hangin'?"

The boy watched in amazement as a smile crossed his father's cracked and broken lips, as his father got to his feet and threw his arms around the man, as they stood in the shade for the longest time, arms wrapped around each other like grown-over vines, heads resting on each other's shoulders for what seemed like hours, until they unwound and sat down side by side on the bench.

"Brought you something, Gunny," the other man said. From the paper bag, he produced a bottle of whiskey and two paper cups. He poured them both a drink and offered a toast. "Semper Fidelis," he said, raising his cup. His father repeated the phrase and drank the whiskey down. For good measure, they did it again.

The boy squatted in the bushes for the rest of the afternoon, until the evening bugs threatened to eat him alive. Near the end of the bottle, the two men cried together for the longest time. As dark descended and a single shaft of yellow light from the kitchen window crept across the lawn, they said their good-byes. His father was unsteady as he walked the soldier back to the Ford. They hugged again before the soldier got in the car and drove away.

His father stood there until the darkness and the dust had both settled to the ground. Had Mother not come out and taken him into the house, he might be standing there still.

45

He walked gingerly, like a man recently recovered from an illness. He kept his eyes on his feet as they slipped and slid across the sanded parking lot, only occasionally glancing at his surroundings. The arrival of a FedEx truck forced him to wait on the far side of the driveway. To steady himself, he put a hand on the trunk of the nearest car. The sheet metal was smooth and cold to the touch. With his other hand, he held his jacket closed across his chest. While he waited for the truck to pass, he looked up at the sky and found a blanket of steel wool sliding across the heavens faster than his sluggish eyes could follow.

He waited until the FedEx truck was out of sight and stepped out into the section of driveway running parallel to the back door. He found it difficult to lift his feet, so he shuffled along, his shoes on the sand sounding something like a train. The curb seemed two feet high. He managed one foot, then the other, paused for a moment to collect his wits and made his way toward the back door.

To the right of the door a blue newspaper dispenser offered morning papers for fifty cents. An elderly gentleman dropped two quarters in the slot and removed a paper. Whatever he was looking for was on the back of the paper. The headline blared: *Police Coverup.* Byline: Carl Letzo. His equilibrium wavered in the morning breeze. He smiled and reached for the door handle, made his way across the floor.

A blast of warm air rolled out of the building. Still clutching his jacket, he crossed the room, got in line, and waited patiently as the people in front of him conducted their business.

"Sir," she said. "Sir, can I help you?" And he realized he'd been standing there. That it was his turn and that he'd somehow lost track of where he was in the line.

He stepped up to the counter.

"Can I help you?" she said again.

He pulled the note from his coat pocket and slid it through the slot. Her eyes were locked on his face.

"I know you," she said with a smile. "You're Frank Corso," she said. "I just love your books."

In response, he dropped his hand and allowed his jacket to fall open. Her eyes dropped to his chest and the numbered key-pad, then back up to the steel necklace holding it in place, then finally to the block-printed note that lay on the counter before her. Their eyes met.

"Please," he said.

Visit **www.panmacmillan.com** to read more about all our books and to buy them. You will also find features, author interviews and news of any author events, and you can sign up for e-newsletters so that you're always first to hear about our new releases.

www.panmacmillan.com

GIFT SELECTOR
YOUR ACCOUNT
WISH LIST
WAITING LIST

HOME   ABOUT US   IMPRINTS   TRADE/MEDIA   CONTACT US   ADVANCED SEARCH   SEARCH   GO

BOOK CATEGORIES   WHAT'S NEW   AUTHORS/ILLUSTRATORS   BESTSELLERS   READING GROUPS

Coming Soon...

Reading Groups

Competitions
Feeling Lucky?

Extracts
Sneak Previews

Interviews

Events
Meet Our Stars

Reviews
What The Critics Say

News & Awards

Editor's Choice
What We're Reading